SPOOKY SHADOWS

Jennifer J. Morgan

Books by Jennifer J. Morgan

Libby Madsen Cozy Mysteries
Shadows in the Forest
Spa Shadows
Shadowed Treasures
Shadow Retreats
Spooky Shadows
The Christmas Fairy - a holiday novella

SPOOKY SHADOWS

Libby Madsen Cozy Mysteries, Book 5

Jennifer J. Morgan

Secret Staircase Books

Spooky Shadows
Published by Secret Staircase Books, an imprint of
Columbine Publishing Group, LLC
PO Box 416, Angel Fire, NM 87710

Book layout and design by Secret Staircase Books
First trade paperback edition: March, 2023
First e-book edition: March, 2023

Publisher's Cataloging-in-Publication Data

Morgan, Jennifer J.
Spooky Shadows / by Jennifer J. Morgan.
p. cm.
ISBN 978-1649141286 (paperback)
ISBN 978-1649141293 (e-book)

1. Libby Madsen (Fictitious character). 2. Arizona—Fiction. 3.
Amateur sleuths—Fiction. 4. Women sleuths—Fiction. I. Title

Libby Madsen Cozy Mystery Series : Book 5.
Morgan, Jennifer J., Libby Madsen cozy mysteries.

BISAC : FICTION / Mystery & Detective.

813/.54

To my daughter—
Everything I do, it's always been for you.

ACKNOWLEDGMENTS

Jerome, Arizona has always been a favorite weekend destination of mine. It's a quaint old town, rich in mining history. For tourists, it's a fun place to walk around, grab a burger and beer, or browse through the shops and galleries. I've stayed at the Jerome Grand Hotel, which was a very cool place. It was originally a hospital back in the late 1920s. Yes, it's rumored to be haunted. No, I never experienced any paranormal activity while I was there. That part was a little disappointing, because I literally seek out haunted hotels to stay in, hoping to have an experience. Sadly, I've never had one. Or, perhaps I should count my blessings … careful what I wish for!

It's been a number of years since I last visited Jerome, and I've lost touch with the several friends I used to go with, but the fond memories will always remain in my heart.

Thank you to my editors and beta readers who take such care with polishing my manuscripts. Sandra, Susan, Marcia, Paula, and Isobel—I appreciate everything that you do. I'm also extremely grateful for my friends and family who encourage me to keep going.

I never truly thought I'd put myself out there as an author. It's been a dream come true, but I won't lie, it's equally terrifying some days. So, I truly appreciate every person who has pushed me along. I'm meeting the best fans and extremely talented authors in the process, all of whom make me a better writer. Thanks for sticking with me!

CHAPTER ONE

The second my hands squeezed the bag of flour, I regretted it. The cloud of white powder engulfed my senses, causing a coughing fit when the one-pound bag crashed to the floor.

Joshua burst into laughter. I ran out of the room trying to catch my breath.

Alexis came over to me with a cup of water; I took a sip. Once I lifted my eyelashes, coated thick in the white substance, I looked at her, horrified. Her expression said it all—she erupted in giggles, too; Joshua, JJ, and Lexi were all laughing, staring at my watering eyes and the flour rivers down my cheeks.

"Oh, sweetie …" Chortling, she lifted a wet rag and gently wiped the mess from my face. "Baking isn't your thing, is it?"

JJ and Joshua bent over in raucous laughter again as I followed their gaze into the kitchen. Through the fog of white dust, I saw that the entire bag of flour was *everywhere.*

"I'm soooo sorry, Lexi!"

She waved me off and opened a nearby closet door, pulling out the vacuum cleaner. "We can fix this—please don't worry. This is the best entertainment we've had in months!"

Still, I was mortified. *Why had I thought it was a good idea to help out Joshua and Lexi baking cookies for the school's fall carnival?*

"Mommy, mommy! Look—" Joshua pointed to Shadow. "She's white now!"

We all laughed while my black Lab looked up at us with her ears back. At least I wasn't in this alone. Of course, my trusted companion was near when I fumbled. Another puff of dust flew into the air as Shadow shook herself and walked out of the room.

JJ handed me a wet rag and I led Shadow out their back door to finish wiping both of us down while Lexi vacuumed. Eventually we got back to the baking—sugar cookies that we spent the afternoon cutting into the shapes of ghosts, goblins, and witches. I didn't feel so bad for the mess I created once I witnessed the black icing finger prints Joshua was leaving all over their white and light-gray kitchen. No wonder Lexi wasn't concerned about my gaffe, she was the mother of a five-year old boy. Nothing compares to that.

Handing me a cup of tea after cleaning up and finally settling onto the sofa, Lexi sighed. "Too much fun." I lifted my eyes questioningly. She laughed and sputtered, "Hey, at least we got to spend the past two hours laughing and not ruminating over all the Love & Mercy drama!"

"Hmm." I muttered, thinking about the spiritual retreat I'd been to earlier in the month. She was right—it was all the talk around the office and among our friend group as well. My roommate, Bella, and I were still processing everything that had occurred. Thankfully, she was handling it well, too busy studying for finals now. By the end of the month, she'd be a certified EMT if it all went well. She seemed to be handling everything—our time at the retreat didn't appear to trigger her past traumas, anyway.

"What's your mother up to lately? I haven't heard much about her," she asked.

"She's off with Margie on a road trip headed north to see the fall colors."

"So fun. I love that she and Margie are so adventurous. Are they still playing neighborhood spy?"

Nearly spitting my tea out with that imagery, I set my mug down. My mom and her neighbor started up a Neighborhood Watch group over the summer. The memory of the two older ladies dressed all in black and stalking around their properties, hoping to find bad guys, was a hilarious sight to see.

"I believe it's settled down over there—she hasn't mentioned anything recently anyway. Way too funny, those two." We had a good chuckle over some of my mother's antics. She's a feisty one, but her heart has always been in the right place.

Lexi hesitated, then asked, "And you and Greg?"

Staring into my mug, I quietly answered, "Yep. Yes—we're fine." The past couple months since we'd been back from Utah were difficult. Long distance relationships are not easy. I missed him and couldn't help but shake the feeling that I was losing him.

"So, when is he coming back for a visit?" she teased.

My eyes perked up. "We're hoping for next weekend," I said, crossing my fingers.

"Very cool. So happy to hear that. And, do you have plans to see him at his place soon as well?"

"We've talked perhaps about skiing over the winter. Not that Heber, Arizona, has ski hills, but they're not far away. That could be fun. It's been years since I've done that."

JJ came and sat down next to me. "When are we going skiing?"

"Ooooohhh, that's a fantastic idea. We need to plan a group ski trip." My mind started formulating plans already.

"Hon, they need time—only the two of them..." Lexi winked at her husband, obviously thinking she was being sly and I wouldn't catch on.

"But, seriously—it would be fun to plan a group trip again. Utah was so much fun." Then JJ's face contorted. "Ok, well aside from the injuries and kidnappings. That won't happen again; let's at least think about it. We can talk it over with Greg when he's here over the weekend."

After I made sure that there wasn't anything else I could possibly help clean up, I ran upstairs and gave my favorite godson a kiss on the forehead. With his attention spellbound on his favorite video game, I barely got a wave goodbye.

Shadow got a little shove when she walked right in front of the TV screen. "Hey...outta my way," he whined. She planted a nice slobbery kiss right on his nose. "Oh gross! Ugh!"

Lexi stood at the base of the stairs as we trotted down, I couldn't stop laughing.

"Let me guess, in the middle of his game?"

I nodded. "Yep, and he got a nice big kiss from both of us!"

CHAPTER TWO

By the time I made it home with my carry-out Cobb salad and bowl of chili for dinner, I was in desperate need of some protein to outweigh all the sugar I had consumed over at the Johnson's. I'd barely sat down to eat when my phone rang.

My good friend, Kirby McDaniel, whom I hadn't seen in several years, was on the line. She went to East Valley Technical Institute with Alexis and me; we all were certified as licensed massage therapists in the same graduating class. The three of us used to be thick as thieves back in the day. Of course, we were younger and had much more energy for going out most nights, then studying and working all day. I considered Kirby the studious one of our bunch, but Lexi came in a close second. I was the adventurous one;

I always wanted to get away and *do something* in our time off. Thank goodness I instigated them; such fun memories. Kirby went on to finish a business degree and we lost touch after a couple years.

During the course of the hour we spent on the phone, we updated each other on how our respective businesses were going. She had spent most of her time since graduation, twelve years ago, in the Flagstaff area working for a franchise massage company, and only within the past year she moved to Jerome, Arizona, and opened her own small business. She explained how she was able to rent a nice accommodation within a historic hotel with great tourist activity.

"*The* haunted hotel?" I wondered.

"Yes, Jerome's one and only. Have you been there?"

"I've driven through Jerome and stopped for lunch somewhere, but I've never stayed overnight. Is it truly haunted? Have you had anything weird happen?"

"No, no. Nothing like that. I put those tales out of my head, actually. They're silly." There was a long pause, then she started again, "Libby, I'm actually calling for a favor."

"Okay, whatcha need?"

"Dad's in the hospital in Phoenix and having surgery next week. I'm trying to find someone to cover massage clients for me while I'm gone so that I don't have to shut down altogether. October is a huge tourist month here. I've tried calling the school to see if they had anyone they could send, but they don't. Plus, I'd be more comfortable with that idea if I only needed extra hands, but as you know, running the business end requires more than a qualified therapist. Do you have any recommendations?"

"Oh boy. We've been quite busy ourselves over the summer—let me discuss with Lexi and see what ideas she may have. I'm sure we'll come up with some way to help you."

"That would be amazing, Libby. And regardless, after Dad is better, we should get together. We're only a couple hours away from each other."

"Definitely. We need to plan something."

* * *

After a long night's sleep, I bounded from bed with Shadow following right behind me to the kitchen. I let her outside and stood in the doorway, stretching my arms high in the air and enjoying the sunshine on my face. Shadow sniffed around the yard while I made the coffee. Soon after, I tied back my shoulder-length auburn hair into a ponytail and changed into my running shorts and t-shirt. Shadow knew the jog was imminent when I finished lacing up my shoes.

We wound our way around the neighborhood at a fairly brisk pace; feeling the cool air and appreciating how great it felt to move. The neighbors were already putting out their Halloween decorations—my neighborhood always went over the top for every occasion. It's probably about time that I participate instead of being the only dark house on the block. Something to think about.

After about two miles, we turned around and started back toward the house. I decided I'd try calling Greg as soon as I got back, maybe I'd catch him before he headed off for work. Other than getting together with Alexis and JJ, I was having a difficult time coming up with other activities we could do during his visit. We've discovered both of us like staying busy. We enjoy the occasional afternoon to sit around and watch movies, but what inspires us more is to stay active, keeping our minds and bodies in motion. Surely, there's something going on in town with Halloween coming up.

At home, I poured a cup of coffee and sat down to read through the news headlines on my tablet. As quickly as I could flip through a couple of the articles, I turned it off. Nothing good happens from reading the news. It's all so depressing. I picked up my phone instead.

After the third ring, I realized Greg was busy and not going to answer his phone. I left a quick message letting him know I'd call him over my lunch break later and I told him how much I missed him.

Bella dragged herself into the kitchen. "Coffee," she moaned.

"Late night?"

"I'm never going to be ready for the tests. The practicals, yes—I'll ace that part. The written test—ugh, I just can't." She poured the warm brown liquid into her mug and then sat down at the breakfast bar.

"I can only imagine. But, if the amount of time you've been studying is any indication, then you're going to do great!" I patted her shoulder as I walked by. "Off for the shower—see you at the spa!" Shadow stayed at Bella's feet, looking up, hoping that she would accidentally drop something delicious from the counter.

* * *

Kathleen greeted us from the front desk as Shadow and I walked in. She had been with us now for several months once we'd been able to finally hire some help. She and Diane were instrumental to Lexi and me now being able to take time off. The first couple of years in business we struggled, as any small business owners would, to find good work-life balance.

"Good morning!" I greeted her as I made my way behind the counter and through the glass doors into the Serenity Room.

Pride flowed through me every time I walked into the business Lexi and I had created together. Would I ever grow tired of the features we implemented? The water elements—a tranquil quiet space for clients. Or the interior design? The warm mauve and gray—soft and comforting sofas, blankets, and meditation floor cushions. It's a peaceful place and I wouldn't trade it for anything. I always remember Alexis' Grandma Kohli's words—"Dharma means 'purpose' and I see that your purpose is bringing your services to those in need. You two *are* Dharma Inspired." Surprisingly, and unknowingly at the time, she was instrumental in our initial startup. Would I ever regret starting a business that keeps me tied to one location? I couldn't imagine that, but that's why I feel fortunate to have a couple more therapists helping out. Everything happens for a reason and I was incredibly grateful.

Shadow jumped up to push the next door open; that's when I noticed there were still paw prints from her doing the same thing yesterday. Oh well. I'll get to it later. First, a hot mug of tea, then I crossed the room to the office that I shared with Alexis.

"Hey there, baking queen!" she laughed, but got up from her desk to give a warm welcoming hug.

"Oh great, I'm never going to live down my clumsiness, am I?"

"Well maybe someday ... but it's still way too soon."

I put down my bag and set up my laptop, pressing the 'on' button. Then, Shadow followed me into the kitchen. Her favorite parts of our days were when she could greet those taking their break. We shared a kitchen with our tenants, Healing Solutions. They provide physical therapy and rehabilitation services which make them a perfect partner with our day spa. At least that's what we've been told by our numerous clients now. It's like a one-stop shop for your body's healing needs.

Shadow ran directly over to Diane who happened to be opening a bag that looked remarkably like dog treats. It wasn't. She poured her granola into a bowl before looking down at Shadow.

"Now, what do you think you're going to get today?" she laughed. She turned to me, "She's too smart. She knows who drops stuff all the time."

"She definitely knows how to strategically position herself, doesn't she?" I put my lunch bag into the refrigerator and called for Shadow. "C'mon, girl. Let's go prep our room. Sasha will be here soon for her massage."

Apparently, my voice sounded as though that would be way more fun. She ditched Diane and bolted toward me as I left the kitchen.

The morning blew by fast. Before I knew it, a group of us were gathered again in the breakroom, noisily opening wrappings and trying to get at our food. For a moment, I got sad remembering my former lunch partner from Healing Solutions. Brian and I had made it a habit for many months to have lunch together. He had made me laugh, but now anytime I thought of him, I was sad. The end of our friendship at the Love & Mercy retreat was extremely unfortunate.

Lexi walked over and pulled up a chair at my table. "What'd you bring for lunch?" she asked me.

"I've got chopped veggies and some garlic lemon hummus…"

"That's it? You're going to waste away."

"I've already had a protein smoothie a couple hours ago. Next snack is peanut butter toast. I think I'll live."

She pulled out a burger and fries from her Wendy's bag and plopped down a chocolate shake. How she manages fast food all the time, I cannot imagine. She's the meditation guru type—you'd think that would lend to a healthier eating lifestyle, but nope. Not every day anyway.

I remembered about the conversation last night. "Oh, that reminds me, Lex—I got a call from Kirby last night. Remember her from school?"

"Oh my goodness, how's she doing? Where is she living? She was so much fun … man, those were the days, weren't they?"

I laughed thinking about the antics we caused in our youth. "Actually, she's right here in Arizona. Jerome," I said, then took a sip of tea. "She sounded really good. She's looking for someone to fill in for her at the famous hotel there."

"Oh, that's the spooky one, right?"

I shrugged. "I'm not sure how *haunted* it actually is … but she was telling me how last year she rented space from the hotel owner to set up her massage business. The hotel was thrilled to offer a new amenity to their guests—so it sounds like a win-win for all."

"And, she's looking for a therapist then—to fill in? Or to hire full-time?"

"Temporary fill-in. She was wondering what we were up to, so I told her all about our Dharma Inspired Day Spa—she was thrilled for us. She asked if I had any recommendations. She had already called the school, but they had no one available. I think she was looking for a personal suggestion from someone she trusted versus a random student from the massage school."

"Where is she going? Why does she need someone?"

"Her dad is ill. She needs to be in Phoenix for several days following his surgery and until her brother can get there to help. You know how it is—don't want to lose the revenue, but there might not be a choice if she can't keep the doors open. It didn't sound like the hotel manager was exactly happy about the prospect of her being away either."

"I'm sure Kathleen would be thrilled to take on some of your clients, if you wanted to help Kirby."

I hadn't even considered that. "Oh, I don't know. I just got back…"

"Libby, you know we slow down. It's that time of year—people are more focused on the upcoming holidays and buying for other people, but not necessarily spending on themselves. We can handle it if you want to go. And, think about it—you can promote Dharma Inspired while you're there. You never know who you'll find as clients who will visit Mesa someday." She smiled widely.

"I'll think about it. I'd rather spend time with Greg … but you're right, Kirby needs help. I'm sure he'd understand if we delayed our weekend together."

CHAPTER THREE

Greg sounded solemn, "Why couldn't we do that together?" As he asked the question, I could imagine his exact facial expression—I missed him so much. His crystal blue eyes, warm tanned face with a light covering of five o'clock shadow. Rugged looking—as a hard-working forest ranger would be—but I'd learned that there was nothing tough about Greg. From how he treated people to his likeable demeanor, he was a gentle and loving man.

"You'd want to go to Jerome?" I asked, surprised. *Why hadn't I thought of that?*

"I love that little town—great place. I'm sure I could find things to do while you are in session. Not a problem. Shadow and I will go find trouble together when you have to work," the mischief in his deep voice made me smile.

My heart swelled. "I'd *love* that! Let me talk to Kirby and find out more. Who knows, she may have found someone already. I'll let you know as soon as I have more details."

As soon as I hung up, I dialed my friend. She hadn't found a solution yet, so we discussed what was involved and I offered myself up.

"Oh my goodness, Libby. I would absolutely love that—there's no one I would trust more than you! But, are you sure? You must be busy running your own business."

"I already spoke to Lexi; between her and our associates, they'll be able to cover. Plus, as she said, it's good marketing for our business, too. Many visitors to Jerome come from the valley."

"Sure! That sounds great!"

She explained what was going on with her father and how long she'd need to be away. Four days for sure, but she'd feel better if she had coverage for five, just in case. During that time, her massage schedule so far included two each day—ninety minutes long. Not bad, although that could always change. She gave me her address; a small cottage not far from the hotel. She'd leave the key with the hotel manager, and she was more than happy for me to bring Shadow and Greg.

"Oh, this will be a nice getaway for you two! There's so much to do in Jerome, and you can walk to everything. There are pubs, great food, and nice artist galleries all over. I'm so excited you've agreed to this—thank you, I'm so grateful!" her voice cracked with emotion.

"I'm honored to help you, Kirby. No worries at all. You focus on your dad and I've got your business covered."

* * *

The early morning ride to Jerome was uneventful—a little more than two hours and I was pulling up to the hotel in my Toyota 4Runner. I looked around for Greg's white Tundra, but didn't spot it yet. It was easiest for him to drive from his home in Heber—which was about a two-and-a-half-hour drive—instead of driving to the valley first.

I cracked the windows and opened the moon roof to give Shadow some air, then I told her she'd get a cookie when I returned. I stepped from the car and stretched my legs, looking up at the massive structure in front of me. The five story Spanish Mission Style hotel with its red-tiled roof was overly done in Halloween decorations—lights, ghosts, spiders, and webbing expertly installed. I looked out over the parking lot again and this time noticed tombstones and huge scarecrows scattered throughout. Beyond, it was an exquisite view over the expansive Verde Valley, the vistas stunning and endless. After a deep breath, I turned toward the entrance to go pick up Kirby's cottage keys.

As I walked under the spider-web covered portal, a small lady bounded through the glass doors, nearly bowling me over. I jumped aside in time to avoid a collision. The short brownish-gray curls all over her head bounced wildly on the short, slight, older woman.

She barely looked up when she barked, "Get outta my way!" Brusquely, she stomped off to the parking lot and I stared in amazement as she slammed the door of a tiny bright yellow Smart car with a black race stripe painted down the center of the itsy-bitsy vehicle.

Still shaking my head in wonder, I crossed through the threshold into the lobby of the historic hotel. A warm congenial smile welcomed me as I looked into the kind blue eyes of an older gentleman wearing gold wire-rimmed glasses and whose wispy thin black hair was combed over in an attempt to hide his balding scalp. He stood rigid; his six-foot-tall lithe body dressed in a smart, perfectly tailored gray suit, crisp white shirt, and a thin black tie.

"I'm sorry, Ma'am. Tricia can be ... well, let's just say, she's a bit abrupt." He smiled politely. "How may I help you? Are you here to check in?"

"I'm Libby Madsen. Here to pick up keys for Kirby McDaniel's place."

"Oh, Ms. Madsen. So nice to meet you. Kirby speaks so highly of you! I'm Bill Longo—hotel manager."

I reached my hand out to meet his. "So happy to meet you, Mr. Longo!" I said as we shook hands.

His eyes were bright and friendly. "Bill, please. You can call me Bill."

He opened a drawer beneath the desk and pulled out a keyring. "Here are her keys—for both her cottage and the therapy room." He handed me the fuzzy pink fluff with a delicate silver chain that held several keys. "Give me a second and then I'll show you around." Bill turned to a young lady sitting at a computer behind him.

While they spoke, my eyes took in the lobby décor. It wasn't large, but it was evident they tried to keep the old-style mining town feel. There was a small sitting area with a forest green velvet sofa and several matching upholstered Queen Anne chairs. Beyond them, I caught a glimpse of a beautiful old elevator—had to be the original.

Then, my eyes caught the man who had walked in the front doors. Before I knew it, I was swept up into Greg's arms. My feet lifted from the ground with the exuberant bear hug. We kissed and when he set me down, I saw that

Mr. Longo had joined us.

"Mr. Longo, this is my boyfriend, Greg," I slightly stepped aside, "Greg, this is Mr. Longo, the hotel manager."

"Bill, please." The tall man reached out to shake Greg's hand. "Ready for the tour?"

"Bill, I have my dog in the car…"

"Oh! Please, go get him."

"Her. Shadow is my baby girl." I grabbed the keys from my jeans pocket. "Thank you. I promise, she'll be good." I love small towns. His soft eyes told me that he always welcomed pets.

Shadow was eager as she watched me approach the vehicle. She jumped down and I walked her to the side of the building quickly to avoid any accidents during the tour. She tucked her tail and sniffed all over pensively. She startled and whined.

"What's wrong, baby?" If I didn't know better, I'd say she was scared. Strange.

Sniffing around along the side of the building, she eventually did her business and we proceeded back to the front of the hotel. She still wasn't wagging her tail and both ears were pinned back as she slowly and cautiously approached the front door. Very uncharacteristic for her.

The second she saw Greg, she perked up. Her tail whipping the air, she bounced up to him whimpering softly and wiggling like her normal self. She sniffed Bill and gave a low woof.

"Shadow, this is Bill … he's going to show us around." The hotel manager gave me a side-eye. I supposed he doesn't have experience talking to animals as though they are people. He smiled though as Shadow sat and handed him her paw. He took it, saying hi to her, and smiling at us.

We'd been working on that one. Instead of jumping up on people, I've been rewarding her when she sits and shakes hands instead.

"Good girl!" I pulled out a piece of her treat from my pocket and she greedily devoured it, looking so proud.

"Wow, she *is* a good girl," Bill admired. "Ok, right this way, I'll show you where Kirby's business is."

He led us directly to the elevator. Both Shadow and I hesitated.

"This thing actually works?" I was skeptical of the brass gate that he opened up to a small, rickety looking elevator car.

He nodded, "Inspected every year. Don't worry."

We stepped in and Greg held my hand as Bill shut the gate and pressed the antique-looking button that read 'B'. After a small bump and some interesting squeals, we watched through the gate as the lobby floor landing passed us and then we could see gray concrete until light appeared again as we settled softly at the basement level.

"See, that wasn't so bad," Greg laughed.

"Ok, only a couple doors down this hall." Bill led the way and as we approached the door, he turned back to me. "It's the brass, older looking key on the ring."

It was easily recognizable. I opened the door and switched on the light. It wasn't a large room, maybe twelve by twelve feet square, but Kirby had done a magnificent job making it comfortable and cute. Closest to us, inside the door, she had a small cabinet area that she'd painted white with delicate drawings of flowers, birds, and butterflies. That reminded me what a great artist Kirby was. Underneath the countertop, there was a sink and a small fridge. At the far end of the counter was what looked like a Crockpot. *Ah, must be to warm the hot stones.* I'd forgotten to ask what type of services she offered—it'd been a long time since I'd done a hot stone massage. I walked farther into the room and at the far end was where she had set up the massage table, close to a cordoned off changing area. The privacy curtain was another Kirby specialty—colorful batiks that displayed nature exquisitely. If I remembered correctly, this technique involved layers of wax and dying multiple times over her intricate design. So beautiful—almost like stained glass in a sense, but on cloth.

Bill interrupted my thoughts, reminding me the guys were still standing there. I was mesmerized by all the details in Kirby's art. "So, if you need anything from me—I'm generally at the front desk." He opened up his wallet and pulled out a business card. "If I'm not, here's how to reach me. All the appointments are set with the front desk. That laptop there—well you'll see the scheduling app on it. Any questions, ask Laurie at the desk. I have no idea how all that works," he laughed.

"Thank you, Bill. Everything looks straightforward."

"Ready to see the best parts of the hotel?"

Greg perked up. "Yes!"

Bill guided us all through the basement area—showing us the laundry room, several staff areas, the original—although overhauled—steam heating system still in operation. After the guys oohed and aahed over the machinery, Bill led us down another hallway that opened up to a huge ballroom. As I admired the old 1920s décor, I noticed a door leading to the outside. I was amazed at how large this building was, but realized we were now in the far eastern portion of the property. The hotel was built into the mining town's hillside; the basement ballroom wrapped around and stair-stepped into the terrain seamlessly.

"Ah! There you are!" a booming female voice sounded. "I've been looking all over for you!" I turned to my right and saw a large woman dressed in a black pantsuit, complete with a beige silk blouse, the delicate collar tied expertly into a bow resting at the base of the woman's throat.

Bill was quick with introductions. "Cheryl, this is Libby Madsen and her boyfriend, Greg Lawson. Libby, Greg, this is Cheryl Basque. She is the President of the Verde Valley Arts Council, serves in the Chamber of Commerce's tourist department, and most importantly, she is the coordinator for our annual murder mystery weekend."

We each took turns shaking the lady's hand when her dark penciled eyebrows lifted and she exclaimed. "Oh! You are the one filling in for Kirby! I'm so happy she found someone to take her place."

Shadow let out a low woof.

"Ohhh, look at you, sweetie," she cooed, with a flash of irritation toward Bill, "Mr. Longo let you inside." It was unmistakable, the distaste settled into the frown lines at her mouth.

I didn't skip a beat. "Yes. It would be a shame if she had to close down for several days. The revenue…"

Cheryl quickly cut me off. "No, no … I meant for the murder mystery weekend, of course. I only learned today that Kirby had to back out. That leaves me in a bind with our opening act happening tomorrow! You are filling in for her, right?"

Greg and I shared a quick glance. I had no idea what to say; Kirby made no mention of this to me.

"Well, I … uh …"

"Oh sure, you'll be great! I can see it now…" she held

her hands up as a director homing in on his shot, "the beautiful harlot caught with one of the town's …."

Bill set a hand on Cheryl's padded shoulder. "Ms. Basque. Maybe someone else can fill in for Kirby. One of the staff here, or…"

"I've already asked everyone. No one seems as interested this year as in the past."

I caught Bill's expression as he moved away from Cheryl and said to me, "Maybe you'd consider? It's always been a grand ole time."

"I haven't seen what the massage schedule is yet. Will I even have time to participate? And, Greg and I were hoping to have some time alone to explore this wonderful town of yours."

Cheryl's hands came together, excitedly clapping, as she did a small hop in place. "Both of you could play along! Oh yes…" then she looked down at Shadow, who gave a quiet low growl, "and I'm sure we can find a role … for this one." She reached out with a couple fingers and barely tapped my black Lab on the head. Shadow ducked.

I wasn't sure how to handle this. "Uh, you know … we just got to town. Can you give me some more information about our roles in this mystery thing? We'll look it over tonight and get back to you tomorrow morning."

Cheryl wanted an immediate answer, that was clearly etched on her face. The other thing I picked up on was that she doesn't take no for an answer. Maybe that was the reason she was finding it hard to find participants these days.

Thankfully, a staff member distracted the coordinator with a question and she was off. Greg and I clearly had similar thoughts as she walked away—his fleeting look gave Bill his opening.

"I'm sorry about that. She is overly exuberant about *her* weekend here at the haunted hotel." His eyes glanced downward as he gently shook his head.

"Is it truly haunted?" Greg asked. "I've always read about that, but honestly … have *you* experienced strange occurrences?"

Bill guided us back down the hallway, as he answered Greg's questions. "I think it's actually good for tourism for the media to keep writing about the hotel's history. Honestly, there have been a few unexplained things my staff have witnessed, but I personally never have. I think the youngsters who come to Jerome seeking work are actually *looking* to be visited by something unexplainable." He laughed as we stopped again at the old steam boiler. "This room here seems to be one that our maintenance personnel avoid. The rumor is that a young man—maybe twenty-something—hangs out here and has startled many when working on the boiler. Seems to always occur in the middle of the night, of course."

Greg laughed, "I suppose anything is scary in the middle of the night when all is quiet."

Tickles of excitement fluttered through my stomach. "I'd love to witness a ghostly appearance! Well, so long as it wasn't dangerous … I don't want to invite that."

The two men looked at me like I was off my rocker.

"You wouldn't be scared?" Greg asked me.

"I don't think so."

Bill cleared his throat. "Well, then, you are in the right place, Miss … the basement is where most sightings have occurred." His voice lowered, and squinting his eyes suspiciously, he ominously added, "Also, the elevator—

many guests have told stories of odd things happening in the elevator. And then, room thirty-two, also a source of many tales."

Greg laughed at his performance. I was even more intrigued now. *I've got to explore this place!*

"Seriously, if you guys are interested in the murder mystery, I know Cheryl could use help. Although, and I don't know the therapy schedule, Kirby has only rarely had appointments at nighttime—and that's when all the mystery weekend activities occur. I would think there'd be the opportunity to do both. One thing Ms. Basque excels at is hosting this annual event. I think you'd have a blast."

With that, he continued to show us around the hotel. Back in the lobby, he pointed out volumes of albums he said were pictures and guests' tales of their experiences. I made a mental note to seek those stories out later. Once we were finished with the tour, Greg, Shadow, and I headed back to the therapy room. I flipped on the laptop and entered the password Kirby had given me. Once I verified my first appointment wouldn't be for a few more hours, we set out to find her cottage and get settled in.

CHAPTER FOUR

We found the cute cottage off Holly St. a mile or so away. As we pulled up to the pale-yellow wood-sided structure, I realized nothing in town was far from the hotel. Kirby sure had it fixed up nicely with flowers pots all over the covered front patio and large planters off the front steps and along the east side of the home. Halloween decorations covered the front of the house and patio, fitting in with the entire town's decorations.

I noticed the planters were filled with vegetables—zucchini, squash, and tomatoes were most prominent now—but it appeared that during summer, she grew much more. Shadow put her front paws on the planter's edge, sniffing at the greenery.

From the garden, Shadow and I took the steps back up

to the porch and looked around. There was a nice propane fire pit and a patio heater as well. She'd decorated so cute—the cushions, the flower pots, and the wooden chairs—all painted cheerfully.

"This is beautiful," Greg said. "Nice place to have coffee in the morning." He'd taken a seat in one of several cushy oversized chairs on the patio.

I opened the metal screen door first, then turned the key in the deadbolt. Shadow bounded past me, sniffing curiously all around. It was a small place—less than a thousand square feet. We walked into the living area—a loveseat and chaise lounge were placed facing a small TV. Turning to our left, there was a small but functional kitchen. Past that, we followed the hallway to the one-bedroom and separate bathroom. *Adorable!*

Inside, Kirby had painted the walls light gray throughout. The loveseat was an eggplant purple and the chaise lounge was dark gray. Accent pillows matched perfectly, and I could see that she had hung her own artwork in each room. The bedroom had a cozy dusty rose fuzzy comforter, pillows and sheets in various shades of gray. It was so serene and peaceful.

I moved our suitcases off to the side in the bedroom as Greg helped to assemble Shadow's crate in the living area next to the small wood stove. I set Shadow's bowls down in the corner of the kitchen and she wolfed down her breakfast. I learned early on not to feed her before we went on a road trip. One experience of cleaning up the contents of her stomach off the back seat of my 4Runner taught me to feed her upon arrival of wherever our adventure led us.

"I think we have time. Want to explore town and find

some lunch?" I asked.

"Let's do it."

We locked up and the three of us headed up Holly St. and over to Main St. Since it wasn't the weekend yet, the town was relatively quiet as we walked along the main drag. I recognized immediately that people took Halloween seriously around here—every single house and business was fully decorated. Residents were tending to daily business—maybe post-office runs, opening their own businesses for the day, picking up some groceries at the market, or strolling through town. Traffic was light, which was what startled us most when we heard tires peeling out from the curb ahead. The color yellow was all we could see as it flashed past. I didn't even know a Smart car could *peel out*, I mused to myself as we passed by several businesses: a bakery/coffee shop, a pet groomer's shop, and then a craft brewery—all decorated for the upcoming, candy grabbin' holiday. The brewery got Greg's attention.

"Hey, up for a burger?" he asked.

"Sure, why not? Looks like they have a dog-friendly patio—let's do it."

Shadow agreed with that. Her sniffer was in full gear, smelling searing beefy scents that emanated from the building. Greg went inside to greet the hostess; Shadow and I walked onto the patio and found an empty table. There was only one other couple at the far end of the patio.

Before we could sit down, Greg pointed out a lively young woman coming toward us. I watched as the perky blonde with her hair in a ponytail, wearing black yoga pants and a camouflaged long-sleeve fitted shirt, bounced on over.

"Hello! Well, look at this sweetie pie right here!" she

exclaimed, and Shadow sat with her paw held up. "Oh, my goodness … what a good girl!" The young woman reached into the pocket of her waist-tied apron and pulled out a dog treat. "Is it okay, Mom? I always ask … I've got myself a big ol' German Shepherd mix and I'm not always thrilled when someone hands him God knows what."

I smiled, relieved she had a cookie with her. "Of course. Looks like I'd forgotten to bring ours. Bad mom. Thank you! Your German —what's his name?"

Greg took a seat next to me.

"Rex—he's sweet as can be, but not everyone sees him that way. Guess he looks and sounds menacing to some. I don't get it."

Shadow raised her paw again, hoping for more. I patted her head and told her to lay down. She did.

"Okay, folks, what can I get you to drink?"

"Whatcha got on draft?" Greg asked.

She went through the list and he chose one called *Snake Venom*.

"I'm fine with water. Gotta work later." I said, secretly wishing I could also have a beer midday.

"Oh, you're not tourists—you work in Jerome?" she asked me.

"Well, technically, we are tourists. We live in Mesa, but I'm filling in for my friend—massage therapist at the hotel."

She stopped writing on her pad. "You're Kirby's friend! Wow, that's fantastic! She told me she had to be away for a bit—her dad; how sad. I didn't know she'd found someone to fill in."

"Yep, I'm happy to help … and I love this area so it's a nice getaway, too."

"Well, let me go get those drinks while you look at the menu. I'm Monica, by the way. I'll be right back."

Shadow watched curiously as Monica hustled away.

Greg chuckled. "I sure wish I still had that youthful energy."

"You're youthful…"

"Not like *that*."

I laughed; he had a point. She could run circles around us.

She was back in a nano-second, placing Greg's brown ale in front of him and a glass of water that she handed to me. She ran over to a side cart where she grabbed a dog bowl that she filled with water. After setting it down for Shadow, she took our food order. We each decided on specialty burgers—I got a green-chile cheeseburger and Greg got the BBQ crispy fried onion burger and we decided to share a basket of fries.

"So, what do you think about joining the mystery weekend thingy?" he asked me.

"It sounds fun … would give us opportunity to snoop around that old hotel. Isn't that the coolest?"

"I think it could be fun, but it's actually up to you since you're the one working."

"I meant to look closer at the schedule for the next few days—I only paid attention to what I've got to do today. Let me do that when I'm back at the hotel, we'll decide tonight and let Cheryl know."

Overhearing us as Monica walked up with our burgers and set them down in front of us, she grimaced. "Oh no, you've already met my aunt, haven't you? And, she's wrangled you into her murder mystery weekend, hasn't she?"

Small community, I thought. *Already meeting the relatives.*

Greg laughed; the tone Monica used spoke volumes. "You've done it before then?"

"Well, no. But, each year, I make certain my bosses give me a *full* schedule for the *whole* weekend. Heck, it's one of our busiest weekends so it's generally not a problem … but Cheryl *always* tries to convince Ted to give me the weekend off. I assist her with some of the preparations—mostly the script writing. She thinks I'd be perfect for the show."

We wasted no time diving into our meal while she talked. Shadow's face watched my every move in anticipation of something falling.

"So, you don't enjoy it—the script writing?" Greg got in between bites.

"Oh no, it's fun and all. But …" she wrinkled her nose and stuck her tongue out, "well, it's hard being around Cheryl that much. Don't get me wrong—I love my aunt and she's helped me out a lot. I mean, after I left Kentucky and drove for days getting here, she put me up and helped me get this job. She's great. But, controlling. I don't think it's a bad thing that we each have our own things to do—separately."

I was curious, "You moved from Kentucky?"

"Yeah. My stepdad. Mean drunk—and I was tired of being his punching bag. Cheryl saved my life; literally." Monica looked at our glasses. "Oh hey, need another beer? I'll bring you more water, too."

Greg nodded yes and she was gone, and then back in a flash.

"You know, if you like mysteries, you probably should do it. My aunt puts on a fantastic show and I understand it's set in the 1920s this year. As part of the arts council, she gets great fundraising—I always love the costumes she rounds up for these shindigs. Oh, lookie … more customers, gotta run. Let me know if you need anything else." She ran off to seat a party of six.

We finished eating, paid, and tipped Monica well. Not only was she a great waitress, we found her quite entertaining, too. We felt like we'd made our first friend in Jerome and looked forward to visiting the Mining Town Brewery again soon.

I looked down at my watch and saw that I had another two hours before I needed to get back to the hotel. "Wanna grab a sweet treat? There's a bakery right over there …" I teased.

We walked up to the cutest shop. The pink and white striped awning over the doorway and picture window was adorable—also decorated with ghouls and goblins. Then, looking into the window display took me back in time, to when my dad and I would drool over baked goods at our favorite bakery. Nostalgically, I saw exactly what I wanted. Before my dad had tragically passed, we always enjoyed turtle brownies together. These looked exactly like the soft, gooey, caramel and chocolate decadence we loved.

Greg stayed outside with Shadow. He wasn't as interested in sweets and decided to pass. As soon as I walked through the door, I was greeted with the two cutest white dogs.

"Snow, Ball … c'mon girls. Get back here and leave the nice lady alone."

After greeting the small fur balls, I looked up at their owner. He was a short, plump man with pink cherub cheeks. He was wearing white pants and shirt, with a pink and white striped apron tied around his waist. He had short black hair slicked back with a light coating of flour all over. I decided in all this pink, he was a confident man.

"What kind of dogs are they? They are soooo soft!"

"Maltese. Super sweet girls. This one is Snow—she has the hot pink collar. And this is Ball—she has the baby pink collar because, well, she's the baby."

I started laughing— "Snow Ball! Way too funny…" The two little girls looked up at me curiously when I called their names. That got me laughing even harder.

"My name is Nate—my wife, Colleen, and I own the coffee shop and bakery. Hey, your husband and dog can come in, too. Businesses here are mostly accommodating to pets."

I didn't correct him about Greg being my husband, but I opened the door and invited them in. Shadow was cautious as she crossed the threshold. I hadn't considered how she'd handle the small dogs. I could see she was extremely curious and her tail was quickly whipping around. The small dogs weren't afraid at all. They bounced all over the place, which had Shadow turning this way and that trying to keep them in her sight. Finally, she sat and the youngest one ran up to her and jumped at the large paw she was holding up. Ball nipped at it.

Nate chuckled. "Aww, she wanted to shake hands with Ball."

Once it was obvious all the girls would play nicely, I made my way over to the bakery counter and chose my turtle brownie and a to-go cup of their house coffee. We chatted with Nate—who also was friends with Kirby and happy to hear she had found a way to keep her business open while caring for her dad.

The bells on the front door clattered; I whipped my

head around in time to see the whirlwind of activity. The same woman, who bowled me over walking into the hotel earlier, blazed her way through the threshold and stumbled over Shadow. She sure gets around, I thought.

"What the hell … what's a dog doing in the pathway!" she grumbled.

Greg had leapt over to the woman. "Are you okay?" He held her arm and she steadied herself. Thank goodness she hadn't fallen.

"Let go of me!" she wrestled her arm back.

Greg held both hands up in surrender. "Whoa, okay. Just trying to help…"

"Then get that dog out of here!" she spat viciously.

By that time, Nate had made his way from behind the counter and over to the lady. I moved over to take a seat at the high-top table where Greg and Shadow were watching intently. I picked off a piece of brownie, eyeing them like a suspense thriller on TV.

"Tricia …" Nate quietly started.

"Patricia Olivia Simpson …"

"Yes, uh … Patricia…" he continued meekly.

"Give me my cookies so I can get out of here!" she snapped.

He scurried behind the counter and grabbed a bag. On the pink and white striped bakery bag, I saw POS on the receipt where the bag was stapled shut. *Piece of sh*— was how I'd heard the initials used. I chuckled to myself—Patricia Olivia Simpson—*POS; that fit her to a T.* I couldn't help but wonder what her all-fired hurry was about today. We seemed to see this one zipping around everywhere. She was a fascinating character, but I wasn't sure I would want to cross her. Thankfully, she had forgotten about us and focused all her attention now on Nate.

She snatched the bag from him and exited in her typical fashion. Shadow emitted a low growl, but I don't think anyone heard but me; we all allowed plenty of room for the Tasmanian Devil to whirl out the door. I no longer saw Snow or Ball anywhere either—apparently, they knew—when that witch blew in, stay out of her way.

I sipped my coffee and watched Nate. He murmured irritably under his breath, *"Patricia Olivia Simpson,"* clearly mocking her correcting him moments earlier. Then his eyes caught ours briefly, before he cast them down at the counter that he'd begun to furiously wipe down. "Sorry about that, folks."

"Oh, we've run into her a few different places during the few hours we've been in town. Who is she anyway?" I asked.

"Patricia thinks she owns this place." His anger was palpable.

"Your bakery?" Greg was curious.

"Well, that too, probably … no, the whole darned town. She runs about like she owns everything and everyone."

"I'm surprised no one has put her in her place yet," I stated.

He scoffed. "The police chief—Jerry—he has a soft spot for her. Not sure why. She treats him no differently either. No respect for authority."

"So, she's broken the law and he does *nothing*?" I couldn't believe that would be the case. "How old is she anyway? The way she dashes all over … but, my first impression was that she's quite old."

"Oh, she's no spring chicken, that's for sure. Has to be mid-eighties. And, I don't know that she's ever done any *actual* law breaking, but plenty of people have called to have her removed from their places of business. She's a nasty little thing. And, I don't know why … everyone in town is nice and welcoming as can be." Nate turned toward the kitchen. "Snow, Ball … c'mon loves, she's gone now."

Shadow perked up when she heard the pitter patter of claws sounding on the tiled floor. She stood up and bounded over to the counter's end as the two fluff balls rounded on her. The two white girls started twisting and turning, flirting with the large black dog. Shadow stretched her front paws forward, placing her face close to theirs. Then she laid down and they were all over her. I'd never seen her play like this, but the three of us got a kick out of the instant canine friendship.

$$* * *$$

Later that afternoon after we settled into the cottage and had unpacked, I set off on foot back to the hotel. Late October was gorgeous in Arizona. Jerome was at a higher elevation than where I lived in Mesa, but still not considered the high country. Afternoons would reach the 80s and overnight temperatures could drop off into the 40-50s. I found the walk to the hotel to be great cardio—all uphill, with the last leg of it being the steepest. Several cars passed me, ascending the long driveway. I stopped shy of the front door and caught my breath while I waited for the doorman assisting a couple with their luggage.

Inside, I could see that Bill and his front desk crew were busy checking people in. I waved to him and then made my way to the ancient elevator. I stood in front of it for a second, reminding myself how Bill had done this earlier. I pulled the brass gate open, stepped in, closed the gate behind me and took a deep breath. The whole thing felt rickety to me—surely, there were stairs I could take instead.

Deciding not to make a scene of exiting, letting everyone in the lobby know what I was doing, I went ahead and pressed the 'B' on the panel. With a jerk, the elevator slowly made its way down. My stomach lurched—I hated this thing. Mostly, I've only ever experienced that confined and claustrophobic feeling in old elevators. My mind couldn't help but wonder—*what would happen if someone called it from another floor while you were getting off, would it start moving? Surely not. But then, how do I know … and what if I got trapped? Yep, I vowed I'd take the stairs from now on.* It seemed as though there should be an operator, someone qualified to use this thing. The contraption squealed and chugged, while I prayed during the whole one floor-length journey. It clattered to a stop and I opened the gate and scurried out quickly.

My heart settled once I'd stepped into a familiar setting and again admired the comfort Kirby had created. I had fifteen minutes before my client would show up so I pulled out the disinfectant and wiped down the table and all touch surfaces. I lit a woodsy scented candle and found the app on Kirby's laptop to play spa music. It had been a while since I'd performed massage with my hands. At my spa, my clients sign up for my specialty which is Ashiatsu—or massage using my feet.

I heard a little tap on the door that I'd left open.

"Hello … I'm Colleen," a quiet, soft voice sounded.

"Welcome, Colleen! I'm Libby Madsen." I reached out to shake her hand. "I'm sure Kirby let you know that she will be gone for a little while?"

She nodded slowly while assessing me. She was a waif of a young woman—no taller than five foot two and couldn't weigh a hundred pounds soaking wet. Her brown hair was pulled up in a bun and she'd worn gray yoga pants and a red tank covered with a light gray jacket. She set her purse down on the corner chair and removed her jacket.

"Has Kirby left notes for you? I'm not sure about her being gone. I've only ever had massage from her."

"No worries. Yes, she has given me excellent notes on all her clients." I continued to quickly tell her my background and experience. She appeared to settle and I asked her to step into the changing area to undress to her comfortability. I stepped out of the room, letting her know I'd give her a few minutes.

The hallway was quiet. It seemed as though housekeeping had finished for the day. I didn't hear the washing machines running, and that end of the hallway was dark. So was the ballroom—Cheryl must have called it a day.

I knocked on the door, "Colleen, are you ready?" When I heard her say she was, I stepped in, dimmed the lighting, and stepped over to the countertop where I had already set out my supplies.

I pulled the privacy covering away, exposing her halfway down, stopping at her lower back. I warmed the lotion by rubbing my hands together and then spread it across her shoulders and upper back.

A loud thump made us both jump.

"What was that?" I wondered. "I didn't see anyone out there a minute ago."

"Probably that old boiler. It makes noise all the time,"

Colleen noted.

"Have you lived in Jerome long?" I asked, trying to ease our minds.

"My husband and I moved here from the Phoenix area about five years ago. We own the bakery."

"Do you routinely get massage from Kirby then?"

"Oh yes. Every couple of weeks. It helps after being on my feet all day—you know, with the bakery."

"Oh, right! Bakery ... we met your family then. Nate, Snow, and Ball."

She giggled. "I bet those two showered you with love ... they are perfect for the shop, they greet everyone."

"We had our Lab, Shadow, with us—my boyfriend Greg and I stopped in for a sweet treat. Shadow and your girls became instant friends. We might need to make a play date. Is there a park around here that you take them to?"

"Sure. Sometimes we go over to Patriot Park. Where are you staying?"

"At Kirby's ... on Holly St."

"Oh, yeah, it's close. Well, everything is close—it's not like this is a huge town!" she laughed.

"So, we didn't get to talk to Nate long, but I take it that he is the baker in the family?"

She grunted yes as I dug into her upper back.

"Our conversation with him was cut short by that fiery lady..." I struggled to remember her name.

"Oh, boy ... that piece of ..." Colleen started to say.

I snapped my fingers. "Ah, yes, Patricia!" I laughed as I remembered the *POS* written on the pink and white striped bag.

"She is a thorn in our sides! That woman complains *all the time* ... you know how, in the city as part of a homeowner's association, there's always *someone* who nitpicks the rules? Well, that is Patricia. Every business owner here has had some complaint—and, although I can't say for sure, my money is on it being that piece of … work."

The vision of her tripping over Shadow flashed through my head.

"Oh boy. Your husband said we could bring Shadow inside. Well, she was in the way when the lady came barreling through the door. She nearly fell. I sure hope that doesn't cause you problems."

Colleen sighed. "I'm sure it will. But don't you worry about that. We'll deal with her."

For the rest of the session, she filled me in on the murder mystery weekend. I had told her that we were considering participating. She highly recommended it— she'd done it several times and although they got tired of it after several years in a row, she said it was always great fun.

By the time the session was over, we had agreed that in the coming days, we'd get our girls together over coffee. Looks like I had met friend number two in Jerome.

CHAPTER FIVE

Later that night, we walked up Main St. and enjoyed the cool evening. Greg had ventured over to a mining museum while I was in my afternoon sessions. Secretly, I was happy he had done that on his own so that I wouldn't be dragged along. I love museums, but have never had much interest in mining … or mechanical things. Art museums are more my thing.

We took some dark steps that appeared to be a shortcut to the next street higher up the hill. It was spooky once we ventured from the main drag; quiet and eerily shadowed.

"Wait, what was that?" I teased.

"Stop it," he ribbed me and then took off running up the remaining steps.

Shadow and I chased.

At the top, we looked down to see the town's lights below and the pitch black of the Verde Valley beyond. We turned right, opposite of where the hotel was located, and continued along the road to where it wound back around to Main St. We both heard the sound of an engine.

Greg whispered, "Over here—hide!" We ducked behind a huge trash dumpster, laughing. Shadow wagged her tail, bouncing excitedly at our silly games. Greg shushed me when the uncontrollable giggles started.

We watched the small truck pass on by and then we stepped out from behind our hiding spot and continued our walk. The adrenaline was pumping; I loved a good game of hide and seek. This brought out the eight-year-old in me.

We found another steep staircase going down the hillside and decided to take the shortcut and see where it took us. When we hopped down from the last step, Shadow darted to my left and off into an overgrown empty lot. With the leash taut, I followed and we left Greg waiting at the sidewalk. Stopping suddenly, Shadow yelped loudly and started to limp.

"Oh, darn it—Greg, she found a cholla," I called out. He started toward us. "Careful, looks like it's shed a ton of clumps on the ground."

We knelt down and tried our best to get them out of her feet and legs.

"They are buggers," Greg commented as he then started pulling the sharp needles from his jacket. "Ouch!" He pulled another from his hand.

I carefully inspected Shadow's paws and felt confident she could walk now. I knew there had to be more to remove from her legs, but it was dark and we needed better light. We guided her off the lot and back to the sidewalk.

Once we got inside the cottage, I could see all the clumps of needles up and down her legs. My heart sunk, knowing how difficult they were to get out. We definitely had our work cut out for us, so I sent Greg into the bathroom looking for tweezers. Between Kirby's and my own that I had brought, we got Shadow resting somewhat comfortably while we spent the next several hours pulling cactus out of her legs.

* * *

By the next morning, I realized we had a larger problem. Shadow hadn't stopped licking at several wounds on her legs; now they had festered. We'd need to find a veterinarian soon, but we left Shadow in her crate while we found some breakfast. Hopefully, we could find a solution this morning.

There was a cute café not far from the cottage that we settled on for breakfast. After ordering, Greg started scrolling on his phone.

"It doesn't look like they've got a vet here—we'd have to drive into Cottonwood."

The waitress set down mugs of coffee and overheard. "Oh, got a sick pup?"

"Our Lab got into some cholla last night. We thought we got 'em all out, but turns out we didn't. We need help."

"Oh! Our local dog groomer is great at removing cactus. She helped my Rottweiler!" The girl who appeared in her teens, but was more likely twenty-something, pulled out a pad from her apron and wrote on it, 'Tricia's Scruffy Solutions'. "Now, tell her Britney sent you and she'll give you a ten percent discount." She smiled and pivoted toward the kitchen, whipping her long blonde ponytail from side to side as she walked away.

I smiled at Greg. "I love small towns. Everyone knows everyone and looks out for their neighbors, too."

Our piping hot pancakes arrived in time for us to get the much-needed refill on our coffee. Over breakfast, we discussed whether or not we'd participate in the mystery weekend and we both decided it would be a lot of fun— We're in!

We thanked Britney for the recommendation, got Shadow from the cottage, and headed to the groomer's, which we had seen on Main St. during our walks. I shouldn't have been surprised, the tiny yellow car was sitting outside the front door at the street's curb, but when we stepped inside, I visibly startled. The little lady who Shadow tripped yesterday was staring directly at us from behind the counter.

"Good morning! How can I help you today?" she smiled and greeted us warmly. I turned around to catch Greg's gaze, confused by her friendly demeanor. I wanted to turn and run, based on past experience with this woman and what Colleen had said. It was too late, though. Shadow was in agony and we quickly needed help.

Greg spoke up, "Uh, yes … good morning! Shadow here, she got into some cactus. We thought we got them out, but this morning she has several spots on her legs that look inflamed. We might not have got them all out." He patted his jacket pockets down and then reached inside, pulling out the paper the waitress had given him. "Britney said you could help…" he read from the note he held and then looked over the counter at her.

Patricia Olivia Simpson walked around the counter and gently approached Shadow who was already side-stepping to hide behind my legs. "C'mere, fella … do you have an ouchy?" she cooed with the baby talk. My brain was having difficulty catching up to this version of Patricia—*where had the cantankerous, fiery, little thing gone?* She was actually being *nice.* "Oh yeah, right here … and oh boy, this leg too. Yes, you did a number on yourself." She patted Shadow's head and stood up.

"Is this something you can handle or should we take her to the vet in Cottonwood?" I asked.

"Oh, you leave her here with me. I've got all the right stuff to remove those pesky bits … I've also got some basic first aid ointment I can put on. I'll wrap her legs up to keep her from licking and she'll be fine in a day or so."

"How long will it take? Should we wait? I've gotta get…"

She interrupted, "Leave her here for a few hours." She went behind the counter again and signaled us closer. "Here, write your number down and I'll call you when she's ready to be picked up."

Greg took the pen she held out and left his cell phone number since we both knew I'd be tied up in massage sessions for most of the day. We kissed Shadow goodbye; neither of us missed the forlorn look she gave us as we walked out the door. My heart sank—poor baby.

* * *

The morning's sessions sped by and before I knew it, lunch time was approaching. I had texted Greg and asked if Shadow was home yet … he hadn't received a call, but would try calling soon to check in. Neither of us were hungry so I decided to wait at the hotel for my final appointment in about an hour.

I ran up the stairs to the lobby and found Bill at the front desk. He was talking to one of his employees when he saw me approach.

"Libby, I hear you're joining the festivities this evening!" he exclaimed. "I think you and Greg will have a marvelous time."

"Yes, we are. I'm surprised how fast the word traveled…" I knew Greg was going to call Cheryl to confirm, but how Bill found out so quickly was amazing.

"Oh, and I have something for you. Cheryl came by to drop off the costumes you'll need, but you were in session, so she left them with me." He turned and opened a cabinet where he pulled two giant boxes from the shelf. "Everything you need for the weekend mystery will be in here. Enjoy!"

"Wow, this is a lot. Okay, I will take these downstairs for now. Do you mind if I hang out in your lobby—to get out of the basement while I wait for my next client?"

"Of course not, Libby … make yourself at home."

After dropping off the boxes in the therapy room, I got excited to read through some of the customer's testimonials about the haunted hotel. I opened the first large three-ring binder. There were pages and pages of white-lined notebook paper where customers gave firsthand accounts of their experiences. Chills ran up my spine as I read some amazing stories. People had reported seeing a young boy at the foot of their bed, only to disappear once they turned the bedside lamp on. Many others claimed they felt icy cold when in the elevator—that one I understood; it was fear, not ghosts!

There were tales of customers having dinner in the

basement ballroom and experiencing various oddities: a breeze through their hair when no one else at their table felt a breeze; a tap on their shoulder only to look around and see no one; or seeing a vanishing young woman in the hallway near the bathroom. Numerous people with similar stories—how could they all be wrong?

"Oh jeez!" I jumped when Mr. Longo sat next to me. "I must have gotten so lost in these stories … I didn't notice you coming."

"Quite amazing, huh?" he pointed to the book I was still holding.

"Do you genuinely think this place is haunted?"

"Oh, I don't know. I suppose it's whatever you believe it to be … right?" he laughed.

"Well, I've got to say … these sound quite convincing."

"Thank goodness. It keeps the ghost hunters booking rooms—all good for business."

"Are you taking part in the mystery weekend, Bill?"

"Oh God, no. Uh, I mean … it's always great fun, but you know… Well, I'm here at the hotel all day most days so my time with the murder mystery games is over. Leave it to the young ones to enjoy, I say." He laughed nervously and then made excuses to get back to work. I watched curiously as the uptight, but amiable gentleman, settled again behind the front counter.

I continued for another thirty minutes, enthralled in tale after tale of ghostly sightings, before I checked my watch and realized I should get set up for the next appointment.

* * *

It was four o'clock by the time I locked the room and

was ready to climb the steps out of the basement again. The rooms off the hallway and the ballroom at the far end were dark. I walked toward the stairs wondering when Cheryl would be arriving for the start of the festivities, and then I heard an enormous clunk. I jumped and whirled around, sure someone had dropped something behind me. No one was there, so I shook it off and kept going, thinking to myself that I shouldn't have read so many of those stories earlier.

After taking two steps, I heard a clang. Chills took over my body and I ran to the top of the steps. I grabbed for the door and then screamed. Greg started laughing, "Jumpy much?"

"Oh, wow," I slugged him in the arm. "You scared me!"

"You opened the door!"

"But, there wasn't supposed to be a man standing there…" I bent over with my hands on my knees, catching my breath.

He was still laughing as he walked me out the front lobby. Several people were staring at us. Clearly, they'd heard my scream.

Once we were outside, he asked, "What were you running from?"

"How did you know I was running?"

"I could hear your footfalls as I approached the door, Libby…"

"I heard a noise … but, now I realize, it was probably only you," I grumbled.

"Sounded like you were in a big hurry!" he laughed.

"Okay, okay … I guess I'm jumpy then. I spent my lunch time reading through stories of the hotel's hauntings.

Guess it got to me." I finally started to find the humor in it and giggled. "Hey, how's Shadow?"

"You didn't get my message, I guess. I told you I hadn't been able to get hold of anyone at the groomer so I'd come meet you after your session and then we'd walk together to go pick Shadow up."

"Oh, alright. No, I haven't checked my phone. That's strange, isn't it—why wouldn't Patricia have called you? Or, answered your call? Earlier, it didn't sound like it would take her long." A tinge of worry spread over my shoulders. We picked up our pace down each hillside staircase.

All the lights were off in the shop as we peered inside from the growing evening shadows. I heard our pup whining, but couldn't see her through the window. We tried the door, it opened and we called out, "Patricia! Hello!" Shadow barked from somewhere in the back of the shop.

We walked up to the front counter and leaned over. The desk was a mess—paperwork everywhere, even on the floor.

"Hello! Patricia … we're here to get Shadow!" Greg yelled loudly.

I walked over to the end of the counter where there was a waist-high swinging door. I pushed through it and then one more at the next doorway before the backroom. As soon as I rounded the corner, my heart pounded and I felt it was difficult to breathe. Shadow was standing over Patricia—bloody paw prints were everywhere. The diminutive woman was splayed out on the floor.

"Call 9-1-1!" I yelled to Greg, who was closer than I realized; he nearly bumped into me when I abruptly stopped.

CHAPTER SIX

It was shortly after six by the time the coroner took her away. The police had finished questioning us when the door opened and several men walked in and headed directly for my dog.

"You can't take her!" I screamed.

The police officer held me back as the animal control guy attempted to get his hook around Shadow's neck.

"Is that actually necessary?" Greg asked him. "Let me put her leash on. She'll go with you—she's not vicious."

"Sir, this dog just killed a woman. We have to protect ourselves."

Greg's face turned red; he tried to reason with the police officer. "C'mon, man. This dog did *not* kill her. I'm positive that's what the autopsy will show. Please let us keep her until that's proven!"

The officer shook his head. "We have to test for rabies. She'll be taken in. *If* the coroner doesn't find evidence of dog bites as the cause of death, then you can come pick her up. Until then, she'll be quarantined."

"Noooooo!" I cried out. "She wouldn't hurt a flea! We have vaccination records. Pleeease…"

None of our pleadings worked. The animal control guy took Shadow away. As we watched her being loaded into the small crate in his truck, I saw that a large crowd had grown outside of Tricia's Scruffy Solutions.

Colleen ran up to where we stood on the sidewalk, "Libby! What on earth happened?"

I couldn't speak as I watched the truck drive away with my baby in it. How had we ended up here? She only had cactus in her legs … now she's hauled away by animal control and what, accused of *murder*? It was preposterous!

Nate joined Colleen and they both ushered us across the street and away from the crowd. When we came upon the bakery, they pulled us inside, locked the door, and pulled down the blinds.

Nate had us take a seat. Colleen rushed off to get the coffee going.

Greg's head hung in despair. "I should have known something was wrong when she hadn't answered the phone. Why didn't I go over there sooner? On the way up to the hotel…"

"You couldn't have known, hon…" I whispered.

Nate sat patiently until Colleen set coffee mugs in front of us. When she returned from the kitchen, Snow and Ball followed her quietly. They sidled up near Greg's and my feet, seemingly knowing we were sad. We all sat around the bistro table in shock. I sipped at the nice hot drink, mulling over in my mind what could have gone wrong at the groomer's.

"Why did they take your dog away?" Colleen quietly asked.

"They think she murdered Patricia," barely audible, I couldn't believe what I was saying.

"That's ridiculous!" Nate stood and paced the floor. "Utterly ridiculous!"

Greg reached out for my hand. "We will get her back. There is no way she harmed anyone—no way! They'll figure this out."

I retracted my hand from his, silently taking another sip of coffee. Eyes around the table were fixated on me. My mind spun in many directions. *What happened to Patricia? Who would want her dead?* I remembered several encounters, including with Nate. Sure, she was a crazy ol' bat, but why would someone *kill her.* We'd get Shadow back—I knew for a fact her teeth marks were not on that woman—and, if all else failed, I'd break into the animal control center and steal her back, if necessary.

"Hon," Greg eyes tried desperately to connect with mine. "Babe, we should get going. It's still early evening. Let's go talk about it—develop a game plan for tomorrow morning."

I looked around the table. Nate, with his cherub cheeks. Where was he earlier this afternoon? Colleen, what did she do after her massage? They clearly didn't like Ms. POS, but deep in my heart, I knew it was neither of them. I needed to figure out who had the motive, means, and opportunity. The faster the real killer was caught, the sooner my dog could get out of jail.

"Greg—we need to go get changed for the mystery weekend. We only have an hour till it starts." I declared.

"Wh—what? Are you serious? We're going to go play a *game* when someone has just been killed?"

"The hotel is the center of everything in this town. Think about it. We need to meet more people, learn what they know—about Patricia, about the town gossip, and all the dirty secrets. I think we could learn a lot by joining Cheryl's event. We have to find out what happened at the groomer's today and we must get Shadow freed."

Greg's eyebrows knitted. "Libs. I think right now maybe we need rest—"

I shook my head, while Colleen and Nate's faces kept following ours back and forth.

"First, Nate … Colleen, can you help think through who in the town could have done this? Maybe we can get together tomorrow after the morning breakfast crowd—" Then, I remembered I had a morning appointment. "Shoot, I have a massage around ten. But, after that, maybe we can gather and put our heads together?"

Nate was the first one to speak. "Shouldn't we leave this to the police?"

Colleen shook her head, "Oh, I want to solve a real mystery! I've done well in the past with the murder mystery game—I think I could be good at this."

Oh boy. "Okay. We're probably not actually going to solve this ourselves, since we're not the experts. However, it doesn't hurt to see what we can come up with. If we can help the police solve it faster, I'm sure they'd welcome the help. For now, put your heads together. We'll be back tomorrow. Here's my phone number…" I wrote it on a napkin. "Call me if you come up with any huge clue before we meet."

With that, Greg and I headed out the door.

"You honestly want to be *on* tonight and socialize?" Greg asked.

I stopped. "Okay, no … no, I don't *want* to be around anyone tonight." Tears started to form in my eyes and my voice croaked. "But, I can't sit still while my baby is in that cage—cold and afraid. But, if we keep doing *something*, maybe … I might get through this. And, like I said before, we might learn a lot."

He wrapped his arms around me. "I'm sorry this is happening, babe. It's not fair. However you want to handle it—I'm right here beside you."

"Okay, let's head to the hotel—the costumes are in the therapy room; we'll change in there."

* * *

Opening the boxes that Cheryl had left for us was like presents on Christmas Day. We pulled out gorgeous 1920s costumes. Apparently, I was playing a flapper girl—dressing up in beautiful beaded and feathery dresses and headwear, along with a black pixie style wig. Greg had a couple stylish tuxedos—one with coat, tails and top hat. There was even a white shirt and bow tie for Shadow. Against her black coat, it would look exactly like a tuxedo. My heart skipped. *We've got to get her out.*

I pulled out a large binder that included the entire schedule for the next four evenings—Friday through Monday. The scene was set: a 1920s speakeasy. My role was a ditzy girl who hung around the bar a lot—my name would be Margaret Davis. Greg would be one of the bartender's best friends who was also quite a player, hitting on all the girls. Nothing here let us know who would be murdered, but we had received an overall character portrait for ourselves and the basics on society's who's-who.

"Ready, handsome Mr. Brown?" I asked.

He turned away from the mirror and gave a long slow whistle as he took in the tight fitting, red sequined ballgown. When his eyes found mine, he squinted. "Libby, you look absolutely stunning tonight. However, I unquestionably like your own hair much better than the wig…" he walked around me taking in every detail, including the beaded headdress that trailed down the right side of my face. "Oh, so fancy, Ms. …" he consulted his cheat sheet, "Ms. Davis." He winked and gently took my hand and kissed it. "Shall we?"

I took the arm of my debonair tuxedo-wearing boyfriend and we headed to the end of the hall, only to find a sign which said to meet in the lobby—it looked like they closed off the basement entrance.

"I didn't realize there was another entrance," Greg stated.

Up the flight of stairs and we stepped into the lobby to find it full of characters. Cheryl was there with her clipboard, directing each person and answering questions. I looked at my watch and was impressed that we still made it five minutes early.

"Ok folks, listen up…" Cheryl's height benefitted her in this role. "Hey, folks—quiet, please!"

A hush settled over the lobby.

"I appreciate your participation tonight—everyone looks so lovely!" Her eyes dropped and her voice solemnly added, "I particularly appreciate you being here in light of the fact that there has been a tragedy in our small town."

People began looking at others around the room. I got the idea that they wondered if this was part of the act. Cheryl continued with a heavy heart, "I want everyone to know that a candle-light vigil will be held tomorrow early evening, in honor of Patricia Olivia Simpson."

There were a few gasps; obviously, not everyone had heard the news yet. She quickly continued, "I've rewritten our scenes tomorrow and we'll honor Tricia by continuing with the tradition the town is known for. She'd have wanted it that way."

I wondered how true that last part was. *Had she previously participated in this event?*

"Okay, let's get into character now!" She picked up the clipboard and tapped it with her pen. "As you know, in the 1920s, speakeasies were a place to let your inhibitions down—dancing, drinking, and women exploring fashion in a whole new light!" She began walking through the crowd, admiring the women's fashion and pointing out key elements. As she spoke, she was organizing us to follow her down a hallway. I hadn't been down this one before and wondered where we were headed. I thought we were going to the basement.

Down the hallway, she stopped at a life-sized framed portrait of a handsome man fully adorned in coat and tails, complete with a top hat and cane. He was sitting for his photo in an elegant maroon upholstered chair with his legs crossed, hands on top of one another, atop his knee. In the portrait, the handle of his cane was in his top hand and actually looked like it protruded from the frame—3-D like.

I was right. Cheryl reached out toward that handle, pushed, and a door opened inward. Everyone gasped.

Ooohs and aahhs all around. Greg and I looked at each other, impressed—we had no idea the picture was actually a door.

"Follow me—remember your code word of the evening, if you want to drink and dance!" she called out as she disappeared into the darkened hallway beyond, and leaving everyone fumbling for their cheat sheets.

"*Bluenose?*" I heard the lady behind us murmur.

Greg and I followed several behind Cheryl as we crossed through the portrait threshold and followed into the dim light. About forty feet down this hallway, we turned and began descending a stairwell. When we got to the bottom of those stairs, there was a black door. A hulk of a bouncer was standing and letting people through one at a time—and only if the code word was correct.

"Thank you. Good evening, Mr. Brown … Ms. Davis," his deep gravelly voice greeted.

Inside, the ballroom was stunning. My eyes scanned the entire scene—there were white clothed dinner tables throughout with porcelain dinnerware set for multiple courses, huge sparkling chandeliers casting light all around, and there was a large dance floor beckoning everyone to it. Louis Armstrong, Bessie Smith, and George Gershwin were sounds that filled the room. My dad would have loved this—he was a jazz afficionado.

A waitress approached. "Please, your seat is over here, Ms. Davis. Mr. Brown, we'll be right with you." The girl led me away from Greg, as I looked back questioningly. I guess we did have different parts—but I hadn't considered we couldn't have dinner together. Then I saw that another lady took him to a table across the room.

I scanned the room looking for anyone familiar. It

wasn't as though I'd met many of the townspeople, but I thought I'd recognize someone—perhaps even one of the clients I'd worked on already. Bill walked through the door as I was about to turn around. He was guided to the table close behind me. I turned to him questioningly.

"She begged," he mouthed, shrugging his shoulders.

I grinned. Ah, he couldn't say no to Cheryl.

In character, I stood and held out my hand. "Hello, I'm Margaret Davis … and you are?"

He laughed. "Owner of this fine establishment … Joseph Adler. I hope you are finding everything to your liking, Ms. Davis?"

"Indeed. Pleased to make your acquaintance." I did a small curtsy, not even understanding why I felt the need to. I got a nice hearty laugh from the hotel manager, though, before I sat back down.

He twisted in his seat and asked me, "I heard about earlier at Tricia's place … what were you doing there?"

"We'd taken Shadow in to have some stickers removed from her legs. When we went back to pick her up. Well, that's when … we found Tricia." I hesitated, then whispered, "They took Shadow from us. Something about what they found has led them to believe she killed Tricia…"

His eyes widened. "No way! Has she ever been aggressive before?"

"No! Never."

"Wow, that is shocking…"

Cheryl's voice came over the PA system. "Ladies, gentlemen … welcome to our annual Murder Mystery Weekend! Glad to see everyone made it through with their code words—good job! Again, it's so great to see many of you returning for more fun, and it appears we've got some new faces in the crowd. How many are attending for the first time?" Several hands went up while one large guy with black plastic-rimmed thick glasses stood up next to me and proclaimed, "I've done dozens of these all over the country—*No one* can beat me!"

Some people chuckled; others I saw gave him a look of irritation. Cheryl rolled right along, "Okay, then! Sir, what's your name—in character, of course—and where are you from?"

"Mr. Harold Davis; I'll be bartending for y'all later on. In real life, I'm from Odessa, TX. I've only recently mastered the Copper Queen Mystery weekend in Bisbee…"

Cheryl quickly stopped him. "Thank you, Mr. Davis … so nice to meet you. And is that your lovely wife next to you?" she teased.

Taking a sip from my water glass, I realized the room had gotten quiet and everyone was staring at me. *Did he say Davis? Oh God, he's not my acting husband, is he? Please no…*

"No ma'am. This here is my sister, Margaret Davis. We frequent this establishment often—in fact, I recently accepted the job of bartender." He looked down at me and I gave him a smirk as I set my glass down. Obviously, he'd had more time this afternoon to study the part. I felt completely out of my element.

"Welcome Ms. and Mr. Davis. Perfect. See, ladies and gentlemen, it's that easy to fall into character and roll with the punches! This year's theme, *as you may have already guessed,*" she chuckled, "is the *Sniper at the Speakeasy.* Mixed in among everyone are also professional actors who are here to keep things moving along. Tonight's first act is a three-course dinner and dancing at the speakeasy. Each night, or act, will bring immense fun and games—please relax, fall into your character, and remember, you can't trust *anyone.*

Who knows, the murderer could be sitting right next you. Alright, let the games begin!"

The wait staff began delivering salads to our tables and conversation turned lively. Other than the characters, Mr. Adler and Mr. Davis, at my table, I realized Britney from breakfast was sitting across from me. She was no longer blonde, but had a dark brown wig styled into a chignon at the base of her neck. She wore a black fringed flapper dress and had long multiple strands of pearls flowing down her front and tied together at the swell of her ample breasts, strategically no doubt, to catch the men's attention. She winked at me, obviously recognizing me from earlier. I returned a little wave; it was too loud to try and converse across the ten-person round table.

After the main course, I found myself getting impatient. I'd never attended one of these before so I wasn't sure what to expect, but everything seemed to be taking *forever* and all I truly wanted to do was go save my girl from the pound. Instead, I was trapped listening to my 'brother' rattle on and on about all the medals he'd won in these competitions. *Sheesh, get a life!*

When I had decided I'd had enough of his narcissism, I excused myself to the ladies room. On the way, I passed by Greg's table and brushed my fingernails across the back of his neck, startling him. I looked back over my shoulder and gave him a little seductive wink, continuing to the corner of the room where I'd seen the sign for the restrooms. He got up and followed me.

"Well, Ms. Davis … enjoying yourself?" he moved in, softly kissing my lips.

"Mmm. Well, that was the best part of my evening so far!"

"But?"

"I'm tired. I can't get my mind off of earlier. And my table mates aren't helping…"

"Oh, that *brother* of yours … what a…"

"Tell me about it. He's *an-noy-ing*! And, I can't shut him up. I'd like to learn more about the others at the table, but he won't stop."

Greg laughed. "I see Mr. Longo is playing along too? I thought he begged off from this weekend."

"Cheryl was convincing, I guess … Bill didn't seem pleased, but…"

The lights went out—a loud shot sounded. Several ladies screamed. We jumped, running down the short hallway, feeling our way along the wall. As we turned the corner back into the ballroom, the lights came on.

"Hurry, over here! He's been shot!" a woman's shrill voice screamed.

Several people were standing around my table. We hurried over there. Harold was pacing back and forth. A lady had moved in and was hovering over someone on the floor. As soon as we got closer, the dead man was Mr. Joseph Adler—or, Bill Longo in real life.

CHAPTER SEVEN

The sunlight beamed through the bedroom window slightly before seven the next morning. It had been a late night; we hadn't left the hotel until after midnight and then we couldn't stop talking about all of the day's events.

Greg stretched and rolled over toward me. "Honestly, we're actually getting up this early?" he groaned.

"We don't have to," I teased, with my index finger moving gently down his arm. I leaned in and gave him a kiss on the forehead. "But, I can't sleep; I've worried all night—I need to hear from the coroner's office."

"I don't think they'll call us—I think it would be the police who would contact us," he replied, still in disbelief that Shadow wasn't home safe with us.

The pain that hit my chest every time I remembered

the look on her face, being hauled into the animal control truck—it was unbearable. "I say we take it into our own hands and show up at their door bright and early this morning."

"Yes. Great thinking … otherwise, we'd wait all day."

We hopped out of bed; Greg headed for the shower and I got the coffee started. Kirby had left us a few provisions like bread, eggs, and fruit. I started to scramble eggs and warm the toaster oven. With some cut-up strawberries, it was coming together as breakfast.

Over our scrambled eggs and coffee, we laughed at the shenanigans from *Sniper at the Speakeasy* the night before.

"I guess we need to make time to read through the material before heading over there tonight?" Greg grumbled.

"Oh good, I'm not the only one who felt lost as can be!"

He shook his head. "Hey, we had a good excuse … like, getting caught up in a real-life mystery and not some acted playhouse thing!"

"Ugh, I'm not looking forward to seeing what's his name again—Howard. Talk about someone who is so full of themselves!"

Greg nearly spit his coffee out. "The look on your face when he first spoke and Cheryl identified him by your fictitious name too! Oh my God, that was the best part of the night! I knew you must have been thinking he was going to be your husband…"

Rolling my eyes, I could laugh about it now. "*That guy* … with the slicked back hair, thick glasses, and spilling over into the seats on either side of him. But, don't get me wrong, it wasn't his looks that turned me off—it was absolutely his *attitude.* 'I'm so experienced… I'm so great… I always win these things…' *Gag!*"

"Wait, I don't remember—what role is he playing?"

"Bartender. Oh, and get this—had Shadow been with us last night, she would have been *his* dog! No way … how unauthentic is that? What narcissist has a dog? Cheryl should have thought that one through."

Greg laughed. "I suppose he could be one of the professional actors, couldn't he? If so, he *is* good—he's got you all wound up."

"Wait a minute—what role do you have, *Mr. Brown?*"

He pretended to grab the collar of a tuxedo and swayed a little. "I'm a playboy—hanging at the speakeasy and picking up on hot flappers like you!"

The faux sexy impression was too much. His cheeks turned pink and he dropped the character, acting seemingly embarrassed.

"No seriously—I've gotta tell you. At my table, I met an interesting man. Real name was Chris; I can't remember the character he was playing though. He's a younger guy, and owns one of the antique shops in town. From what I gathered, he knows a lot of people and always participates in Cheryl's annual production. The interesting part though is that he wasn't too keen on Mr. Longo … *or,* Patricia." His mouth sipped from the coffee mug; his eyes held mine in suspense. "He was quite forthcoming with the gossip— apparently, Bill and Patricia were married! Some time ago, but there's bad blood between them and everyone knows it."

"Bill? He's the nicest guy…" I was shocked, but then remembered when I first saw her, she had stormed out of the hotel. *Wonder what that was about?*

"Yeah, when his character got shot in the speakeasy—Chris later said to me, 'about time Bill got his due.' I didn't know how to react so I sat back and listened to him ramble on."

"That's disturbing. I've never had anything but good feelings about Bill—he's quiet, meek, and introverted. But, he's super nice and seems like he'd do anything for his staff at the hotel. And, I haven't heard him gossip or speak ill of anyone since we've arrived." Of course, we'd barely been here twenty-four hours—definitely not long enough to truly get to know someone.

"Oh, at my table ... Britney, that cute waitress from the café ... she sat across from me. I didn't get a chance to talk to her. And, you know, once the murder occurred and we rushed back to the table, I don't recall seeing her again the rest of the evening."

"Blonde girl, right?"

"Well, last night playing her role, she had on a long dark wig—pulled into a knot at the base of her neck. What was she wearing ... Umm," I struggled to remember, but then snapped my fingers. "Tight short black dress with that fringe across the top and mid-waist ... you know, when she moved, the whole dress came to life moving along with her. She looked gorgeous."

"I don't recall seeing anyone like that ... and for what it's worth, you were the most gorgeous woman in the room last night. Hands down."

"Aww, you're sweet."

"Okay, we can talk murder mystery later—let's get to the police station and demand our Shadow back!" he said, standing up and taking his dishes to the kitchen sink. My eyes followed him admiringly, and I loved that he called

Shadow *ours*.

Before I had finished showering, Greg called out. "Police called—they want us to come down!" I was surprised we had heard from them so early, but was relieved. It had to mean they had news—I prayed it was positive about Shadow.

* * *

Greg opened the front door at the police station for me. We introduced ourselves and asked the gentleman at the front desk for Chief Smith. He knew who we were and showed us into a small office around the corner from the front lobby.

"The chief will be with you in a few minutes. Care for some coffee?" Officer Matta, according to his badge, asked. We both declined.

I stood and paced the small area, not able to sit still. Deep in thought, neither of us wasted energy on small talk. I couldn't imagine that my dog actually bit someone to their death—seemed so preposterous. So, what happened then? Who hated Patricia so much that they killed her so viciously? Or, had it been an accident? No, unless it was suicide or something—the blood came from her neck. We saw that ourselves. Would she have literally slit her throat during the middle of the work day—at her place of work? Seemed unlikely.

Before the door opened, I swore I heard claw taps on the linoleum flooring. Chief Smith opened the door, and first through was Shadow. My heart leapt. Her tail whipping around, she started wriggling and whining, her claws sliding frantically on the flooring, trying to get to me.

The chief dropped the leash and Shadow nearly bowled me over after I dropped to the floor, reaching out to her. Hot tears stung; I embraced her as tightly as I could. She didn't stop her squeals until Greg joined me on the floor and had given her lots of love also. I sat back to look— she looked okay. Her front legs were bandaged with white medical tape.

The chief noticed me inspecting. "The vet has checked her over and I guess she had some cactus in her paws and legs. She removed them and put the bandages on because there are a couple open wounds," the chief explained. "If you two would have a seat, I'd like to get a statement. You were first on scene—I know my officers interviewed you, but I'd like to get an official statement for our investigation."

We looked to one another—clearly thinking similarly: *do we need a lawyer?* We got up off the floor and selected chairs next to each other at the table. Shadow sat on my feet.

He sensed our hesitation. "Folks, you are not under suspicion—don't worry about that. And the coroner has confirmed—there were no bite marks anywhere on the victim. Now, I can't tell you much—but what I can tell you is it looks like the weapon was a sharp object. She was stabbed in the jugular. We believe your dog actually tried to help her. But, there'd be nothing anyone could have done once that artery was severed—she died within minutes," he sighed.

Greg started, "I don't know what we could tell you any different than yesterday when we found her. As you know, we took Shadow to her so she could remove the cactus bits—and when she hadn't called by the end of the work day, we got concerned. We thought she would only have her a couple hours at most. In fact, that's what she told us to plan for. When we arrived, it was dark inside. We heard Shadow bark; we called out for Patricia … heard nothing. Finally, we entered her back room because no one was answering us. That's when we found…" he cleared his throat.

I put my hand on his shoulder and squeezed. It was an awful scene we saw and I knew I was having a difficult time getting it out of my head. I hadn't realized until now Greg was having a hard time too.

"How did you meet Patricia?" the chief asked.

"We were recommended to her from…" Greg looked inquisitively at me.

"Britney—at the café…"

"Oh, right … the vet tech. She's the one who actually ultimately fixed Shadow up," the chief pointed to Shadow's bandages.

"She's a vet tech?" I asked.

"Yes, works in Cottonwood. But, also helps out at the café on occasion. A couple years back while still going to school, she also helped Patricia with grooming."

Interesting, I thought. Something about that was nagging me, but Greg and the chief continued talking about that day so I dropped the thought when Chief Smith turned to me.

"And, you're working up at the hotel," he rustled through a stack of papers, "filling in for—Kirby McDaniel, doing some ma—ssage?" he exaggerated.

I nodded.

"Where is Kirby while you're here doing her work?"

I was thrown off for a second. Was that an accusation toward my friend? "Uh, her dad's in the hospital down in Phoenix."

"I see. Do you know which hospital?"

"Honestly, I don't."

"Phone number for Kirby?"

I wrote it down on a piece of paper he stuck in front of me.

"And, what's your relationship with Bill Longo?"

"Relationship? He owns the hotel. I'm working in the hotel basement for a few days. That's it." I felt myself getting defensive—I didn't appreciate the tone he'd taken.

"Has he mentioned he's the ex-husband of Patricia Olivia Simpson?"

Why does everyone insist on using her full name? Irritating. "Um, I just learned that this morning—but, no, he didn't tell me that."

"How did you learn that information?"

I looked to Greg. He added, "We're participating in the murder mystery weekend. Last night one of the participants, Chris—don't know his last name—antique shop guy, he mentioned it to me."

"Out of the blue? In what context was he telling you about their marriage?"

I saw Greg's reaction—we both were growing increasingly uncomfortable with the line of questioning. We don't know anyone in this town well; we certainly don't want to get innocent people in trouble.

"Uh, well … as part of the *game*—the murder mystery— Bill was, well, killed." Greg swallowed hard. "Chris said— 'finally, he got his due', or something along those lines."

The chief's eyebrows lifted. "He said that?"

"It was part of the *acting*—the *game*. Bill didn't die or anything!" Agitated, Greg shifted in his chair. Calmly, he leaned forward and said, "Listen, we don't know any more than what we've already told you—twice now. Can we please take our dog and leave?"

"Of course, of course ..." the chief gave a little sigh. "Listen, I'm sorry folks. This is a small town and we're protective of our tight-knit community. Murder doesn't happen here every day like it does where you're from. We need to make sure we're covering all our bases and that we find this maniac. Be careful out there—a murderer is still on the loose." He stood and ushered us to the front door. We all shook hands and he added, "I've got your numbers, we'll be in touch if anything else comes to light. Thank you for your time."

We walked our dog out of the police station and made it about a block away before I couldn't hold it in any longer.

"You don't think we interrupted the murderer, do you? If he, or she, thinks we saw something—are we in danger now?" I couldn't catch my breath.

"He didn't say anything about *how long* she'd been dead when we found her. I suppose he wouldn't give us that level of detail."

"Wait, when was the last time you called Patricia before we headed over there?"

"As I walked to the hotel to meet you. Let's see ... that was shortly before four, I suppose."

"And you called earlier in the day also?"

"Yes, around two ... could have been two-thirty."

"Doesn't mean she had already been attacked; she probably was busy and couldn't answer the phone." It dawned on me then that I hadn't paid attention to whether I'd seen or heard other animals when we dropped off Shadow. The details were getting murkier and by that evening, once the police got there, it became chaotic. *Had she been super busy that day? Or, had we been her only client?*

We saw Snow and Ball coming up the street, being walked by Colleen. Shadow pulled on the leash and we could see Colleen was having a time keeping her two under control as well.

"Good morning!" she greeted. "That park is right this way—it's a dog park so we could let all the girls run around and play there, if you have time?"

"Sure! Sounds good … Shadow would love that," I said.

"I'm so happy to see her here this morning. Clearly not the right suspect—they came to their senses, I see."

"Thankfully," Greg added.

"C'mon, through here," Colleen opened the first gate, and we all walked through. Once that one was closed, we opened the next one and then took the leashes off all our girls. "Normally, I take them to the small dog area—right over there. But, since no one is here this morning, this should work out. We'll have to watch if more large dogs show up—don't want my little ones getting trampled." Sweet as can be—Colleen seemed jovial and considerate. The familiarity I felt was as though we'd known her for a lifetime.

Shadow didn't seem to mind the bandages on her legs—but Snow and Ball inspected them. They knew that vet smell and if I wasn't mistaken, they sympathized with Shadow. It didn't take long before our dogs ran around in circles, thoroughly enjoying themselves. The three of us sat down on a park bench and watched.

"Did you get her back last night?" Colleen asked.

We filled her in on the whole story—as well as our evening being cast in Cheryl's murder mystery. Greg broached the subject of the hotel manager being married to Patricia. Colleen appeared surprised we had that information. She was hesitant to gossip, though, so all we got out of her were pleasantries. I understood she didn't necessarily *like* Patricia, but she didn't speak ill of the dead.

"We were thankful when they split—Bill is too nice of a man. So, when we heard he started seeing Cheryl—well, we've been secretly cheering them on. He's such a lovely man and Cheryl, although highly motivated and driven business-wise, does seem perfect for him."

I nearly choked on my own saliva. Coughing, I tried to ask, "Cheryl … and, *Bill?*" I looked over at Greg who appeared as surprised as I was.

"Oh, yes. I believe they still think they've kept it underground, but, no. In a town this size, everyone's talking about them. So, in public, you'd never see them all chummy—strictly business, and that's it."

"Because of Patricia?" Greg asked.

Colleen twisted her nose and mouth. "Welllll, let's just say … Patricia has thrown a couple temper tantrums over the years—I'm sure she knew about their little thing. Perhaps they all came to an understanding. It's possible."

Snow let out a little squeal. When we all looked over to them, we saw she was on her back with all four paws in the air. Shadow was about a foot away, so I was relieved she wasn't the cause of the squeal. Colleen saw my concern.

"Oh, no … she does that for attention. She's teasing Shadow!"

We watched the funny antics for a few minutes; laughing. It felt good to laugh after such seriousness over at the police station earlier.

"Do you happen to know Chris? Owns the antique shop…" Greg wanted to know.

"Oh, yes! Lovely guy … and you should check out his shop—gorgeous stuff in there. I've picked up a few pieces myself."

"He doesn't seem to like Bill that much—I couldn't figure out why."

"You'd have to ask him." She changed subjects and turned to me. "Do you think it'd be possible to get another massage while you're here? I loved what you did yesterday—I mean, I adore Kirby and all, too; don't get me wrong. But, the way you worked out the kinks in my neck…" she rolled her neck to demonstrate.

"I'll check the schedule, but sure, if there's time, I'd be happy to." I checked my watch, then stood. "Speaking of which, we need to go. I've gotta get to work!"

We pried Shadow away from the cute white fluffballs. As we left, Colleen moved them over to the small dog area. Shadow whined and kept pulling me in their direction. "No. C'mon, Shadow—time to get some food for you. We'll play again another time." We waved to Colleen and headed down the street, back to the cottage.

As we rounded the corner to Holly St., Shadow abruptly stopped—a low growl rumbled from her throat. A blue sedan held her attention; it was parked across the street from Kirby's place.

"C'mon, girl … let's get home."

Greg eyed the car suspiciously as we passed and made our way up the walkway to the front door. Slowly, the car pulled away from the curb and left.

"Did you see who it was?"

"Tint was too dark—couldn't tell."

Shadow stood vigil at the door for a minute after we let her off the leash. Greg went to the front window and continued looking.

"They're driving back the other way now—slowly. Wait, looks like the car has stopped." Shadow ran to the window and then began barking ferociously. Paws on the window sill, her voice was deadly serious. "Oh, now they're pulling away again." Greg let the sheers fall back into place.

From the kitchen, I could see the car as it drove in front of the cottage. Greg was right—those were dark tinted windows. "What kind of car was that?"

He hesitated a moment, "Genesis—I believe. New model. Couldn't quite see the plates though; too far away."

"Should we call the police?"

"Why? It's a public street—anyone can drive on it. Plus, they could be lost looking for someone's house."

"Then why was Shadow so upset?" He couldn't answer. It wasn't like Shadow to bark at every car that passed. And, it certainly wasn't normal for her to stop during a walk and bark at a vehicle.

"I'm heading to the shower…" I called out halfway to the bedroom.

CHAPTER EIGHT

My walk to work was uneventful, but Greg had insisted on escorting me after feeling like someone had been watching our residence earlier. Shadow, Greg, and I took the short cut, up the stairs alongside businesses, which got us up the hillside quickest. We passed by Monica walking her German Shepherd mix, Rex. We waved from across the street and I made a mental note that I'd like to go back to the brewery—maybe this afternoon before we got all caught up in the mystery again.

They followed me inside; Greg wanted to grab his costume for tonight and his binder with all the details about Mr. Charles Brown, the playboy. I chuckled with the imagery of that. Greg was a handsome forest ranger, but a playboy? Nah.

In the massage room, Greg packed his box and shut the lid. "I didn't see Bill at the front desk when we walked in, but I'll ask for him as I go out. Ugh, maybe I should have brought the car?" He questioned as he hefted the box to his shoulders.

"Be careful," I said, watching him leave the therapy room. Only then did it occur to me, *I didn't get a chance to ask why he wanted to meet with Mr. Longo.*

My client arrived on time. It was Britney.

After she changed and we started our session, I tested whether this client would be a talker or perhaps she'd want quiet time. I never know which type I'll get.

"Enjoying the mystery?" I asked.

"Oh, yes. Every year—it's so much fun. Just wait until we can start exploring the hotel next!"

"You do this each year? Wow."

"I think if I didn't love animals so much and hadn't pursued veterinary work, I would have moved to Hollywood to become an actress. I find such joy in role play."

"Hey, speaking of animals … I hear you used to work for Patricia Simpson. Is that true?"

She tensed. "It helped put me through college. The day I left that place wasn't a day too soon."

"Really? Why?"

"Tricia is not a nice boss."

"Why did you recommend us to go to her then?"

There was silence for a full minute.

"Well, just because she wasn't a good person to work for doesn't mean she's that way with the animals. I guess."

"Wait, had you started to question her ability with the dogs?"

She squirmed. "Uh. I saw a few things that rattled my nerves, but seriously, she was still the best one to help remove the cactus from your dog's leg."

"What had you seen?"

"You know, I honestly don't want to speak ill of the dead. I'm sure she was having *one of those days* … as we all do; it was probably nothing at all."

Over the next hour, she told me about working in the Verde Valley—mostly she liked it, but she had considered moving back to the city as well. She spent her late high school days caring for her mother, who sadly passed away from cancer. She briefly mentioned a boyfriend who was older than her, but she didn't elaborate on who it was or what he did for a living.

After that appointment, I had one more, then my afternoon was free. I texted Greg and asked if he'd like to meet at the brewery for a late lunch and he agreed.

As soon as I sat at the bar, I scanned the beer list, looking for the one Greg chose yesterday. With no more appointments, I decided that's exactly what I wanted.

Monica set a napkin in front of me, smiling, "What can I get for you, Libby?"

"Pint of Snake Venom, please."

"Will that hunky boyfriend be joining you?" She teased.

"He will. Should be here any moment." She set down another cocktail napkin and turned to pour my beer.

"Menus?" she asked as she set my glass down.

"Oh yes—famished." She set two menus down and then turned to help another customer several stools away.

The restaurant was full—tables of chattering customers and most of the bar stools taken too. A voice behind me caught my attention. I turned to look and saw Cheryl sitting with another lady and two men, none of whom I recognized. She was a busy lady.

Across the room, I saw the chief and a couple of deputies finishing their lunch. At the bar, there were two guys chatting it up over beers, and that's when I noticed my fictitious brother on the other side of them. He raised a couple fingers from his hand resting on the bar as a hello when we made eye contact. Thank goodness, he made no move to get up.

Greg startled me as he touched my back and leaned in for a kiss.

"Finally, what was the hold up?"

"Oh, I ran into Nate on the way over. For such a quiet guy, he's sure a talker with me." He pulled out his chair and bellied up to the bar, raised a finger to Monica, pointing out he'd like what I was having.

"Was he walking those two precious ones?"

"No, he was outside the bakery, clearing a couple of their sidewalk tables. I assumed he was closing up for the day." He looked at his watch, "I think they close at two. Anyway, it sounded as though they were quite upset about Tricia's death."

"I would imagine. It's a small town and all." I felt compassion for others even though our interactions with this lady were never exactly good.

"Well, that's just it. I didn't get the sense that he was necessarily upset over her death so much as…"

Monica interrupted and asked what we'd like for lunch. We both chose burgers. I turned back to Greg and reminded him where he was in his story.

"Apparently, they were in the middle of a lawsuit with Tricia."

My eyes widened. "What was she suing them for?"

"You mean, what were *they* suing *her* for…"

"Really? The bakery owners?"

"According to Nate, Tricia doesn't have a great reputation in town. Probably why there were no other dogs at the shop when we took Shadow in. She had lost a lot of clients—they preferred to make the drive to Cottonwood rather than to deal with her anymore."

My eyebrows lifted as I took a sip of my beer. Again, I thought, *why would Britney recommend her to us if this was true?*

"Nate said that she injured Snow during a grooming session. It wasn't an isolated incident either—they were willing to overlook a questionable encounter another time with Ball, but when Snow ended up at the veterinarian for signs of possible strangulation, that was it for them. Using the veterinarian's report, they hired a lawyer and sued her for negligence that could have led to the death of their dog."

Completely stunned, "I can't believe they didn't tell us this that night of the murder. You know, when we sat in their bakery—they were consoling us over Shadow."

"I might be wrong, but I think they're nervous that the police are going to see their lawsuit as motive. They're probably trying to lay low. Not sure why then he felt the need to tell me about this—maybe because he sees me as someone who isn't a local?"

Our food arrived and each of us were alone in our thoughts as we devoured the scrumptious hot cheeseburgers. I heard Cheryl's laughter, and the man at her table said something along the lines of, "We'll make more out of that property than she ever could!" All the occupants lifted their glasses to cheer the man.

I took the final sip of the beer in my glass and signaled to Monica for another one. When she set it down in front of me, I asked her, "How's Rex? Enjoy his walk earlier?"

"Oh, he loves our daily jaunt, that's for sure. We'll have to get our kids together…maybe tomorrow? I'm sure they'd enjoy each—been to the dog park yet?"

"Yes, we have. It's a nice one. Colleen introduced us and Shadow played with their little fur babies."

Her face sobered, "How are their little ones?"

Since Greg had already related this story to me, I played along as though I knew nothing. I looked at her confused, "They're playful—so cute. Why? It seems like there's more…"

"Oh, Snow wasn't doing so well for a while. I don't know all the ins and outs, but heard through the grapevine that she was injured …"

"At Scruffy's?" She nodded her head, wiping up the counter top.

"Have you taken Rex to her?"

She hesitated, "He doesn't require all the grooming as those Maltese would. I bathe him myself."

"She seemed friendly enough to us." A little white lie, but maybe it'd get her to open up.

She sighed loudly, shaking her head. "When you live in a town this small, you learn quickly who the problem ones are. She was a handful for a lot of people around here."

And there it was—the police had their hands plenty full of potential suspects, right here in the small town.

Monica got back to her job and Greg and I finished our beers, then paid our bill. Turning around and hopping down from our barstools, we noticed Cheryl was staring right at us. She curled an index finger, motioning for us to come to her table.

"Well, howdy guys—how are you enjoying the event so far?" she purred using her perfect tourism and hospitality voice.

"It was loads of fun last night…" Greg answered.

Cheryl looked to her tablemates, "I'd like to introduce you to some friends of mine—you might have seen them last night, they're all participants too!" She went around the table and made her introductions. I hadn't recognized any of them, but I paid attention when she came to the man that I thought I'd overheard earlier. He was an older gentleman, thinning hair, and wire-rimmed glasses— looked similar in stature to Bill Longo, but was much more extroverted with a booming voice and large presence. She said Doug Lister worked for the area's Chamber of Commerce. We exchanged pleasantries and then Doug mentioned, "I heard you were the ones who found that … er, found Patricia?"

We looked to one another and then I answered, "Yes, unfortunately. God rest her soul." His expression confused me.

He smiled widely. "Well, the town will never be the same, that's for sure." He picked up his water glass and took a long drink before setting it back on the table.

Cheryl stood and put an arm around each of us, as if we'd been lifelong friends. Perhaps that was the act she was putting on for her colleagues. With her cheery voice, she said, "We'll see you two tonight—don't be late!" as she steered us toward and out of the door.

Greg scoffed, "Wow, is it me, or are the townsfolk not all that sad over Tricia's death?"

I disappointedly shook my head. "And I thought small towns banding together in a time of need was commendable, something I'd like. Now, it seems as though that can work against you as well."

CHAPTER NINE

We arrived fifteen minutes early that night, all dolled up—Greg in his tuxedo, me in a short green fringed and sequined dress, and Shadow in her tuxedo-looking shirt. She was so cute, I kept doing a double-take as we walked the sidewalk to the hotel's front doors. The white bandages against her solid black front legs looked like little boots that matched perfectly with her shirt and bow tie.

Everyone met in the lobby again, dressed to perfection and in good spirits. Who knew a real murder had occurred? The festive atmosphere was in full-swing. There were small clusters of participants gathered whispering—no doubt testing their theories about Mr. Adler's death. I glanced around behind the hotel lobby's front desk and only saw a young woman working. I supposed it wouldn't work out so well for us sleuths to see Bill Longo behind the desk after his character died last night. However, I hadn't seen him all day and that was odd. He was always at the hotel.

"Ladies and gentlemen—" Cheryl's voice called out. "So good to see everyone back! It's time to solve this mystery. Mr. Joseph Adler, 1920s wealthy businessman and well-known about town, was shot during a gala dinner last night in his own speakeasy. For his friends attending, it was no secret that he ran an underground gambling operation and broke prohibition laws regularly. In fact, we learned that he was distributing alcohol to several other local businesses."

Theatrically, she held her hand to her open mouth and gasped. Rolling her eyes first and then pointedly fixing them on each one in the audience, she continued, "What other illegal activities was he conducting? Who else knew about it? *Who* wanted him *dead?*" She looked around the room, obviously satisfied that she held all our attention. "Well, let's go find out! We'll gather first in the ballroom for some light hors d'oeuvres and cocktails. That's an excellent opportunity to network—there are a lot of questions to be asked. Once you've obtained the clues you need, feel free to roam the entire hotel looking for more—they are everywhere! Well, I will warn that hotel guests are only staying on the third floor this weekend, so please … no disturbing anyone on that floor; the elevator is already set to bypass it. I wish you all luck, and may the best sleuth win!" She started walking down the hallway toward the portrait and we all followed.

The ballroom was transformed tonight into a gambling hall, with the same bar setup, and a dance floor. All the great big band hits were playing. Many of the participants headed straight to the dance floor. Others picked a poker table, and several went over to the craps table. Greg, Shadow, and I headed to the bar where we saw my fictitious brother, Mr. Harold Davis, tending bar. The large Texan smiled broadly as we walked up.

"Well, lookie there—you brought my dog tonight!"

We both smiled as we took a couple bar stools. I asked Shadow to sit beneath mine. I was nervous about having her, even though Cheryl insisted, and so far it didn't appear anyone minded a dog around. I didn't trust *Harold* as far as I could throw him, so I'd already made up my mind that I wouldn't leave Shadow alone with him.

From our mystery bible binder earlier, we learned our roles entailed hanging out at the bar most of the evening. Greg, or rather, *Charles Brown*, was required to flirt with all the women and I'd be back and forth dancing with the guys. *Not exactly the weekend away with my boyfriend that I'd planned, but here we are.* We'd make the best of it and so far, it seemed like a great bunch of people.

Within no time, a lovely young man, clean shaven and hair slicked back, walked up to me. "Ma'am, may I have this dance?" he said shyly.

I automatically looked to Greg for permission, before realizing that this was my role, after all. I simply gave him a quick signal to watch Shadow and then took the young man's hand, following him to the dance floor.

The song was a quick tempo and I was quite surprised how well the young man moved. Me, however, well I'm not a dancer, so it took me several minutes to get my feet under control. Thank goodness Edward Blakely, as he had introduced himself, was a great leader.

"You're a great dancer," I commented. "Sorry about

your feet—I'll try to be better."

"You're doing great, don't worry."

"So, are you from Jerome?"

"Moved here a year or so ago, from the Midwest." Then he turned to whisper in my ear, "But, I think we're supposed to stay in character."

"Oh, okay … yeah, you're right. Then, *Mr. Blakely*, how long you been coming to Mr. Adler's establishment?" I wasn't sure what type of accent that was, but whatever it was came out as a high pitched, sappy, woman's voice.

"I moved to the region recently; have my own *establishment* about thirty miles down the road—Mr. Adler and I were supposed to meet this weekend to discuss some business."

"Oh, the competition?"

"Well, I'd like to look at it as a lucrative business deal." He winked and then spun me around right on cue.

"May I ask what kind of *deal*?"

"Oh, little lady … you don't need to concern yourself with such things." He spun me for the final time as the song ended. I decided the 1920s were not for me—*little lady?*

"Thank you kindly for the dance, Mr. Blakely."

I turned and walked back to the bar, where I found Greg in full playboy mode talking with Britney—or, for tonight, Mary Moore. She looked stunning in a dark red long beaded gown with spaghetti straps that hung over her slender shoulders. She winked at me as I approached the bar and ordered myself a gin and tonic. I gave a quick smile, but otherwise ignored them while I sipped my drink.

I leaned into the bar, asking Harold, "Hey, do you know that guy I was dancing with?"

The big lug's eyes squinted at me. "You mean in real life?"

"No! Do you know *Mr. Blakely*?" I asked impatiently.

"Oh. Right." He cleared his throat and then leaning on his right arm, getting closer to me, he spoke softly, "Mr. Blakely … he had a meeting scheduled with Mr. Adler last night. Never happened—since, well, he was *murdered*." I nearly broke out laughing with his dramatic emphasis. He was ridiculous.

"Do you happen to know what the meeting was about? I know you were Mr. Adler's right-hand man. Surely, he confided in you."

"Well, little lady…"

Both of my hands slapped down on the bar and startled him, as well as Greg, Britney, and Shadow.

With my jaw clenched, I hissed, *"Don't call me little lady!"*

"Okay, okay. Jeez!" He nervously wiped down the counter.

Greg smiled at me and turned back to talking with the flapper. Shadow sat staring at me to be sure I was okay.

"So … what was the meeting about between Mr. Adler and Mr. Blakely?"

He leaned in again. "Mr. Adler learned that Blakely was running an underground operation in competition with him. He wanted to discuss some *boundaries*, if you know what I mean." He cleared his throat. "Word is that the Chicago mob bosses weren't happy when they learned about the competition—could harm their business, you know."

"Mr. Adler was in with the *mob*?"

He gave me the *little lady* look for a half a second before changing his mind. "Of course, he was! How do you think he's getting the alcohol? Or any of this—look around," his hands swept out toward the gambling tables. "All this takes money, Ms. Davis," he winked and then moved over to take someone's drink order.

Well, this was new information that I hadn't read in our instructions. I was beginning to see how detailed Cheryl was in organizing this game. Every participant must have specific details no one else had and that's why her instruction to network was so important. *Alright, then I've got to get away from the bar and mingle.*

Before Greg and Britney ventured out to the dance floor, Greg had the four of us pose for a selfie. I finished my gin and tonic, told Shadow to stay when Harold agreed to watch her. As much as I hesitated, I left her with my Texan brother and headed over to the gambling tables.

I hung out behind the five who were seated at the poker table. There were four men and one courageous older woman. I didn't recognize anyone at the table, everyone was a stranger to me. Two of them could be playing mobsters—one had a handlebar mustache that made him look more high society though, so maybe I was wrong about that. I found myself staring at the older woman, wondering if perhaps there were makeup and costume effects at play. She looked up and smiled kindly at me.

"You gonna stand there, or you want to be dealt in?" one of the mobster-looking men asked me. The dealer pointed to an open seat, inviting me to join them.

"Oh. Uh, I'm lousy at poker," I tried as an excuse.

"It's a friendly game … no harm getting some practice," the handlebar mustache man said.

It would be a good way to converse with the five of them, I could learn a lot. "Well, if you're sure…"

"C'mon little lady, sit right here." The man wore a fedora, kept his face downward and spoke with a southern drawl. He got my best scowl as I took the seat, even though he never looked up to see it. The lady at the table chuckled.

"Five card stud ..." the dealer said. He handed me some chips to play with and dealt the cards.

"I'm Mrs. Brandish—and you are?" the nice lady asked.

"Oh, I'm Lib ... uh, I mean, *I'm Ms. Margaret Davis.*"

Everyone around the table took a minute to introduce themselves.

"Nice to meet you all. Thanks for letting me join in."

The gentleman next to me asked, "Where were you last night when Mr. Adler died?"

"Wow, okay ... let's get right to it then," I said surprised. "Why, I was in the washroom when I heard the gunshot. And, where were you?" I shot back, giving him the side-eye.

"Mrs. Brandish and I were on the dance floor," he winked across the table at his partner.

"Are you two married then?"

She gave a nod and added, "Twenty-five years now."

I looked to the dealer, "Were you here last night for the gala dinner?"

He shook his head no. All the others at the table looked at me like it was a crazy question; I figured it didn't hurt to ask. I had read where every person in the room, whether wait staff, dealers, or whatever role, were participants and potential suspects. I wondered if these players overlooked that bit.

Fedora man, who concentrated only on his cards, was my next target. I pushed a chip out to the center and when my turn, played my card before asking him what he was doing during the murder.

He slowly looked up, and that's when I saw he had an eye patch over his right eye. His hat's small brim was positioned to shade that side of his face so I hadn't seen it previously. In a gravelly, but quiet voice he stated, "I was at the bar—like me a good whiskey before dinner."

There was something about him that was terrifying. Was it the eye patch? Regardless, I took the chance and asked another question. "How'd you know Mr. Adler?"

"Who says I did?"

"Well, I figured we all knew him or we wouldn't be invited to his gala, right?"

"How'd you know him?"

Ah, busted. I hadn't remembered from the character notes if I had actually known the man. *Why exactly was I invited to his party?* Deciding to ad lib and play along, "Guess I was invited as one of the town's flappers who were sure to keep the party lively, dancing!" I laughed.

No one else joined in the laughter, even the nice lady. They all stared at me as though I was their new suspect, but I couldn't understand why. I grabbed one of the passing waiters and ordered a gin and tonic. The tension was too much at this table. *Wasn't this a game?*

Mrs. Brandish won that round. As soon as she scooped up her chips, she and Mr. Brandish got up and walked over to the craps table. Fedora man, again with his gaze facing the table, sighed. Slowly, his eyes found mine.

"Mr. Adler and I, we're in business together."

"What type of business—gambling or booze?"

"Hotel business."

"Ahhh. Nothing illegal going on here."

"You need to mind your own business, little lady."

This time I decided not to press it. The man scared me. Either this murder mystery weekend is taken *way too seriously* by some, or he is actually a terrifying man. Well played, I decided, as I chose not to stick around to find out which. Thankfully, my drink arrived as I stood and plucked it from the tray.

I turned back to the table, "Thank you again for letting me play." I left him staring at a new hand of cards, ready to take on the other two men still sitting there. No one said goodbye as I walked back to the bar.

Shadow was sitting where I'd left her; Harold was still pouring drinks. She was the center of attention as patrons came to order, and she loved every moment of it. When I strolled up, she stood and started wagging. I looked around for Greg and saw that he was now dancing with three ladies and Britney was nowhere in sight. I leaned onto the bar.

"You win anything over yonder?" Harold asked me, pointing his chin toward the poker table. I shook my head no. "I'm surprised they invited you to sit with them at all. They're a rough crowd over there."

"The guy in the hat—have you met him yet?"

"Oh, the one who lost his eye in the barroom brawl? Yeah, he's a nasty little cuss."

I leaned in and whispered, "Is that true? Or, part of the game..."

"Oh, c'mon! All this is part of the mystery weekend, Libby! Play along..."

"Sorry. Okay. It's just that he is legitimately *scary*."

"He's good, huh?" he laughed.

"I'm going to take Shadow outside—I'm sure she could use a break. Let Greg ... er, I mean Mr. Brown know I'll be right back."

"Will do."

We walked to the far end of the ballroom, where there was a door that exited to the lower hillside parking lot. I opened the door and as we stepped into the cool breeze, it reminded me how late it'd gotten. I checked my watch, it was already eleven thirty. Shadow startled and began barking at something at the far end of the building. Foolishly, I hadn't brought her leash, thinking we'd sneak outside quickly and go right back in. Her tail tucked and the hackles on her back stood on end.

"What is it, Shadow?" I squinted to see that far, as I knelt by her side, holding around her neck to keep her close to me. I faintly saw someone there—looked like a child. I glanced all around, no one else was nearby. Where was this child's parents?

"Shadow, heel," I commanded and we slowly walked down the sidewalk that ran along the hotel. "Good girl, heel."

"Hello! Are your parents inside?" I called out to what appeared to be a little boy. He had older style clothing on. *Was he part of the production?* "It's pretty cold out here— maybe we should go in and find your parents?" He stood staring in our direction, but didn't make any movement or answer my questions. Shadow barked at him.

"Shh, good girl. Stay close." I had my fingers tickling the top of her head, reminding her she's with me. We were now no farther than twenty feet away and, all of a sudden, the boy vanished.

Shadow ran.

CHAPTER TEN

That's just great. I slipped off my high heels and started running barefoot after Shadow. When I rounded the back of the hotel, it was pitch black and I saw no sign of Shadow or the small boy.

"Shadow!" I heard something moving behind a large dumpster. "Get over here!" Thankfully, it was her and she came right to me. "What are you doing running off like that? Let's get back inside."

As I reached to open the door, two men walked out, pulling cigarettes from their breast pockets and lighting them. I recognized one of them. Shadow began sniffing them.

"Chris, isn't it?" I broached. "From the antique shop…"

He turned to me. "Yes, have we met?"

"You met my boyfriend earlier—Greg. My name is Libby Madsen. You may know Kirby McDaniel? I'm filling in for her for several days."

"Oh yeah, of course … this dog was with him too. Good boy," he said patting Shadow's head. I decided to ignore the incorrect gender when he noticed my costume. "You've also joined the infamous murder weekend too—that's brave," he chuckled.

"Yes, not quite sure how I got wrapped up in this … but well, here I am." I started to put my heels back on my cold feet. "Have you figured out who the killer is yet?"

"Nah. We only come for the camaraderie."

"I had no idea Bill Longo was going to play the victim … have you seen him since last night?" I was curious; I assumed he was staying out of sight because of the game. Then again, I found it unlike him to be absent from the hotel business. And, I knew directly from him that he didn't want to join as a participant. Was he an unwilling victim?

Chris took a long drag on his cigarette. "Nah. Can't say I have." The smoke enveloped his face as the words left his lips.

The other guy hadn't been introduced and had moved away from us, leaning against the building. I was about to introduce myself when Chris abruptly ended our conversation.

"Well, gotta get our cig break in before Cheryl finds us…" He walked over to his friend. Shadow and I watched as they walked off into the front parking lot, directly toward the Halloween graveyard headstones.

"Okay, girl. Let's get back inside." When I opened the door, she barrelled on through and skirted the crowd, right back to her place at the bar.

Harold noticed how long we'd been gone. "That was some potty break!"

"Hey, we saw a young boy out there. It's cold—what if it's one of the participant's kids? I sure hope not—but... Should we have Cheryl make an announcement?"

"Was he wearing brown knickers and a tweed beret?"

I nodded.

"Ah, that's the resident ghost!"

"No, c'mon ... it was a real boy!"

"That's what everyone thinks, but the boy has been around this hotel since the thirties or forties. I read all about it before coming here. Legend has it that he and his mother died here and he roams the property looking for her to this day. You know this was a hospital—built back in the mining days in 1926. Shoot, he may have thought you were his mom ... in that get up and all."

I looked down at my dress, then back up at him. "You don't truly believe in ghosts, do you?"

"Well, I've been in my share of haunted hotels over the years ... and, yes, I have seen some unexplainable things. You know, there's a lot of history about the old hospital found in books there in the lobby," he pointed his finger up to the floor above us. "You'll find stories about this boy."

I remembered reading numerous accounts of hotel guests' experiences, but couldn't recall reading about the history of the former hospital. "Thanks. I think I will do some research while I'm here." I twisted around gazing at the dance floor; *where was Greg?*

I saw a lively bunch dancing, but Greg wasn't one of them. That's when I found him over at the craps table. Mrs.

Brandish had found someone to talk to apparently—they were deep in conversation.

"You okay with Shadow hanging here again?" I asked Harold.

"Of course, no problem."

I hoped to convince Greg that it was time to leave. I wasn't quite sure what to expect—if Cheryl would be calling a close to the night or not. I searched the room and didn't see her anywhere and quite honestly, I was exhausted after so much had happened in the past twenty-four hours. I was more concerned about figuring out who the real-life murderer was than this fictitious stuff anyway.

Before I reached the craps table, I was intercepted by Britney. "Oh, Libby! Thank goodness I found you!" she was breathless.

"What is it? What's wrong?" My hand found her shoulder. She was shaking.

"It's Bill. He's been arrested for Patricia's murder!"

My jaw dropped. Bill Longo? There was no way the man was capable of murder. "Is that where Cheryl went, too?"

She nodded slowly. "On her way out, she told me to find you—Bill was asking for you."

I couldn't imagine why, but I raced over to Greg and told him we needed to leave. He actually looked relieved when I pulled him away.

When we retrieved Shadow, Harold was quite animated, "Hey, Britney was looking for you guys. Something about Bill being arrested," he quickly related.

I nodded, "Yes, that's where we're headed now."

He seemed legitimately concerned about the hotel manager. I don't know, I think my mystery brother was beginning to grow on me. I quickly gave him a hug. Even in his narcissistic ways, perhaps I was seeing a new side to him—who knew, maybe he'd been character acting all along.

On Main St., as we walked past Scruffy's dog grooming, we both saw a light on inside.

"Think the police have security in there?" Greg asked. "There's still yellow tape up."

I shrugged. "I suppose there could be some automatic nightlight. Or, maybe, someone mistakenly left a light on. Who knows." We continued walking slowly away, however, through my periphery I saw a shadow; there was movement inside the window. I halted again. The light went out.

CHAPTER ELEVEN

We quickly continued to the cottage, left Shadow to sleep, and we got into Greg's Tundra to head over to the police station. Once again passing by the shop, we noticed it was completely dark.

"Must have been security," Greg reasoned.

Once we got to the police station and tried the front door, we realized there was no way to see Bill tonight. Or, was it already morning? I looked at my watch—it was one o'clock. We drove back to the cottage and I was officially on my last legs.

"I can't imagine that nice, quiet guy being a murderer," Greg said, shaking his head.

"And, why would he want to see me? We hardly knew each other—I mean, we only met two days ago." I realized how it sounded. "Of course, I'm concerned about him and no, I also do not think he's capable of killing. But, why has he asked for me in jail?"

"Well, it's been a long day. Let's try to get some sleep and maybe things will become clearer later this morning."

* * *

I slept fitfully. Dreams of people swing dancing and small apparitions breezing by. In the pre-dawn light, I laid there listening to Greg snore, my mind full of last night's casino activities. Mr. and Mrs. Brandish seemed nice enough; the other two thugs at the table not so much. Were they suspects? But what exactly made me think that? Because I was tired of being called little lady by older men? Because the one guy wore an eye patch? Hardly damning evidence.

That brought me to the fact that Bill Longo had been arrested for Patricia Olivia Simpson's death. My stomach lurched. Something was wrong; he couldn't be the killer. But, after learning that the couple had a contentious divorce—perhaps? No, but, *really*? He seemed so non-confrontational. I couldn't even imagine him yelling at someone, much less viciously murdering them. No, something was nagging me. He had to have been set up. I mean, isn't it obvious that they'd go after a former spouse? Wait, had she remarried after her divorce to Bill—I'm fairly sure we'd heard she'd been married prior to him. He probably wasn't the only ex who could have done it, right? I'd have to ask around. It seemed like there were plenty of people in town that she had rubbed the wrong way—had they even checked into any of those grievances?

I couldn't lay in bed any longer. Coffee would help. I

got up, let Shadow out of her crate, and started the coffee maker. Not long after I'd taken Shadow out and the warm aroma of coffee filled the house, Greg emerged from the bedroom. His muscular chest was bare; he wore flannel pajama pants that hung low on his hips. My heart skipped watching him as he stretched, yawned, and then rubbed the night's sleep from his eyes.

"Why are we up so early? Do you have an early appointment?" he asked, yawning once again.

"No. Couldn't sleep. Sorry to wake you though," I snuck in for a hug and kiss. His large arms embraced me, making me wonder why I had crawled out of bed.

"No, no. Coffee smells good. I'm up." He did another tall stretch and then moved for the cabinets to find a coffee mug. "You're worried about Bill, huh?"

I nodded my head. "I'm completely astounded that he's been charged with murder. It doesn't make sense to me."

"Do we honestly know the guy, though?"

"Yeah, I know what you mean. But…"

"I agree, it seems out of left field. But, what has JJ told us in the past … a *huge* percentage of homicides are at the hands of loved ones, or at least former loved ones. Spouses and exes are the first people they look at."

JJ was our dear friend and detective, and I had remembered him saying all that.

"I wonder if there are other exes of Tricia's though? Is Bill the only one?"

"And, she certainly had her fair share of people in the community whom she had run-ins with. Shoot, in the last two days, we've learned about Nate and Colleen's grooming complaint… sounds like Britney is a disgruntled former employee, and it seems like there were others, right?"

"Hadn't Monica—over at the bar—told us something as well?" I added.

"There has hardly been time for an investigation—has it even been thirty hours yet? Had they even interviewed those in the community? Seems to me they jumped right to Bill being a suspect—but, we have to consider, maybe the evidence was pretty conclusive?"

"No, they jumped to the conclusion that *Shadow* had done it initially. Remember? Talk about poor forensics on the scene! Seriously, they couldn't tell a stab wound from a dog bite?" My blood started to boil again, thinking about them taking Shadow from the scene. "What was that about? Honestly!"

He wrapped me in a giant hug again. It was decided we should get to the police station as early as we could.

* * *

When we walked into the lobby of the station, the lady at the desk looked up over the rim of the glasses hanging near the tip of her nose. "Can I help you?"

"Yes, we're here to see Bill Longo."

"Sorry, visitor's hours haven't started." Dismissing us, she went back to the paperwork in front of her.

Greg stepped closer to the counter, "Is Chief Smith in yet? We have some information for him."

She looked up again, annoyed. Sighing, she pushed her chair back. "I'll have to go see…" We heard her footfalls exit through a door behind her. *Was she honestly stomping away from us?*

We paced around the small lobby area while we waited. There was a coffee station set up along with three chairs for visitors. We'd been offered coffee here before and I wondered if it was any good. I decided to take my chances. I took a tiny sip to test how much doctoring it would take to make it drinkable. Greg laughed as he saw my recoil.

"That good?" He decided to pass as I poured a couple teaspoons of sugar and a few creamers into the small Styrofoam cup.

The chief entered the room from the hallway. "Good morning, folks! What can I do for you?"

"We were here to see Bill Longo, but understand that visiting hours haven't started yet," I mentioned.

Greg continued, "But, before we left, we thought you should know that last night—er, well, early this morning, we saw a light on in Tricia's grooming salon. We found that suspicious, but figured it must be security that your department arranged."

Chief Smith appeared to know nothing of the sort. "Hold on." He turned to Ms. Friendly at the front desk who had returned to the paperwork she hadn't wanted to be distracted from. "Sherri, please get Officer Tan for me." Of course, with the chief asking, she jumped right to action, calling the officer.

The youthful Asian officer rounded the corner and approached the chief, "Yes, sir?"

"Do you know anything about a security detail at the murder scene?"

"No, sir. We locked and secured the place. It's marked with crime scene tape."

The chief looked back to us. "Is it possible the light was actually a reflection from one of the street lamps or something." I shook my head. "No. I also saw the shadow of someone moving around in there. The light went off as we were walking by, so I assumed their job was done and they had exited from the back of the building. We didn't see cars around—that's why I assumed that. We went on home and got our vehicle and drove over here, to the police station—after one a.m. The light in the shop was still off as we passed by again.

Officer Tan gave a hmmph. Chief Smith's eyes squinted as he asked me, "What were you both doing out so late?"

Greg quickly responded, "We were walking home from the hotel. We're participating in the *Sniper at the Speakeasy* … uh, the murder mystery weekend. It's right on the route home—Tricia's shop, that is."

"And you came *here* that late?" Officer Tan asked.

I nodded my head. "Cheryl Basque had left us message that Bill wanted to talk to me."

"But, Cheryl runs the murder mystery event … why would she have had to 'leave a message' for you?" the chief seemed surprised. He looked to Tan, "Did you see her here last night—you were on duty?"

Officer Tan shook his head no.

That was news to Greg and me. I quickly added, "But Britney, and the bartender at the casino night, told me Cheryl said Bill needed to talk to me right away—he'd been arrested."

"Casino night?"

"Yes, part of the murder mystery event…" I was getting impatient with them.

"So, Ms. Basque wasn't at the hotel last night then?" Office Tan asked.

"Well, she was … to kick it off, but honestly after that, I don't remember seeing her." I looked at Greg, questioningly.

He shook his head, too. "Yeah, that's accurate. After her initial speech, I never saw her again."

"Once Britney and Harold told us Mr. Longo had been arrested, we assumed that must have been where she was all evening," I added.

"Wait, who's Harold?" Chief Smith wondered.

Oh boy. "Uh, you know … that is his character's name in the mystery. I'm not sure I know his real name. Do you, Greg?" He didn't know either.

"Does this Harold reside here?"

"Hmmm. I didn't get the impression that he does. He mentioned several times traveling around to various mystery weekends." Then, it dawned on me, "Cheryl mentioned the first night that they hire a few actors to help keep the mystery moving along—and they'd fit in like any other character. Perhaps he was hired help?"

"Well, here's the problem, Ms. Madsen. None of this adds up. Officer Tan was on duty last night. Mr. Longo was not arrested—at least not by our department. Cheryl Basque never came to the station last night either. So, again, I'd like to ask what business you had going on at Tricia's in the middle of the night?"

My mouth opened and I couldn't find the words. *Bill hadn't been arrested?* I looked to Greg and he was equally perplexed, but he did find the words.

"I'm sorry. We must have been misinformed then. We were under the impression that Bill Longo had been arrested for the murder of Patricia Simpson. Otherwise, we'd have no business coming over here in the middle of the night. And, again, we passed by Tricia's shop because it was on our walk home from the hotel after the mystery game. We didn't *stop* there—we simply observed lights on.

We hadn't expected anyone to be inside her business. Now we're here to relate that information to you."

The chief appeared satisfied with that. He turned to Officer Tan, "Please check in at Scruffy's to see if the seal on the door has been broken. That'll let us know if someone was in there last night." Then he turned to us. "And, we're not going to find your finger prints in there, are we?"

We both shook our heads no, but then I reconsidered. "I suppose they could be. Remember, we were there when we found Ms. Simpson deceased. But I can guarantee there are no new prints—we did not go in the shop or touch any of the doors or windows last night. Promise."

With that, we exited the police station. *Unbelievable. What the heck happened?*

CHAPTER TWELVE

Shaking our heads in disbelief, we stopped off at the bakery for breakfast. Nate was helping customers behind the counter and Colleen came out to seat us at one of the few window bistro tables.

"Snow! Ball!" I cheered as they hurried over to greet us.

Colleen set our menus on the table. "Good morning, friends! Where's Shadow?"

"We left her at the cottage this morning. We've come from the police station," I informed.

Her hand moved to her mouth. "Oh, please tell me they are off their kick that Shadow had anything to do with Patricia's death!"

Greg shook his head. "No, she's been cleared.

And, our trip there turned out to be misinformation—unfortunately."

"Well, I'm happy to hear that our friend, Shadow, is no longer a suspect. Coffee for both?" We eagerly said yes, as my stomach churned thinking of the station's coffee I hadn't finished.

When she returned with steaming mugs, Snow and Ball following her closely, we placed our orders for the special of the day: Quiche Florentine.

"Why would Britney or Harold send us on a wild goose chase?" Greg asked, while doctoring his coffee with fresh cream.

I couldn't think of a reason, but it was a crappy thing to do. We were seriously worried about Bill. "I definitely have a question or two for them tonight—that's for sure!"

Nate's customers had left and he came around the counter to our table. "Howdy, folks! So glad you stopped in this morning—good to see you again."

"Hey Nate, have you seen any activity across the street?" Our heads turned to stare out the window and over at the grooming shop. "I mean other than the police coming and going." Greg asked, then lifted his mug carefully taking a sip of the hot coffee.

"No. No activity—it's been closed."

"We saw someone in there last night," I informed.

"Last night?" he shook his head. "We aren't here after about four in the afternoon so we wouldn't see anything on this street at night. If they're investigating until late in the night—well, that'd sure surprise me!"

"Yeah, that's what we thought. Have you seen security guards around the place—any time of day?"

"Nope. Not a one."

Colleen brought us hot plates and the quiche looked

delicious. "Want any hot sauce or anything else?"

We didn't and they left us to enjoy our meal. Once we were done, we talked ourselves into a little sweet treat to take home with us. I chose one of the beautiful patisserie slices—layers of dark and milk chocolate, raspberry, and covered in a ganache with berries resting on top. Greg picked out a few donuts.

"Let's get our girls together again at the park before you all leave town, you hear?" Colleen shouted as we started to leave.

"Yes, of course. Shadow—well, all of us—would love that!"

* * *

A few hours later, I walked into the hotel lobby and straight to the front desk.

"I'd like to see Mr. Longo, please. Is he in?"

The woman on duty was not one I'd seen working before. Not surprising. We'd only been here for a couple days and I'm sure they have many staff members to fill multiple shifts that make up the twenty-four-seven schedule.

"I'm sorry, Mr. Longo has the day off. Is there something I can help you with?" The lady spoke eloquently—was that a British accent? Her black hair, streaked with beautiful silver strands, was pulled up tight into a high bun on the back of her head. Her complexion was impeccable and beautifully enhanced with natural-looking makeup. She wore a smart black pantsuit with a light blue silk blouse. Her name badge said, "Mrs. Brandish, Assistant Manager."

My eyes flew open. "Ah, Mrs. Brandish! We met last night…"

Her face remained stoic. She apparently had no idea who I was.

"We met at the poker table last night … the murder mystery…" Nope. She still waited to know how she could help me. "You aren't part of the murder mystery weekend?" I asked.

She gave a tiny grin. "I'm afraid not. Now, are you a guest at the hotel? How may I help you today?"

Still confused and trying to place the face of the woman I met last night, I answered, "Oh, I'm sorry. I'm Libby Madsen, licensed massage therapist, and I'm filling in for Kirby McDaniel for several days," I pointed downward toward the basement.

"Nice to finally meet you, Ms. Madsen. I have heard splendid compliments about your services whilst covering for Ms. McDaniel. I hope her father is doing well."

"Thank you. Anyway, I was hoping to get hold of Mr. Longo … sooner than later. Can you tell me when he'll be back?"

The look that crossed her face was identical to the lady I'd spoken to the night before. *It was the same person—I was sure of it! Why was she pretending to be someone different today?*

"Ms. Madsen, Mr. Longo was called away on unexpected business last night. But, I'm more than happy to assist with your needs while you're working here." The smirk was chilling and not at all fitting with the polite spiel.

"Uh. Okaaay. Um, well, I hope he's okay. I guess it can wait. Thank you." I smiled and turned toward the basement staircase.

She called out, "The elevator—there's one this way…" she pointed opposite of where I was headed.

"That's okay…" I murmured as I continued to the stairwell.

Before heading into the therapy room, I decided I'd go to the end of the hallway. Was the ballroom door open from this side today, I wondered. I pulled the handle, it opened, and I stepped into the dark room. I felt along the wall until I found the light switch. Illuminated, I saw that casino night had been cleared away and the room was completely empty—including the bar that had been set up at the far end. There wasn't a table or chair anywhere. Part of me was hoping to find Cheryl or someone from her team setting up for tonight.

I shut off the lights and headed back to my room, when I was startled by a noise near the boiler room. I backed up a few steps and craned my neck to see if there was a staff member in there. No one was around. *It indeed was creepy around here alone. And, shouldn't the washers and dryers be running? Doesn't housekeeping have to get an early start to get all the rooms done before check-in time this afternoon?*

I shook it off and opened my room to get everything ready for my first client. The light was on inside. *That's strange, I swear I double checked before leaving yesterday.* I pulled out disinfectant from under the sink and starting sanitizing everything. I lit a lavender candle and turned to pull the sheets from a cabinet. When I turned around, the candle was blown out. *Weird.* There was no fan or air conditioning running. *Hmmm, I suppose I created a breeze with the sheet.* I relit the candle and waited to be sure the flame took hold. Once assured, I finished with the bedding on the massage table and then double checked the changing area. Everything was tidy; ready for the client. Back at the countertop, the candle had blown out again. *I give up.* Instead, I sprayed some essential oil mist that I found under the sink.

"Good morning," a man stood outside the open door;

I startled.

"Oh! Wow, it's so quiet down here—I didn't hear you!" I was looking at a middle-aged man I thought to be slightly older than myself. "Mr. White?" I asked.

"Yes, please call me Ted."

"Oh, are you the same Ted who owns the brewery?"

"Indeed."

"Nice to meet you finally! Monica has mentioned you … she's lovely, by the way. We've agreed to get our dogs together sometime—run around in the park."

"Hopefully nice things…"

I stared absentmindedly.

"Monica mentioned me…" he prompted.

"Oh, yeah, of course … she had said she particularly likes to work a full schedule over the murder mystery weekend and you always accommodate that." I laughed nervously. "I think you've met my boyfriend … you're participating in the weekend festivities here, right?"

He nodded. "Who is your boyfriend?"

"Greg Lawson—we are here from the valley. Mesa. Well, and Heber—he lives on the Mogollon Rim."

"Oh yeah. Great guy. Forest Ranger, right?"

"Yep. Well, let's get you on the table…" We discussed what areas on the body were troubling him. Then, I let him know I'd be back in a few minutes to allow him time to change. I stepped out of the room, closing the door behind me.

Again, I was struck by how quiet it was in the basement. No equipment running—*eerily quiet*, I thought to myself. After a few minutes, I turned to tap on the door when there was a loud metallic screech. I jumped—my heart leapt. I looked around, from one end of the hall to the other. No sign of life. Then I heard the familiar bubbling and squealing—*damn boiler.* I tapped on the door and heard 'ready' from the other side.

"What was that noise out there?" Ted asked.

"Oh, this place has lots of creaks and sounds—namely that ancient elevator and the enormous boiler that resides across the hall from here."

"Have you seen the young boy running around the hotel?" he asked, his voice muffled in the headrest.

I hesitated, wanting to learn more first. "What little boy?"

"Oh, legend has it that there are quite a few occupants of the hotel that visit guests. Best I understand it, they do harmless pranks. Most people see them from a distance and nothing actually happens, but I guess it would still scare the … well, frighten some."

"Do you know what the boy looks like?"

"I've never witnessed myself, so I'm only going by the rumors. I've heard he wears 1920s clothing … some trousers with suspenders, a white shirt, with a cute little vest and bow tie. Oh, and a cute cap on his head. What do you call those?"

"A beret…?"

"Something like that. I've heard he's a real cutie."

"Yep, I saw him the other night outside of the hotel, but still on the grounds. When I went toward him to talk, he literally vanished."

"Yes, indeed … you had an encounter!" Ted got excited.

"I guess I thought he was one of the guests' kids, however, when I went looking for Cheryl to make an announcement, she wasn't anywhere around. I mentioned it to someone who told me he wasn't real—the boy was a ghost."

"Wait, Cheryl left her own party last night?" He sounded surprised.

"I guess. I couldn't find her anyway."

"That makes sense then…"

"What does?"

"Well, I was closing up the bar. It was a slow night and I decided to close early. When I was taking out the trash, I swore I saw her car pass by."

"Which direction?"

"Oh, down the hill. Quite fast too!"

That was interesting. Where was Cheryl going so fast? Must have been something important to pull her away from her beloved event. But, we already knew that she wasn't bailing Bill out of jail. Where did she go?

Once the hour-long massage was over, I stepped back into the hallway while Ted got dressed. This time I could see that the ballroom door was open and the lights were on. Before I stepped back into the room, I made a mental note to try and find Cheryl before the next client arrived.

Ted handed me his credit card for processing. "You and Greg should come by the brewery again—today's special is smoked pulled pork sandwiches. We've been slow smoking the pork since yesterday."

"Ah, that's what I've been smelling about town. Sounds fantastic. Let me check my schedule and get with Greg, we might see you there later."

"Thanks, Libby! And, if I'm down in the valley, I'll make sure to look up …" he read from the card he held, "Dharma Inspired Day Spa. That Ashiatsu you were explaining sounds amazing."

"Excellent, hope to see you there!"

I watched him walk down the hall to the elevator. After making some clanging metal sounds, the squeaky old thing transported him to the lobby. I walked down the hallway and peeked my head into the ballroom. Several staff members were hurrying around setting some tables in place and stocking the bar again. I couldn't believe they moved everything out and then back into place each day— seemed like much unnecessary work to me.

Across the room, with clipboard in hand, Cheryl was busily writing something as I approached her.

"Oh, Libby—you frightened me!" Her eyes were wide, then softened a touch, "How are you and Greg enjoying the mystery weekend?"

"It's been fun," my voice hit that fake high note.

"Know who did it yet?" she ribbed.

"Uh, no … I have no idea. But, I do have a question…" I started before she interrupted.

"Oh, you know I can't divulge anything, Libby … no cheating!"

"No, no. Not that. Last night, Britney and the guy who tends bar—over there," I pointed. "They sent Greg and me away, saying that you said Bill Longo had been arrested and he wanted to see me."

Her smile faded. The eyebrows narrowed, but she said nothing.

"Well, we went looking for Mr. Longo and learned that no, he hadn't been arrested. Why did you have them give us that message if it wasn't true?"

There was an awkward pause before she started thumbing through papers clipped to her board. She looked back to me. "Do you mean *Harold?*"

"Yeah, I don't know what his real name is … but yes, Harold."

She chuckled. "That guy will do *anything* to win at these mystery weekends! I suspect he felt you and Greg were on to something and he decided to send you off track." Her pen tapped the clipboard nervously.

I thought about that for a moment. "But, why would Britney be in on it then? She initially told us, then Harold."

She tapped the board with more fervor. Her icy glare was unnerving.

I ignored that and pushed the point. "And, I couldn't find you—where had you gone? There was a boy I saw outside the hotel," I pointed to the door that led outside. "I went looking for you for help."

She hesitated for a minute, then hissed her words pointedly, "I'm a busy woman, *Ms. Madsen*. It takes a lot of my time to run this whole thing," her arms swept around. "I don't have time to be running down parents of a missing boy. Did you tell someone at the front desk?"

I felt stupid. Why hadn't I gone to the front desk? Was it because Harold had already told me he was a ghost? What if it hadn't been a ghost? Oh, poor boy. I shook my head slowly, "No. I didn't."

She tsked. "If I'm not available, please check in at the front desk. Now, is there anything else, Libby? I've got work to do!"

"Yes. One more thing. Where's Bill? The personnel at *the front desk* told me he's unexpectedly been called away and I have some business things to discuss with him."

She caught my sarcasm and her stare indicated I had hit her last nerve.

"Now, why would I know what business Bill has been

pulled away on? If that's what they told you, then that's what it is!"

"Oh, well, given that you two are in a relationship and all, I thought you'd know exactly where he is. My mistake. Thank you for your time." I turned to walk away, but couldn't help but briefly glance back at the flustered Cheryl Basque. Was her look evidence she truly was in a relationship with Bill? It seemed so.

I hurried down the hall to close up shop. The moment I stepped into the room, I sensed someone had been in there while I was away. I'd left a candle burning and now it was out. I also swore I'd put the sheets into the laundry hamper in the corner, but I found them tossed about—half on the floor and partly on the table. I peered back down the hallway but didn't see anyone nearby. The few people I had seen were in the ballroom. I quickly picked things up, turned off the lights, closed and locked the door. Managing the steps two at a time, I pushed through the door at the top of the stairwell and nearly bumped into one of the porters.

"Oh, I'm sorry…" I touched his arm to see if it was hurt when the door got him.

"No worries. I'm fine." He was in a hurry.

"Hey, you haven't seen the big boss recently, have you? Mr. Longo?" I asked as he tried to get by me.

He shook his head, eyes down, never making contact with me. "I've gotta get to work."

My phone rang as I watched him go through the doorway and disappear down the basement stairwell.

"Hi Kirby! How is your dad doing?"

"He's recuperating well and should get out of the hospital tomorrow. He'll still need help for a bit while they get him strong enough to walk again."

"Oh, good … glad he won't have to stay in the hospital long."

"Hey, I got word about Patricia—"

"Oh no, I totally forgot that I should have called you."

"Don't worry—I'm sure you've had your hands full. Had you met her?"

"Oh yeah. In fact, my dog Shadow was accused of murdering her."

"What?!"

I explained the situation about taking Shadow there and then how we found Patricia dead later that evening.

"Oh, wow … I'm so sorry, Libby. That had to have been horrible."

"Not my most fun day ever—but I'm thankful that the coroner at least exonerated my dog. I feel for Patricia, though. I'm not even sure if she had family around locally or not. I mean, I learned that she and Bill had once been married…"

"Oh yeah. Those two. I think her kids lived somewhere in the south … I can't remember where she's from. Texas? Georgia? Alabama? I don't know, something like that…"

"Then the strangest thing happened …" I told her all about the murder mystery weekend: Bill's character who got killed off the first night, the young boy I saw that everyone said was a ghost, how Britney sent us on a wild-goose chase by saying that Bill had been arrested for Tricia's murder, only to learn he hadn't, and also that I still hadn't seen or talked to him since that night.

"Wow! You sure have dived right on in, haven't you Libby?" She laughed.

"I guess I have," I said, laughing along with her. Only

when telling a story aloud does one realize how ridiculous it all sounds.

"Well, I wanted to check in and make sure everything was going smoothly—the clients are showing up, right?"

"Yep. I'm fairly sure they're happy—guess we'll find out on Yelp, won't we?" I chuckled. "No, genuinely, it's gone smoothly and Greg and I are enjoying ourselves. Despite the drama."

"I'm sorry Cheryl roped you into her mystery weekend. I *completely* forgot about that when I asked you to cover for me at the spa."

"Oh, no … no worries at all. I think it's enhanced our time in Jerome actually. We're having a ball with the acting. I absolutely love the outfits. Greg looks so handsome in his tux."

"We need to get together when all this settles down. I'd love to meet this man of yours. Maybe I'll find myself in Mesa someday soon?"

"That'd be great!"

We chit-chatted while I walked through the town: down the hillside stairways, along the shops of Main St., and back to Holly St. where I walked up to the cottage to find Shadow and Greg sitting on the front porch enjoying some sunshine. We said our goodbyes and I looked at my watch—two o'clock, lots of daylight left to explore around.

"First, let's check Shadow's bandages, we may need to replace them with clean ones." I unwound the self-stick stretchy bandaging and we both examined her legs. The festered cuts from a couple days ago looked healed. "Let's take these off—give them some air. As long as she doesn't start licking, we should be good."

Greg thought similarly. "Now, let's get out and see

the town and its surroundings," he prompted. We loaded Shadow up in his white Tundra, which he now called Whitey. He drove along Main St., up the hill toward the old mining site. I marveled at the decades-old tailings that appeared as long horizontal steps that graduated down a huge hillside. One could see it as an eyesore, or marvel in the various sediment layers that illustrated the types of earth found in the hills.

From there, we took a ride out highway 89A. I remember during my childhood, my dad took me camping somewhere in this region, but nothing looked familiar now. The winding, twisting road led us through Mingus Mountain, up over the summit, and then ultimately it would lead down into Prescott Valley. There were several turnoffs where Greg was telling me of great hiking and camping. He'd spent some time in the area several years ago with the forest service doing restoration work—similar to that which he'd spent most of this past summer doing.

"Let's head over to Woodchute Trailhead, I think you'd love it. Shadow certainly would," he suggested.

"Sounds great."

We parked at the trailhead and set out on a nice hour-long hike. Once sure that we were alone, we let Shadow off the leash to explore around more. She traversed the trail, sniffing one side, then quickly the other side, wagging her tail the entire time.

"My client today was Ted, the brewery owner," I started. "I learned a couple things. First, he also thinks the boy I saw outside was a ghost. Second, he saw Cheryl speed by his place last night as he closed up early. It would have been while the mystery party was still going on."

"Well, we know it wasn't because Bill was arrested..."

"Exactly. I can't wait to question Britney and Harold about that more tonight. I believe they passed along the message Cheryl told Britney. But, here's the other thing I learned today—I told Cheryl I was looking for her last night and couldn't find her."

"Did you tell her *why* you were looking for her?"

I nodded, "Yes, about the boy ghost *and* that Britney had said Bill was arrested for Tricia's murder."

"Oh, wow—you confronted her? Wish I'd been there … what'd she say about Bill?" He got excited.

"She denied it all! She mentioned that Harold would do anything to throw us off track—that's how bad he wants to be the winner. Then, she got angry when I mentioned it had been Britney who initially gave us the message."

Greg shook his head and then stopped. "You mean to tell me Britney made that up? That rat…"

"I know! But, here's the thing—Cheryl was guarded, became defensive talking about it. She started telling me what a busy woman she was and doesn't have time for my…" I caught my breath, thinking back to her scolding. "Hey … she never answered me on where Bill actually was. And, when I called her out on having a relationship with him, I caught the shocked look."

"You mentioned that too?" He was surprised. I smiled and nodded deviously. "Ohhh, Libby … you are asking for trouble." He pulled me in for a hug and kissed the top of my head. Shadow sensed the pack togetherness so she squeezed in between our legs too.

CHAPTER THIRTEEN

The late afternoon return journey through the switch-backs on Mingus Mountain and into Jerome felt even more scenic. We both marveled at the beauty of the forest as the light cast long shadows. The contrast of that with the high desert scrub and artful vistas as we descended in elevation appeared as a never-ending landscape, a portrait many artists had created.

"Traffic going the other way seems much heavier. I wonder how many people live in Prescott Valley and travel to Jerome for work?"

"Hadn't thought of that—figured most worked and lived in Jerome. It's also a weekend, so could be weekend traffic is often heavy this direction."

"Oh yeah," I cut short and my head spun around and I

turned in my seat. A little yellow Smart car sped by. "Hey! That looked like Tricia's…"

Greg caught the flash of yellow too. "What are the odds there are two of those little things up here?"

"Do you think a relative may already be clearing out her belongings? I wonder if there's a service being planned?"

"It is a little strange we haven't heard anyone talk about plans…"

I made up my mind that I needed to hunt down Bill Longo and ask some questions. He was her last husband and appeared to have stayed in touch with her—surely, he'd know. Then it occurred to me, *what business is it of ours? We're only here temporarily. Would we actually want to attend a funeral of someone we didn't know well? Did it matter what the family had planned?*

* * *

We had learned from our mystery binder that no dinner service was planned for tonight—only one more formal dinner and that'd be the final night. So, we decided we would have dinner at the Mining Town Brewery before we had to get all dolled up for seeking out clues.

"Howdy folks," Monica greeted as we walked through the door. "Good to see ya again!"

She grabbed a couple menus and led us to a table at the far end of the room, near the bar. Shadow settled in the corner between our two chairs and Monica brought over a small dish of water.

"Ready to try something new from the beer menu?"

We both took her suggestion for a brown ale called Sidewinder.

When she placed our beers in front of us, she informed, "The special tonight is a half rack of smoked ribs, blue cheese potato salad, and a biscuit, all for 12.99"

"Oh, Ted had mentioned earlier about pulled pork sandwiches being the special today?"

She explained that had been the lunch special, but ribs were now ready from the smoker for dinnertime.

"That sounds delicious, we'll have two orders then," we both agreed.

"See over there—that's Chris, the one who owns the antique shop and was at the same dinner table the other night." Greg tilted his head to a table several over from ours. "Isn't that Britney with him?"

I slightly shifted in my chair, trying not to call attention to myself. From my periphery, I could tell that it was her. The two youthful adults appeared to be deep in conversation. Neither looked happy.

"Yes, I met him outside the hotel when I took Shadow out last night. Forgot to tell you about that." Britney's hands flailing caught my attention. "Must be serious," I commented turning back to Greg. He nodded.

We tuned them out and tried to figure out who killed Mr. Adler. We had two more days to complete the mystery weekend. Were we even close to figuring anything out? *No.*

Greg theorized, "Of course, whoever did it, had to have motive and opportunity. He runs a speakeasy—during prohibition. That means that the mob is probably the money behind the operation. That could provide the motive."

"But, if the speakeasy is earning the mob money, why wouldn't they want to keep that gravy train going? Kill the owner, bring attention to the illegal activities—this doesn't bode well for their business. At least, kill him outside of the establishment and disappear him!"

"'Disappear him'," he laughed out loud. "Listen to you—as if you're mob-like." He took a sip of his beer. "It's not that I disagree though. You're right, they wouldn't do it in the middle of dinner in the speakeasy."

"So who else would have motive to kill him?"

"We need to learn more about the family. Who *is* his family? Who got greedy?" Greg's eyebrows wiggled.

"Oooh. Or, who is skimming from the top? That would pull the mob guys right back into play."

"I still don't think they'd *off* someone in such a crowded room," he teased with his own mob-like language, clearly proud of himself. We couldn't stop laughing after that.

"You two are sure having fun!" Monica appeared from nowhere with two huge platters and set one in front of each of us. "More sauce on the side maybe? Anything else? Another beer, perhaps?"

"Sauce and beer sound good to me," I said.

"Oh, and more napkins for sure," Greg added.

She ran off and was back in a few seconds. "Y'all headed for more mysterious events at the hotel tonight?" We nodded as we dived right into the food. "I hear there are surprises planned..." she teased as she walked away.

Both of our eyebrows lifted and we also reached for napkins. The smoked ribs were as delicious as they had sounded. We mowed our way through the platters and sat back completely satiated. That's when we saw that Ted was working—he waved from the bar and indicated he'd be right over.

Shadow gave a low growl when he approached the table. I gently patted her head and assumed that he must have startled her awake.

"Another beer for you guys?" We both said no.

"This was delicious, Ted," I said. "You've got something great going on here." I glanced around the room full of patrons.

"Yeah, business has been pretty good. Love the weekends—people come from all over the state for a little getaway."

"Are you from Arizona originally?" Greg asked.

"No. I moved here after college—grew up in Washington state. Tacoma area."

"What brought you here?"

"Visited with friends of mine that went to ASU at the time. They brought me here to Jerome one weekend. I fell in love with it. Up in the Northwest, microbrews were all the rage then—but there were soooo many of them. When we visited here, there wasn't one yet. Against my father's wishes, that's what I decided I wanted to do. Live in a small town and run a brewery."

"I love when people follow their dreams—even against what everyone else thinks they should do," I commented. "My dad was always supportive of my dreams ... I was lucky. He wasn't one who pushed me to live my life the way *he* wanted it to be. That's probably because he was the quintessential dreamer himself."

"I'm sure he's proud of you then, Libby ... it's clear you've followed your passion."

"I certainly hope so..." my voice caught in my throat. "He passed away when I was sixteen. But, I'm confident that somehow, from wherever he is, he knows." Greg reached out and took my hand where it rested on the table.

Ted smiled, then added, "Definitely—I believe our

deceased loved ones are always with us. My grandma is, and that's what gives me my strength and determination. Until her passing, she supported me along my journey; always was there to listen, and I do believe she still does. Unlike her son. My dad barely speaks to me, even to this day. He was convinced I needed to be a lawyer—when I went and did this after he paid for law school. Well, I'll probably never live that down."

"That's too bad about your dad, but I think it's cool that you've persevered anyway." Greg pushed back from the table. "Sorry, folks … time to recycle some beer."

Ted and I laughed as he walked toward the restrooms. "So, your grandma visits you from beyond … does that mean you believe in the afterlife? I know we talked some earlier about the hotel ghosts—do you personally believe in the stories?"

"I don't discredit those folks, that's for sure, but I haven't experienced similar occurrences. With Grandma, it's a *knowing*. I feel her, but it's not as though I've ever *seen* her visit me."

Greg snuck back into his seat. "Speaking of ghosts … we saw Tricia's driving her little car out of town—towards Prescott Valley—earlier."

Ted's eyebrows knitted. "Serious?"

I chuckled at his expression. "Well, we saw a little yellow Smart car. Not sure who was actually driving it."

"Ah, her daughter. More than likely anyway." Ted looked around the bar. "She used to come in her quite a bit before she moved away."

"She used to live here?"

"Yeah, until she paired up with some richy-rich and moved away to California with him."

"Do I detect jealousy there?" I asked, teasingly.

He smirked. "Light years ago—yes, we dated briefly. She's a handful— 'poor guy' was my only sentiment when I learned she'd been cheating. No jealousy, but a huge sigh of relief."

"I could only imagine. Guessing that the apple doesn't fall far from the tree?" I added.

Ted's eyes widened, "Doesn't take long to pick up on, does it, Libby? Monica could tell a story or two on that subject—her poor dog, Rex." He gave the table a couple raps with his knuckles, "Folks, gotta get back to the bar. You enjoy your evening and hope to see you back soon."

I sat considering his last words before I turned to Greg. "Maybe two beers were too much for me? Did he mention that Monica *had* taken Rex to Tricia's shop then?"

Greg clearly wasn't understanding what I was talking about.

"I thought I'd asked Monica that question…"

"What question?" Monica appeared at my side with the check in hand.

Caught off guard, I stammered. "Oh! Didn't see you there. Ted mentioned that something happened to 'poor Rex' at Tricia's shop … but I swore you'd told me he hasn't been there for grooming?"

Monica's smile melted into a grimace. "Ted, Ted, Ted. Always sticking his nose where it don't belong."

"Oh, okay, so he misunderstood then." I waved it off—no big deal.

"Rex didn't go for *grooming*. Tricia hit my dog with her car. Speeding around town as she always does!"

My hand went to my mouth. "Oh, jeez! Sorry … no idea!"

"Not your fault, Libby. That woman was a menace. She had the *audacity* to fault ME for having my dog off leash! I'll never forget that little *alt-er-cation*." She patted the black folded pad that held our receipt, and smile widely, "Let me know when you're ready—no hurry. Can I get you another beer?"

We both shook our heads no.

* * *

Back at the cottage, all three of us changed into our nightly attire. Tonight, we drove to the hotel—after a full day and being tired from our earlier hike. Even Shadow seemed like she'd rather have a night in than to hunt down mythical killers.

As we entered the lobby, I told Greg I'd be right back. Since we were here, and the laundry room was probably less busy, I thought I'd throw in a couple sets of sheets from earlier massages. He nodded and led Shadow off to talk to a few participants who were standing aside, waiting for Cheryl to direct everyone.

Cautiously, but quickly, I hurried down the stairwell in heels and the tight dress. *Get to the room, unlock the door, then grab the sheets and throw them into an empty washer—shouldn't take long,* I thought. My plan was delayed as I rounded the corner and discovered the door was wide open. My heartbeat thumped—I knew for certain that was not the way I'd left it earlier that afternoon.

I reached around the doorframe, flipped on the light switch, and called out, "Hello!" without stepping inside.

No one answered. I cautiously rounded the corner, ready to karate chop someone. The room was empty and nothing looked to be disturbed. Letting out a sigh, I quickly grabbed the sheets from the hamper and made my way down the hall to the laundry room. I could hear the guests all gathered now in the ballroom, but the door remained closed. My sense of urgency increased. Being back in the crowd would be better—it was too dark and creepy in the basement.

I poured in the detergent and set the appropriate dials, then smashed the sheets into the washer, and hit the start button. I turned around and nearly ran into him.

I jumped back and held my fists up, ready to fight in high heels. "What are you doing here?" I yelled out, hoping someone from the ballroom might hear me.

No such luck.

CHAPTER FOURTEEN

Whoa! Little lady, just calm down now," one of the mobsters I'd met at casino night was standing in the doorway.

"Don't call me '*little lady*'!" I seethed. "Now, back up and let me out of here!"

"Jeez. I'm only looking for clues, Ms....."

"Madsen. Er, uh … Davis," I rolled my eyes.

"Ms. Davis. We're *supposed* to be looking for clues to solve the mystery. Why are you…" he pointedly looked over my shoulder, "doing *laundry*?"

Okay, in hindsight, I supposed I did look like the ridiculous one. Why was I doing laundry late at night during mystery weekend? I didn't feel like I owed him an explanation, so I pushed my way past and went back to my room. He followed.

"This is where you work?" he questioned, looking into the small room.

"Yes, it is. Now, would you please get back to looking for clues and let me be. You do understand how frightening it can be for a woman alone in a basement to be confronted by a man, don't you? Especially one that looks like ... well, that looks like a thug!"

He scoffed and backed away from the door. "Sorry, ma'am. Thought we're all here to solve a mystery. No harm intended." He walked off down the hallway.

I shut off the lights, locked up the room—double checking to be sure—then headed to the stairwell. Running up the steps faster than I was comfortable wearing heels, I grabbed the door handle and twisted it hard. The door didn't budge. I tried again—it was locked! Ugh!

I turned and went down the stairs a little more carefully this time. I hated the elevator but it looked to be my only choice now. I briskly walked down the hall and stood before the brass gate in front of me. *How does this work again?* I pulled the gate open, stepped inside, and gasped when the car shifted slightly. I began to pull the gate across when a hand stopped it.

Mr. Mobster was back.

"Mind if I join you?"

"I actually do, but do I have a choice?" I sneered.

He came in anyway and latched the gate before he reached across me to push the 'L' button. The timeworn machine whirred into action—clunking along slowly. My fists clinched and, as much as I wanted to close my eyes, I didn't dare with the stranger next to me. A loud bang sounded and the lights dimmed. The antiquated deathtrap had stopped—mid-floor!

Beads of sweat started at my hairline. A grip-like vise enveloped my chest.

"HELP!!!" I began to scream. Banging the gates. Someone had to hear me.

"Now don't get all hysterical…" the man dared to say.

I turned on him and scowled. "I'M *NOT* HYSTERICAL!" Hearing the voice that couldn't possibly have been mine, I realized his point. I couldn't catch my breath—it only got faster. Panting—I felt dizzy and I began to sink to the floor.

"Okay, lady. It's not my favorite thing either, but please … let's stay calm now." His voice actually sounded human for once.

Sitting down helped and my breathing began to slow. "I'm sorry. I don't do well in confined … spaces. Especially those that are suspended in the air. My whole life— claustrophobic—not my favorite thing." I rested my head back against the wall. Images flooded my consciousness remembering when, only a few months back, I was trapped in a small confined space, frightened by the intimidating homeowner.

The elevator lurched and I gasped again. The lights brightened and it was slowly moving upward again. The man held out his hand and offered me help. Carefully standing, I faced the see-through gate, waiting for the lobby to appear. Slow and steadily, it finally made it.

I frantically grasped for the latch, but fumbled. "Hurry. I need to get off this thing!" I cried out.

The man effortlessly opened the gate and I jumped out, nearly slipping on the tiled floor. Shadow began barking furiously. I looked to my right and saw Greg and her approaching the elevator.

"I was getting worried," Greg started, giving the man next to me an inquisitive look. "We were coming to find you. Shadow was insistent."

The mobster guy side-stepped around, avoiding my barking dog, and hurriedly making his way down the hallway toward the speakeasy entrance.

"Are you okay?" Greg nervously asked. "Who was that man?"

After several more seconds trying to find the words, "That, *that stupid elevator*, broke down on us! I *hate* that old thing!" I cried out.

He pulled me close to him. "Okay. It's going to be alright, sweetie." He looked down at Shadow, who sat pressing her body into my leg and sitting on my foot. Then his eyes met mine. "You have quite the partner there. Shadow knew something was wrong—she actually grabbed my hand in her mouth and began to pull me. I've never seen her do that. I thought she needed to go outside urgently. But then, I heard the commotion in the elevator…"

"He scared the bejeezus out of me downstairs … that's a long story. But, no, I think he's harmless—taking his role a little seriously, but otherwise, an innocent bystander." My humor was finding its way back. I chuckled slightly, thinking about how I must have totally freaked him out. "Okay, c'mon, I'm ready now; let's solve this mystery."

"Are you sure? We can leave…" Greg offered.

"No, honestly, I'm fine. I just have to stay off that elevator. That's all. Let's go have some fun."

Still skeptical, he took my hand and we walked down the hallway to the secret passage into the ballroom. We entered as Cheryl wrapped up her spiel and boy, did we get a look from across the room. *How dare we be late!*

Harold was behind the bar, so we quietly moved in that direction while the rest of the group seemed to pair off. Most of them left the room quickly. Some milled about the ballroom whispering their theories.

"What can I get you two to drink tonight?" Harold asked as we walked up. "Where've you been? You missed the part where Cheryl instructed to work in partners and clues are hidden throughout the hotel."

We chose bottles of water. I ignored the question about where we'd been.

"Why did you send us on a wild goose chase, Harold?" I asked matter-of-factly.

He scoffed, "What, uh … what are you talking about?"

"Bill Longo was never arrested." My eyebrows lifted, waiting for an explanation.

Harold's eyes scanned around the room. "That's what she told Britney … *I swear!* Honestly—I'm not lying. I overheard Cheryl and Britney! Then, Brit went off to find you and she asked me to relay the message if I found you first." He crossed his heart.

"You actually thought Bill was arrested for *murder?*" Greg asked.

"Honestly, no. I was stunned. But, also, I didn't have a reason to question Cheryl or Britney. Dammit—what are they up to?" His face reddened and his fists clenched. "I've gotta find Britney!"

We took our water bottles and turned to see him leave the ballroom. Britney appeared not two seconds after he went outside—they'd missed seeing each other.

"Oh, exactly the one we were looking for," I said to her, before she could say anything.

"Yes, where have you guys been?" She looked directly

at Greg, "Guess we get to go look for clues…" she smiled widely. "Did you find your partner yet, Libby?"

I ignored her question. "Why did you send us off looking for Bill Longo last night? He was never arrested!"

The shock of my words hit her. "What? Cheryl …" she looked around the room. "That's exactly what Cheryl told me to tell you! Harold was there—he can back me up." Her eyes wildly shifted back and forth between the two of us. "Honestly! I'm not making this up!"

Greg reached out and touched my arm. "She's telling the truth. It's Cheryl we need to talk with again."

I felt like a pawn in some game and couldn't figure out the motive behind it. After a few seconds of awkwardness, I agreed with Greg. Britney was most likely being used also. *But why? Were Cheryl's actions all a part of this mystery weekend?*

I couldn't make sense of it, but decided to drop my line of questioning for now. "I missed the introduction. Do you happen to know who my partner is?"

"Nope, but you should get your little piece of paper …" she held hers up, it read *Charles Brown — playboy.* We all looked to the pulpit where Cheryl had been standing earlier.

"Okay, I'll go see if she left mine there … good luck you two!" I hesitantly smiled at Greg.

I found two small folded pieces of paper sitting on the lectern—one was Greg's that had *Mary Moore—flapper* written on it. I opened the next one and found *Harold Davis—bartender* and *Rascal—bartender's dog* in the same beautiful script. Along with the names appeared to be a short poem. A clue? It read: *Two by two, stairs lead to two, it's there to find the two.*

What? I read it again and then stuck it in a corner of my

bra and looked down at my dog. "Well, Shadow … you are officially a *Rascal* now. Guess Cheryl didn't know you're a girl. Oh well. Let's go hunt down my *brother*, shall we? Then 'two by two', we'll find a bunch of… two's? *What?*" She wagged and wiggled, so excited to hear 'go'. We headed out the door I had seen Harold leave through several minutes earlier.

I looked out into the darkness and didn't see or hear anyone——only saw scarecrows swaying in the light breeze, darkened shapes that certainly were the headstones, and then the witch floating within the nearby a tree. We walked to the back of the building as we had the other night, rounded the corner, only to find two cars parked back there. One was a dark sedan. The other was a white pickup truck. Both were unlit and I couldn't detect anyone in them. We turned and walked toward the front of the building. No one there either, so we went back inside.

As we walked through the threshold and the door was closing, I swore I heard a car door slam. *No one was out there though, maybe that wasn't it.* I noticed the ballroom had completely cleared out now, so we headed down the hallway, ascended the secret staircase, and then out into the lobby.

There was a girl at the front desk. I stopped and asked if she'd seen Harold Davis——I got a blank stare. Of course, even if he was a guest at the hotel, he wouldn't be registered under his fictitious character's name. *What was his name anyway?*

"Well, Shadow … er, Rascal … looks like it's just you and me, kid! Let's go find us some clues…" Again, she bounced around at the word 'go.' We found the stairwell and moved up to the second floor. The lighting was dim and seemed smoky as well. *A fog machine? Really, Cheryl? She doesn't miss a thing, does she?* I had to give her credit though—it was spooky.

Shadow sniffed along the baseboards as we crept down the hallway. I wondered where everyone else had gone—we hadn't run across anyone on this floor yet. The next door we came to—number thirty-two—was slightly ajar. Shadow pushed her way inside and I followed. Immediately she sat, barking at the closet. I turned on a light in the darkened room.

"Honestly? We need to look in there?" I asked her. She jumped at it, her paws flat on the wooden door.

I reached for the doorknob and turned it. *Squeeaak …* I twisted harder and finally, it came open. Shadow pushed her nose into the opening, sniffing and wagging her tail wildly. I pulled the door toward me and screamed when a scarecrow fell on us unexpectedly. Shadow wiggled more, her nose prodding the stuffed Halloween decoration until she turned it over. Pinned to its shirt pocket was a note. Shadow looked up, then pawed at my leg.

"Okay, okay … I'll get it." I knelt down to remove the note from the scarecrow's ratty clothing. Before I could unpin it, a frigid breeze blew the guest room's door, slamming it closed. I jumped up; Shadow moved next to the bed, growling a low guttural warning.

I couldn't see anything—no one was in the room with us. There wasn't an open window. I had no idea what caused the door to slam like that so I turned back to the closet and ripped the note from the scarecrow, and unfolded the small piece of paper. It read: *Scarecrow.* Hmmm.

Shadow was fixated on the area between the bed and the window. Still growling and her tail tucked, she appeared frightened. Her nose was furiously sucking air, pointing up toward the window. I pulled back the sheer curtains. This room looked out over the upper parking lot—the guest parking area, it appeared.

"What is it, Shadow?" I noticed she had stopped growling. She sat now, staring at me. I took in the view: rows of cars, a hillside beyond that, and there was lighting throughout—yellowish, not bright at all. I could see where the hotel staff had made a graveyard, decorated to the hilt. Then something caught my eye. There was a scarecrow right in the center and it appeared to have a similar note pinned to its chest. "Ah, ha! I think I've found the next clue, girl—good job!"

We hurried from the room, down the stairs to the lobby, then out into the guest parking lot and over to the graveyard. Shadow ran right to the scarecrow, not even paying attention to the Grim Reaper she'd passed. I gave that thing a second look—extremely unsettling late at night in a graveyard.

I pulled off the note and read it out loud to Shadow, who was sitting on my foot. *"You're lost—get back inside. What's meant to be will be.* Ah, jeez—that's *no help* at all!

Shadow's head dropped disappointedly. She stood and began sniffing around. That's when she discovered Mr. Reaper and she began barking wildly at it. "Yeah, I get it girl … that thing is creepy."

A man's voice spoke, and I screamed. Shadow stopped barking at the Grim Reaper.

Harold laughed, "Where have you been? I've been looking for my partners this whole time." He waggled his little piece of paper in front of me.

"Where have *I* been? You're the one who left the

building … looking for Cheryl?"

"I came back and everyone was gone," he claimed.

"Well, I went outside to get you and didn't see you anywhere—where'd you go?"

"Not important. I'm here now—what clues have you found?" he pointed to the paper I was holding.

"Apparently, nothing to find out here. It says to get back inside. *What's meant to be, will be.*"

"What's that mean?"

I shrugged. "Let's go see…"

When we walked back into the lobby, there were a few clue hunters milling about. I didn't see Greg and Britney, but there were a couple detectives I hadn't seen before. They didn't stop us—inattentive officers, I'd say.

I filled Harold in on what we'd found so far, in addition to the graveyard note.

"I know that Room 32 in this hotel is the most haunted one—legendary, actually. Is that where you said you found the note?"

I nodded, and told him about how it suddenly got freezing cold in there and the door slammed. Shadow was growling.

"Ah, it was the ghost—had to be!"

"Should we head back to the second floor then and pick up where we left off?" I asked him. He agreed, and after discussion over *not* taking the elevator, he reluctantly huffed and puffed up the staircase. "Maybe you should be taking the stairs more often, Harold?" I teased.

"Funny… ha, ha…" He wasn't amused.

Shadow quickly made her way back to Room 32. She pushed her way in and we discovered another pair of sleuths in there. The scarecrow was still on the floor where we'd left it.

The man mentioned, "Looks like someone else already beat us to this room and got the clue already—we haven't found anything here."

I didn't let him know we'd been there previously. We nodded and, after Shadow sniffed the place again, decided there was nothing more to find. We moved on to the next rooms. Shadow sniffed through several—no reaction at all. Harold and I didn't find any little slips of paper.

As we headed to the fourth floor—knowing that the third floor was off limits—we ran into those two detectives in the stairwell. Now they started to grill us.

The one with the long black overcoat and hat wanted to know how old Harold was—he said thirty-two. They asked me the same—thirty-eight.

Where were we both when Mr. Adler was murdered? I was in the bathroom; Harold was behind the bar.

Then they shocked me. "Mr. Davis—on what date had your father explained you were no longer part of his business?"

Confused, I questioned Harold, "Father?"

Laughing, he told the detectives, "My father left me the business in his will."

Father? This means Mr. Adler was my father too?

"Exactly. Which gives you motive to kill him after he told you he was writing you out," They said it in a *gotcha* manner.

"That's ridiculous. Doesn't prove a thing because he never told me anything of the sort!"

"We'll see about that. Don't leave town—you are on the suspect list." The man's partner jotted a few notes in his small notepad, tipped his hat, and then we watched them go through the door and proceed down the fourth-floor hallway.

We stood for a couple seconds staring at one another. We'd learned more clues to the mystery, but weren't sure what to do with them yet.

In unison, "We're related to the victim?" we started, then busted out laughing. He held the stairwell door open for us and Shadow led the way.

Door after door, Shadow nosed them open and we scoured the rooms. Some had already clearly been picked through. Others had not. We never ran into the detectives again, but as we were nearly done clearing the fourth floor, Greg and Britney appeared through the misty fog-like hallway.

Shadow was excited and ran to Greg. She sat and held out her hand and he shook it, then praised her enthusiastically. We hadn't brought cookies, but she didn't even seem to notice as Britney started her adoration as well.

"Figure it out yet?" Greg asked Harold and me.

"Not even close … how about you guys? Wanna share any insight?" Harold asked.

They looked between themselves and then decided that would be cheating. We all kept our clues to ourselves and proceeded our separate directions. For Harold and I, that meant a stair climb to the fifth floor. Shadow enthusiastically jumped at the stairwell door as though she could push it open. It didn't budge until I punched my thumb down on the lever and pulled the handle toward us. She pushed her way through and traversed the hallway loudly, sniffing her way to the first doorway. This door was closed.

"Feels weird opening a closed hotel room door, doesn't

it?" I said to Harold. "They did say we could explore *all* rooms on any floor, except for the third one, right?"

He nodded and reached for the handle, turning it to the right and slowly pushing it open. Fumbling for the light switch inside, he jumped backwards, nearly stepping on my toes to get out of the room.

"Whoa, what was that?" his voice quivered.

Shadow barrelled on through the doorway and then ferociously began barking.

"Hello?" I called out, before stepping inside.

No one responded.

Then I saw what spooked Harold.

I screamed.

CHAPTER FIFTEEN

Many participants came running when they heard me scream. They found us still trying to catch our breath—but now, it was because we started laughing hysterically. Shadow was still dismayed, sniffing around the bed and confused as to why we weren't taking this more seriously.

Greg and Britney were the first ones through the doorway. They looked to the bed and then over at Harold and me.

"What on earth is goin' on in here," Britney called out.

We pointed to the ridiculous looking dummy that scared the life out of me.

"Guess we have another dead body?" I cracked up.

"Oh jeez, what's this about?" Greg walked over and

lifted the limp, plastic body.

"Cheryl's idea of fun, I guess."

Several other pairs of mystery-goers were standing in the doorway, spilling out into the hallway. Harold noticed something and walked over to where Greg was holding the dummy. He reached out and ripped off a note. A clue! He held it up and read: "*warm water runs—*"

We heard footfalls now running away from us. Harold yelled out, "The boiler!" and we all joined in on the chase for the next clue.

Now that everyone was learning the clues at the same time, it felt like we were chasing each other around the hotel. Up the stairs, down the hall, in this room, and then over to that one. Back down the stairs—some were wasting time with the elevator, but I wasn't complaining, it helped us to beat them to the next clue. I couldn't stop laughing at the sight—like the movie Clue. *Colonel Mustard, in the library, with the candlestick.* I'd actually loved the board game as a kid and found myself enjoying this mystery weekend more and more. I also discovered that I had a whole different appreciation for my big lug, narcissistic, character brother—by now, I'd learned that he happened to have great humor and we were getting on much better than at the beginning.

The rest of the night flew by as we continued to collect the many clues. Once we were done, Harold and I tried putting our heads together to figure out what they all meant. We overheard several other groups in the ballroom doing the same. Was it the mob who killed Mr. Adler? Or maybe his ex-wife—or girlfriend? Some were sure that he was killed by family, and I even caught the whisperings of a theory that he killed himself. I hadn't thought of that. In the middle of dinner? Seemed unlikely, but *what if?*

What we were assured of was by this time tomorrow evening, the final night of *Sniper at the Speakeasy*, someone would have to come up with the right answer to win.

* * *

The next morning, we headed over to the café for breakfast. Britney set down two coffees in front of us and then scooted in the booth next to me. "Wasn't that a hoot last night?" she chuckled.

"Cheryl sure knows how to throw a party, doesn't she? It's been great fun, and I'm almost sad it ends tomorrow," Greg said.

"I'm actually learning to like Harold," I said softly. Both of the others gave me a questioning look, but said nothing. Then I added, "But aside from the mystery weekend festivities, I still can't believe that we haven't seen Mr. Longo around the hotel. And, who killed Tricia?"

Britney hung her head slightly. "I *know.* I keep wanting to forget there was a real-life murder right here in our little town! Maybe Bill did have something to do with it and he's on the run? I mean she'd always been a pistol. But, what she did to Bill—well, that was just not right."

"What do you mean by that?" I asked.

"What did *she* do?" Greg questioned at the same time.

"Well, you know that she was cheating on her former husband when Bill first moved to town and took interest in her, right?"

Our eyes widened and we both shook our heads no.

"Oh, yeah … he didn't even know she was married. Until it was too late. He was smitten with the feisty little firecracker. Then her truck-driving husband came home one weekend, unexpectedly mind you, and all hell broke loose."

"He found them…?"

"Well, no … not exactly, but word had gotten around that she was spending time with the haunted hotel manager. He marched right up there and socked Bill in the nose." Her hands found her hips. "At least, that was the rumor around town at the time."

I flinched, imagining what that'd be like for someone like Bill. I also wondered if the former husband had come back now and taken his anger out on Tricia instead.

Britney glanced around to see if anyone had overheard, then she turned back to us, using a lower voice. "Anyway, it wasn't long after that Tricia's husband was on the road again for weeks. Shockingly, Bill never stopped seeing Tricia. Then one day, months later, we started hearing that Tricia's husband had died in a horrific trucking accident."

"No!" I exclaimed.

"The guy wasn't well-known around town—he was gone much of the time. But, all the same, it was tragic. In no time, Tricia had money to open up her shop. She and Bill—again, astonishingly—continued to see each other."

Greg and I were riveted. We had no idea the little— what did she call her?—*firecracker* had *so much* drama surrounding her.

"We understand she has a daughter … was that with the truck-driving husband?"

"I'm not exactly sure how they all relate. She also had another husband before the truck driver—back before she moved to Jerome. I think they lived somewhere down south …Texas, Louisiana, or something like that? Can't remember. I *think* her daughter is from that marriage—she'd be oh around fifty-something now, I believe."

That didn't sound like the one that Ted mentioned. At most, his former girlfriend was probably around forty-ish. "Did she have other children?"

She nodded, "Oh yeah. At least one more daughter that I know of, and I'm fairly certain a son as well. And a slew of grandchildren and great-grandchildren—all she ever talked about. But, again, not sure how they all relate with all her marriages and such. She was super cagey whenever asked about her family. I could never make heads or tails anyway." She looked behind her and realized the café owner was staring her down. "Oops, guess I best get back to work—looks like your breakfast is up!" She hurried to grab it. Once we were settled with our food and refills on coffee, she went back to helping her other customers too.

We stared across the table at one another. "Sheesh, sounds like there's a lot more to learn about good ol' Tricia…" I marveled.

Once we finished, I glanced at my watch; still a few hours before I had to be back at the hotel. We decided to get Shadow and go for a walk around town—for exercise, but also, we both were getting antsy to learn more. We should be able to figure things out by meeting people. So far, everyone we met was sure eager to talk.

* * *

Nate and Colleen were busy cleaning up from the breakfast rush when we walked through the door at the bakery. Chief Smith and a deputy were sitting at a table located right inside the door.

"Mornin' folks," he greeted. "Say, did ya ever catch up with Mr. Longo?"

I shook my head, "Nope. His assistant manager told us he'd been called away on business."

"Ever find out why Cheryl said he'd been arrested?"

I shook my head again, remembering that I never had gotten to the bottom of that. Cheryl or Britney—one of them was lying. I took my turn with the questions.

"Any leads on Tricia's murder?" I asked him.

He looked to his deputy first. The young man tilted his head slightly. Whatever that meant, the chief decided to share a bit with us.

"We're getting a number of tips and following every lead. Should have something to announce publicly soon." He took a sip of his coffee. When he looked back at us, he frowned. "The problem is—well, this damn mystery weekend. Too many people playing amateur sleuth, if you know what I mean," he winked at me. I took that to mean he was specifically talking about me.

"I'd think that'd help your department out..." I suggested.

"Yeah, you'd think. Except, it can also distract. We'd appreciate it if the public took that part a bit more seriously."

"Are you accusing me of something here?"

He gave a slight nod. "I've been hearing you're asking a lot of questions around town. Please be careful." He raised his chin toward his deputy, who seemed to understand that meant they needed to leave. They both stood.

"Have a good day, Ms. Madsen."

I turned to Greg, confused. "What'd I do?"

"I hadn't thought you'd gotten in their way. But, I took

that as a stark warning."

We turned to see that we were now the only customers left in the bakery. Nate came over and asked if we'd like a seat.

"We wanted to stop in and say hi, but looks like we got reprimanded from the police instead."

"What could you two have possibly done?" Nate chuckled.

I piped up, "Guess I ask too many questions?"

"About Tricia … her murder?"

"Apparently. Which, by the way, did you know she and Bill were carrying on while she was married? We found that a bit shocking—didn't seem characteristic of him."

Nate laughed. "Oh, Bill's an interesting fellow. All buttoned up tight and *professional* at the hotel. But, he is not a saint—trust me."

That surprised Greg. "Oh yeah, how so?"

Nate moved us over to a table in the corner. He went to grab the coffee pot, poured us each a mug, and brought Shadow a small bowl of water. Then he took a seat, "Now, mind you … I haven't lived here near as long as either Patricia or Bill. But, *that woman* always got what she wanted. That's the first thing to consider. Bill wasn't all high and mighty as one might think, but he never saw it coming with that leech. She was all over him right from the beginning. I heard that she thought he was affluent. Rumor around town was that she had always been after money and the second he set foot in town, she was gonna get her some of that."

"He doesn't *own* the hotel, though, right? He manages it?" I asked.

"Yep. No money in managing a hotel—but she

apparently didn't know that. No one ever accused her of being the sharpest knife in the drawer—but she was manipulative. Crafty as hell."

"We heard she had several dead husbands..." Greg mentioned.

"Yep, apparently. And, from what I gathered, she was wrapped up in lawsuits with several of her former husband's heirs. Again, manipulative and feisty."

"So, when she died, she was still fighting these battles in court? I wonder if that was a motive for her murder?"

"And maybe that is what the chief doesn't want *you* to know..." He looked to the door that the chief had walked out of ten minutes prior.

I sipped my coffee and pondered what he'd said. "Wait, *why* wouldn't the chief want me to know about Tricia's history?"

"You didn't hear it from me, but I happen to know that the deputy he was sitting with—well, he's married to one of the in-laws."

"One of the heirs?"

He nodded.

"They're from here? Was this the truck driver's family then?"

Nate looked confused. "Uh, no. I don't think so. Don't know about a truck driver."

"The husband she was with when she started seeing Bill Longo."

"Oh! Ok, no ... this was before that one. She was married to a man who lived in Prescott Valley. He died of cancer from what I was told. He has a daughter and she's married now to the deputy that was in here. They live in Prescott Valley—he commutes here for work."

"So, his wife was fighting Tricia in court over what? Is she also Tricia's daughter?"

"I don't think Tricia was blood related—but she was stepmom for a number of years. Pretty certain that lady was from a previous marriage of his."

"Did you know what the court battle was about?"

"We heard that Tricia wanted her fair share of the estate…"

"She wasn't in the will?"

He shook his head.

"Wow, her story keeps getting more and more convoluted, doesn't it?" Greg marveled.

Colleen came out from the kitchen with Snow and Ball following closely behind. Shadow jumped up and greeted her new friends. They spun about yipping, tails wagging, and happy.

"Now, what are you all gossiping about over here?" she chided.

Nate filled her in on the chief's warning. She laughed. "Since when is it against the law to ask questions?"

"Exactly!" I added.

"Have they discovered who killed Tricia yet?" She got curious.

"Not that he'd tell us—but, he did admit they're following up on leads."

"Well, I sure hope they look up all the court cases she was involved in—she was a horrible business owner. Aside from that, from what we've heard, she made it a sport to keep people in court for years. Always appealing decisions against her and *never* happy until there was money in her pocket."

"Colleen, have you seen or heard from Mr. Longo?" I

asked, changing the direction of conversation.

"No. Why?"

"We haven't seen him in a few days and thought it was odd. His assistant manager said he was called away on business. We thought his business was the hotel. Anyway, he hadn't mentioned to me that he planned on being away while I was covering for Kirby."

She stood shaking her head. "No, his life *is* the hotel. So that is strange. I'm sure he'll be back soon."

The dogs stopped their play and all focused on the front door where Monica walked in. She was now the center of attention—all three were demanding her love.

"Well, what a greeting today at the bakery!" she exclaimed. "I love how they all have become fast friends."

Colleen went with Monica over to the counter and helped put together an order of goodies, and I decided to join them. Nate continued bending Greg's ear about the lawsuit they'd opened against Tricia.

Monica ribbed me, "You couldn't help but get in on the sweet-treat action, huh?"

"I was eyeing the cute tartlets from over there. But, also, those cupcakes are gorgeous!"

I picked a pumpkin spice cupcake and got a coffee refill. Monica completed her order with half a dozen donuts and a mint fudge brownie.

"The guys should be happy with the donuts," she smiled.

"Headed into work?" I asked.

"Yep, last day on shift and then I get a couple days off. You all are done with that mystery thing tonight, right?"

I nodded, while trying to take a bite of cupcake. Cream cheese frosting dotted the tip of my nose. Colleen handed me a napkin.

"Cheryl treating you all decent?"

I nodded again. "Last night was the most fun—it'll be interesting how this all wraps up. I have a couple theories, but also feel completely lost so who knows?"

"Who's your partner?"

"Um, I know him by the name Harold…"

She shrugged her shoulders, "Hmmm. No idea." I wasn't convinced she was as clueless as she said.

A thought crossed my mind. "Cheryl must be beside herself since Bill went on the run."

Monica's eyebrows crossed. "I'm sorry? Bill … what?"

"Well, the other night Cheryl told our mystery partners that Bill had been arrested. But, we've learned since that wasn't true. Then we discovered he had left town unexpectedly." I paused, then said, "Sorry, my mistake … I must have misinterpreted that as meaning he bailed out of town. If he actually was accused of killing Tricia, that's how I could've gotten that wrong."

She stammered. "Oh, gee … I don't think … I'd heard that."

"Well, with him being gone and all—I'm sure Cheryl misses him anyway." I played coyly.

"Why would my aunt *miss* him?" I had to give it to her—she played stupid on this subject expertly.

Colleen distracted us, giving me a pointed look as though I'd let the cat out of the bag, "I'm sure being the *friends* that they are and all … she must be worried about him, right?"

Monica picked up her bakery bags. "I'm sorry, ladies. I'm going to be late for work." She hurried out of the bakery, tip-toeing around the dogs who ushered her out.

Nate and Greg's stare went from the front door back over to us at the bakery counter.

"Libby, I'm not sure *everyone* knows about their relationship…" Colleen quietly informed.

"Monica didn't, that's for sure…" I stated. Then I spotted it. The dark blue sedan we'd seen across from the cottage. I swore it drove past, but by the time I'd made it to the front door, it was long gone.

Greg, Shadow, and I thanked Nate and Colleen for the coffee and goodies as we headed out of the bakery to continue our walk. My mind was milling around all the newest information like a whirlpool spinning out of control. Something about Cheryl wasn't sitting well with me and Monica's reaction hadn't made that any better.

We slowly made our way down the main drag when I saw the antique shop.

"Think we can take Shadow inside?" I asked him.

"We can ask. If not, I'm happy to sit out here with her while you look around."

I opened the door and popped my head in. I saw the man of average height, tanned skin, and jet-black hair. He looked and waved me in.

"Libby, c'mon in!" he shouted.

"We've got Shadow with us. Is that okay? I'll keep her on a tight leash."

"Should be fine."

I motioned to Greg, then took the leash from him and wrapped it around my hand several times. I looked down at her. "Be good, you hear? Heel." We all walked up to the counter. Shadow tensed. She started barking wildly. "C'mon, Shadow. Behave." She tried intently, pulling to get behind the counter.

"Sorry," I said to Chris.

Greg reached out. "Here, give me her leash. I'll sit with her outside." They left the building and I turned back to Chris.

I felt my cheeks flush red. "I'm so sorry about that. She's normally sociable and has never been a problem."

He shrugged, but I got the idea that he was happy she'd left. "What can I do for you, Libby? Enjoying the mystery fun?"

"Oh, yeah. I wasn't sure about it at first, but now, I think both Greg and I are actually enjoying it."

"He seems like a nice guy," Chris stated, looking through the window where Greg and Shadow sat on a bench.

I nodded. "Hey, I wanted to find a little something to take back home as a gift. Got anything like that?"

He showed me over to a display close by that had numerous jewelry pieces along with various odds and ends. "You might find something here that interests you." He stepped back behind the counter several feet away as I browsed the selection. By now, I discovered that I was the only customer in the store.

"I love small towns," I ventured, trying out the small talk on him. "But, man, everyone knows everyone, don't they?"

Curiously, he asked, "How so?"

"Well, in the couple days we've been here, I'm pretty sure we've been told several times that Bill and Cheryl have a *thing* going on," I teasingly offered.

He shrugged. "Yes, you are correct. The whole town gossips. That's why I try to stick to myself."

"So, it's not true?"

"Oh, who knows … could be true. The other truth about small towns is how everyone gets around. It seems they've all slept with one another, married and divorced, or are somehow related. Can get old very quickly."

"Do you know Bill well? I've found him to be accommodating at the hotel."

He climbed up a short ladder and turned away to dust a nearby shelf, avoiding eye contact. "Yep. Everyone loves Bill," he lamented.

"Do I detect that you're not one of them?"

He twisted around on his ladder. "Is this about the mystery weekend—or, what exactly are you asking?"

I thought about that for a second. *What exactly did I want to know from Chris?*

"I heard he and Tricia were divorced. You don't think he could have killed her, do you?" I asked innocently.

"Nah. No way could Bill have killed Tricia." Shaking his head adamantly, he added, "Bill is a good man. I may not always agree with him, but he's *not* a murderer."

"You've had a disagreement with Bill?" I asked, rummaging through a box of trinkets, noticing a particularly beautiful brooch—simple old world Scottish style. The Celtic knot appeared to be pewter with a simple pearl in the middle. I thought of Jordan—my sister would love this.

"You sound like a cop," he chuckled.

Laughing, I tried to keep things light. "No! I only find your mention of it funny since he seems so … docile?"

"Yeah, I see what you mean. I guess whenever you borrow money from someone—it changes everything."

"He borrowed money from you?"

"Other way around. It hasn't been easy running an antique shop." He hung his head slightly. "Bill's been great though—sure got me out of a pickle."

I moved back to the counter and Chris came down off the ladder. "Did you find anything you'd like?" he asked.

"Oh, I found several things … but I need to think on it." I couldn't help but notice the dejected look. "Thank you. I've got to get going, but we'll be back. Great talking to you, Chris!"

Outside, Greg asked if I bought out the store. I showed him my hands—nothing today. As we walked home, my thoughts went back to how Shadow had reacted to Chris. Or was it the old shop that spooked her?

CHAPTER SIXTEEN

That afternoon, after we'd been back at the cottage researching a few things online, we decided to venture over to Prescott. I'd learned Tricia's stepdaughter's name was Olivia Chavez and she worked at a bar. I was certain that if we found her, perhaps she could clear a few things up. I also suspected she was the one driving around in Tricia's Smart car.

Within an hour, we had made our way over Mingus Mountain and found the cute bar downtown off Gurley St. on what was known as Whiskey Row. We left Shadow in the 4Runner, with windows cracked and sunroof open, while we popped in. Stepping inside, it took a moment for my eyes to adjust. When they did, I saw there were the few regulars at the bar talking to the bartender. The four of them looked up when we walked in. You could have heard a pin drop had the jukebox not been playing.

We walked on up to the bar and I ad-libbed. "Hi! I'm looking for Olivia Chavez—friend from way back. She told me to look her up in if I were ever in town. Well, here I am!" I gave the bald-headed, long-bearded, muscular man a huge smile. He didn't return it.

"Her shift doesn't start till eight…" he grumbled.

"Oh, darn. I'll miss her then. We aren't staying in town—only here for a few hours." I stomped my foot, "Darn, I know she'd want the goodies her mom sent with us…" I looked over to Greg. "What was her address again…think it was on…" I stumbled trying to remember some of the street names I'd seen when looking up the bar on google maps. "Oh dang, my memory is horrible!"

The burly man said, "Not far from here…Pleasant St."

"Yes! That's it … excellent, I'll see if I can catch her now. Thank you!" We turned and left the less-than-inviting place.

I pulled out my phone, typed in Pleasant St. into Google maps before I forgot, and it directed us further east on Gurley St., where we found Pleasant. We decided to begin by turning right. Turns out, it is a long street on either side of Gurley. We slowly passed houses, looking carefully for the yellow Smart car. Once we got to the end of that street, we slowly went back the other direction to be sure we hadn't missed anything. We crossed the main street, and ventured north, continuing to look for the unmistakable yellow vehicle. We felt defeated once we had made it to the other end and hadn't found the house.

"Now what?" he asked.

"Let's explore the neighborhood—the shopping centers nearby. Maybe she's running errands before her shift tonight? Groceries, gas, or somewhere?"

We found a Sprouts market around the corner off Montezuma St. Driving slowly, surveilling the parking lot, we saw a lot of SUVs and trucks but no small cars. We pulled out onto Montezuma and chose to check out Sheldon St. I kept my eyes peeled while Greg navigated traffic. No luck.

He pulled into another parking lot, where there was a hardware shop, a credit union, and some other businesses. "Any other ideas?" he asked.

"I sure thought this would be easier. It's not a huge city! Well, it's not as tiny as Jerome either—I'm not sure what I was thinking. I'd hate for this to be a wasted trip." I checked my watch. It was approaching two … we had to be back for the finale dinner by six and also plan for the hour's drive back. "Need anything while we're in the big city?"

"Not really … are you hungry? Breakfast was hours ago."

"I could eat. I looked in the back and saw Shadow staring at me. "How about back at that town square— where the bar was—there's a park. Let's walk around a little first and check it out. If I'm remembering correctly, there were tons of restaurants, surely there's one with patio seating. How about that?"

Greg agreed and got us turned around, headed back to Whiskey Row. Circling the town square for the second time, my eye caught a flash of yellow down one of the side streets.

"Look! Go back around—I think I saw the car." I called out. Shadow jumped up to her backseat window and barked excitedly, startling both of us.

Slowly driving down the street, we found the little race-striped Smart car parked in front of a municipal building.

Greg pointed, "Interesting—look at the car parked next to it."

"Genesis. Isn't that similar to the one we saw near the cottage?"

"Uh, yep, same make and model. Coincidental—think the owners of these two cars know one another?"

Greg shrugged. "Still want to get out and walk?"

"I do. But, hold on a second," I opened the passenger door and slipped out. Casually walking by each car, I glanced at the parking meter's time. I turned and quickly climbed back into the vehicle. "Seems as though each car arrived at a similar time—both have ten minutes left on their meter. Let's give it a few minutes to see who comes back to these cars."

It didn't take long—within five minutes, a young lady with long brown hair covered with a green stocking cap, dressed in baggy jeans, loose t-shirt, and black combat boots approached the tiny vehicle. She was a petite girl—five foot tall, if that. I quickly jumped out of my car and called out, "Olivia!" She turned my direction. "Wait…" I shouted.

Her facial expression changed from curiosity to irritated quickly. I hurried over to her. Greg and Shadow stayed in the 4Runner.

"Hi. I thought it was you!"

"Do we know each other?" she asked.

"We haven't met—but I knew your mother, Patricia."

"Patricia is not my mother." She still had one hand on the car door. "What do you want?" she asked, nervously looking around.

"Oh. Wow, I've been misinformed then. I guess I

assumed … Olivia … her middle name," my voice trailed off. "Patricia Simpson from Jerome," I pointed toward Mingus Mountain. "This is her car, right?" I asked, glancing at the tiny vehicle.

"Who are you?" she questioned, as she opened her car door and threw a bag on the seat.

"Right. Should have started with that, sorry. I'm Libby Madsen—your mom, er … I mean, Patricia groomed my dog. Uh, well, that was before she passed away. I'm so sorry about your loss, by the way." Struggling to determine how this girl was related to Tricia, I found myself having a heck of a time conversing with her. "Anyway, I saw her car as we were passing by…" I pointed to Greg in the car, he waved at us, and she scrunched her face into more of a scowl. She sure *looked* like a mini-me of Patricia. "I mean, the car is quite distinctive. When I saw you, I figured you're her daughter so, well, I'm wondering how the investigation's going and wanting to give our condolences. That's all."

She stammered for a second. "Tricia is dead?"

Oh crap. What the hell? "Oh, wow. Okay. You didn't know this? But, you have her car…"

"My dad bought this car for me. Well, he and *that piece of work* signed a loan together to give it to me for my twenty-first birthday," she informed, as her body language shifted to downright irate. "During their *divorce*, she took it! Dad and I fought her ever since to get it back." She twisted around, looking back at the building she'd come from. Her lawyer's office, I presumed. "Unfortunately, it's taken *years* … she's driven the shit out of it, and Dad never made it to see me finally win that battle."

"Oh," I started solemnly, "your dad has passed, too?" I shifted my weight nervously from leg to leg. "I'm very sorry."

"I don't need your pity! And I still don't understand why you're here? Did you have unfinished business with Tricia, like nearly everyone in that town had?" she spat. "Because if so, none of that is *my problem*. You hear? Leave me alone!" She turned to get into her seat.

I put my body in front of her open car door. From her seat, she looked up at me irritated. "Wait. Wait, please give me two more minutes and I promise ... I'll leave you alone."

"What!" she yelled.

"You hadn't heard that Tricia was murdered?"

Her face fell. "Murdered?" she said quieter, contemplating what I'd said. She looked back up at me, her eyes were fiery, "Well, I guess all of her shenanigans caught up with her finally!"

"Shenanigans?" I asked. "Can you share? Sounds like she's put you through a lot—I'd love to help your family find justice, if that's what you've been seeking. It's not easy losing your father, especially when you feel as though someone's wronged the family?"

Her eyes softened slightly. "Who are you again?"

Still trying to figure out how to get her to talk, I told her, "The police are looking at *all* current and former family members—of course, you probably know that, being married to the deputy and all."

"Who told you that? I'm not married to no *cop*!"

"Oh, my mistake, sorry! Well, you won't believe this—" I turned and pointed again to the 4Runner where Shadow had her nose pressed against the backseat window. "They've even accused *my dog* of killing Tricia. And, I can tell you for a fact, she didn't. I'm sure you'd like to be cleared and I'd certainly love to keep my family out of this mess. Can we buy you lunch and hear your story?"

"And you're not the police?"

"No, not at all." I held my pinky to her. "Pinky promise." She stared me down, but ultimately lifted her pinky and twisted it with mine.

"Okay," she gave in.

"You're from here, what's your favorite place?"

She pointed to a sandwich shop around the corner and said we could eat outside on a dog-friendly patio. I ran over and told Greg what we were doing and we unloaded Shadow. He filled both parking meters with quarters and we were on our way. I noticed that no one had come back for the blue sedan yet.

Olivia was correct—I had a Reuben sandwich and it was amazing. Greg opted for a turkey, bacon, cheese melt and Olivia swore by their roast beef with grilled onions and mushroom. Shadow sat at my feet, drooling.

"I'm sorry I was so short with you earlier. Ever since Dad died, and that witch has served our family time and again with lawsuits, I don't trust *anyone*."

"Do you mind if I ask how your dad died?" Greg asked.

"He spent all his time on the road—truck driver. Well, several years back he was headed back east on a run and his brakes failed. He was on a mountain pass and they found it on fire at the bottom of a deep canyon. Told us he died instantly."

Both Greg and I grimaced at that image, and remembered hearing about a truck driving previous husband. "Your father didn't die of cancer, then?"

"No, where'd you hear that?"

Obviously, small town gossip. Greg turned to me, "So, how long was Tricia married to Bill then? I thought it had been longer than a few years."

Shrugging, "Yeah, I was thinking it was longer—but who knows, everything has been coming in dribbles from the townspeople. And it sounds like we're caught up in rumors. Do they actually know?"

Olivia's eyes caught mine, "I don't think she ever actually married Bill. They lived together for a time—called each other husband and wife, but while going through the court battle, we learned she was collecting on Dad's death benefits. When I questioned how, since she supposedly quickly remarried, well, that's how we learned they were never 'legally married,'" she finished with air quotes.

I took another bite of my sandwich, followed up with a few sour cream and onion chips. My attention suddenly diverted to a large man standing across the street and a couple businesses down. If I wasn't mistaken, he stood staring directly at us. He wore a long dark trench coat, a black stocking cap, those dark mirrored sunglasses, and leaned against one of the building's pillars.

Greg was still pondering what Olivia divulged. After a moment or two, he asked her, "What year did your dad die, then?"

I took my eyes off the ominous man and engaged back in our conversation.

"2015," she said quietly. "Worst year of my life..."

"Okay, and we learned that Bill and Tricia split up when?" he asked me.

"I don't know that we have that information. We only know that they did break up—and supposedly he's secretly dating Cheryl now. And Tricia was upset about that."

Olivia's eyes grew wide. "Arts Council Cheryl? The mystery weekend coordinator?" She wiped her mouth and sighed loudly when we nodded affirmatively. "Wow. That's a tight circle of … *friends.*"

"How do you mean?" I asked, distracted when I realized that the man was no longer across the street.

"Well, Cheryl and Tricia used to be close friends—at least from what my dad told me, I assumed they were. Sure hope she ended it with Bill before Cheryl moved in on him…"

"How do you know Cheryl would have pursued Bill?"

"Oh, c'mon, Bill doesn't chase … he's a weak mouse. Guy's a complete wimp. My dad could have pounded him, you know, when he learned the witch cheated," she scoffed. "Even dad realized who was responsible for that. He went easy on the guy—almost pitied him. She was … well, something else. So, yeah, *if it's true,* Cheryl would have been the pursuer."

"Was it a pattern then? With Patricia…" Greg wondered.

"Oh yeah. That woman has *no* scruples. Not even one!" She slammed her hand against the table. "She killed my father. I know it! She is a money-grubbing piece of shit!"

"Do you have proof?"

Olivia's eyes questioned.

"That she killed your dad?"

"Oh. Well, no. She wanted him out of the picture once she realized she wasn't going to get any money from our family. My dad wasn't stupid. He worked it out perfectly— my brother and I were sole beneficiaries in his trust. Plus, it's not like he had a fortune anyway, but he was smart that way and wanted to protect what he did have. I'm not sure what she thought she could get out of him actually. Maybe because he was the type that treated the ladies special. He'd have done anything for her—wined her, dined her. For some reason, he truly loved her—spoiled her rotten."

"So, you don't actually know that she had anything to do with your dad's truck malfunctioning?"

"No," her voice lowered, and she hung her head, staring at the table. "But, right after the accident, we hired a private investigator to help us determine foul play. There was nothing conclusive. Then we got wrapped up in years of litigation—greedy old ..." She sipped her soda from its straw, squelching her foul language.

I reached out my hand and patted hers. "I understand how difficult it is to accept the death of a parent. I can't imagine being haunted daily by someone so greedy and wanting to take more from you. That's horrible." The lingering question in my brain was whether this gave Olivia motive to kill Tricia. She was most certainly an angry young woman. And understandably so, but angry enough for murder? I couldn't be sure, so I asked, "Olivia, where were you the night of October twenty-ninth?"

"See, I knew it!" she seethed. "You are cops! I knew it!" She started to move back from the table.

Greg quickly stepped in. "No, no. Olivia, we want to help. You were here in Prescott, right?"

"Yes, I was! But I cannot believe you would even suggest..."

"Sweetie," I said to her, "the cops will eventually get over here and question you. We can't be the only ones who have seen you driving Tricia's car..."

She swiftly interrupted, anger flaring, "*MY car!!!*"

"Yes, of course. But ... there will be questions. You should be prepared to answer them."

She looked between both of us, collecting her thoughts. Then her eyes cast down again, "I'm sorry. You both do seem nice—but, I don't know who to trust anymore."

"That's understandable," I empathized.

We paid the bill and gave her our phone numbers in case she remembered anything else. We all walked back to our cars; I noticed immediately that the blue sedan had already left. Before saying goodbye, I recalled something she'd said earlier.

"Olivia, does your brother live here too?"

"Nah, I think he's in Texas now. He was moving … but he has to be settled in by now, I'd think."

"Would he be angry enough to kill Tricia?"

"Of course not!" She was offended.

"Okay, yes, of course. And, what is his name?"

"Dale …"

"You may want to tell him about her death. You know, so he's also prepared for any questions…" I suggested.

We said goodbye to Olivia and headed back to Jerome. But not before covertly following her home so we'd know where she lived.

* * *

As we entered Jerome and made the loop around on Main St., we saw that Nate and Colleen had their dogs at the nearby dog park.

"We are still early enough, wanna let Shadow out to play with her buddies?"

Shadow bounded up to the window, saw the little white dogs in the distance and let out a bark.

I laughed, "I think that answers your question. Sure, it would be good to get out of the car—seems like we've sat all day long."

"Because we have!" Greg chuckled.

We parked the vehicle and grabbed Shadow's leash, securing her for the short distance into the park.

"Good morning!" Colleen said as we arrived. "We'll come over there—"

They were the only ones in the park, but it was better for them to join us in the large dog section than the other way around.

All the girls, once together, started yipping and wriggling all over. They ran and chased down Shadow. She then turned on them and chased them across the grassy area, and they kept up this play on a repeat loop.

"Good timing. We were getting ready to leave, but we have a little more time—this will be fun for them," Nate said, watching the dogs as they made their way to the other side. "What have you guys been up to today?"

"We went over to Prescott for a while."

"Oh, to do some shopping or something?"

"No, actually ... we went looking for Tricia's daughter," I started.

"She has a daughter in Prescott?" Colleen looked confused.

"Well, apparently, no. Would have once been her stepdaughter..."

"Oh, that one. I think I remember her. Was she the mini-me?"

I nodded and laughed. "She's the one who we saw the other day driving Tricia's car—not sure if I told you about that?"

"Yeah, we saw the little yellow car flash by too...can't remember whether that was before or after Tricia though," Colleen's eyes cast downward and her thoughts trailed off.

"It's a long story for sure … but helped us understand why someone was driving the car," Greg added.

We answered Colleen's questions as we all walked around the park while the dogs played. Nate was particularly quiet and didn't add much to the conversation. Watching him, I wondered whether he knew more than he'd let on.

My phone sounded from deep in my jacket pocket. I pulled it out and excused myself from the group as I stepped aside and punched the button.

"Hi, Kirby!" I answered.

"Libby— how's everything going?"

I continued walking across the park while she told me all about her dad's recovery. I assured her everything was fine and we looked forward to seeing her in a couple days. As she continued talking, I decided to find out what Shadow was fixated on at the far end of the park. She and the two white fluff balls were intent on something in the corner, near bushes that lined the other side of the fencing.

As I got closer, I saw a large bush outside the fencing. Shadow was pawing at the chain-link fence trying to get at that bush. I pulled her away and bent down a little to see what was grabbing their attention. I couldn't see anything, so I pointed them back toward our group several yards away. Greg saw and started calling for them.

"…And then, one day he wasn't living there anymore," Kirby finished her sentence.

I had to admit getting distracted, but she had been filling me in on the whole Cheryl and Bill drama with Tricia and her former husband. It sounded like quite the friendly 'circle' amongst those three—something felt strange about it all. Cheryl sure hadn't let on how good of friends she and Tricia were. In fact, she barely skipped a beat when the woman was found dead. That sure seemed suspicious to me.

Shadow came running back, and following farther behind her were the little ones. I finished my conversation with Kirby and got them to chase me back to the others.

"They must smell some varmint over there," I huffed when I got to Greg.

Colleen and Nate picked up their two and let us know it was time for them to go. They wished us good luck in the finale later that night, then we watched them walk down the street and into the surrounding neighborhood.

"I didn't realize they lived so close," Greg mentioned. "Who called?"

"Kirby … confirming she'll be home in a couple days. Can't wait to meet you!" I smiled and reached up to plant a kiss on his lips.

"It doesn't feel like we've been here that long already. Guess we've stayed busy…"

"I like this little town."

Shadow ran back to the spot in the fence.

"Ugh. That dog … one track mind!" I turned to start walking back across the park again.

Greg said, "I'll go out—to the other side down there. Let's see if we can drive away whatever it is."

He left through the designated gate. I jogged down to where Shadow was now digging the grass up. "Hey, girl … stop that!" I knelt down to her level as she pressed her nose at the bottom of the fencing and pawed at it incessantly. "Can you see anything over there?" I asked Greg.

He kicked at the bush, hoping to send something scampering. Nothing ran out. Or rattled. He crawled down on the ground, and squared up exactly where Shadow was looking. Carefully, he began to move aside branches of the desert sage.

"Wait, there's something shiny … metallic…" he scooted closer. "Hmmm."

"What?"

"They are scissors—it looks like." Outside of his reach, he laid down on his side and stretched out his arm. "Got 'em" He sat up. "Oh shit!" He dropped whatever he was holding.

"What? What happened?" I pictured him getting a snake bite, or something cutting him.

"There's dried blood…" he stood up, looking me in the eyes, "Call the police. I think we found the murder weapon."

CHAPTER SEVENTEEN

The ballroom was exquisitely decorated for the finale. Another three-course dinner would be served, the final clues discovered, and the grand prize winner announced. Considering I was clueless in the Mr. Adler murder investigation to this point, I felt sorry for my 'I always win these—' partner. I would most likely be the cause of his downfall this time around.

Dressed again in coat and tails, Greg was astonishingly handsome. Shadow wore her tuxedo shirt and tonight, a beautiful red sparkling bow tie, too. The dress provided for me tonight was a long sleeveless, tight-fitting, black gown. Greg admired it, and although it was a beautiful evening gown, I couldn't imagine how I was supposed to make my way around the hotel looking for clues. I could only take baby steps—my legs felt tied together, trapped in the fabric.

We found our seats and then went to grab a drink.

Harold was smiling and cheerful as we approached. "Ready to win this whole thing, Libby?"

I gave him a small nod, guiltily concerned that he'd regret being placed with me as his partner. "Have you got it all figured out?"

"You know I do," he winked.

Well, that was news to me. From last night's wrap-up, it hadn't appeared to me that we had *anything* to go on. "Glad you're my partner, then…" I smiled up at him.

Britney walked over to us. "Last night of this shindig…" she uttered, sounding as though she wished it were already over with.

We all got our drinks from Harold and then went to sit down for the dinner. Before it was served, Cheryl took the microphone and after a few high-pitched screeches, we could finally hear her. "Is that better?" she said, and everyone nodded.

"Okay! Well, this is it folks! We're going to learn once and for all, who killed Mr. Adler… and *why*. Aren't you excited?" She cheered us on. There were several enthusiastic game players who hooted and hollered, including Harold, as I looked back and caught him jumping up and down with his arms in the air, yelling, "Yeah!"

Greg squeezed my leg underneath the disguise of the white tablecloth. I smiled in his direction. Looks like we both agreed, Cheryl and the exuberant players were a bit much.

Appetizers were placed in front of each of us. I started to dip my coconut shrimp into the sweet and spicy sauce they'd included on the plate, and listened carefully to our host.

Cheryl gave out the evening's instructions—only the fourth and fifth floors were where clues would be found tonight. The first team back to the ballroom with the correct findings: *who* did it, and *why* (we already know it was done in the dining room with the revolver) … that team would win a free weekend's stay at the hotel, along with a free hour-long massage for two, a nice dinner at the local steakhouse, along with a free scenic train ride on the Verde Valley Railway.

She finished up by introducing the local businesses who were, "All proud sponsors of this weekend's murder mystery—they've happily donated. It's a great winning package, so I hope you give it your *all* so you can be the big winner!"

I excused myself to go to the restroom before the dinner was served. I walked in and heard a couple ladies talking to each other between stalls. At the stall on the far end, I struggled for a minute trying to figure out *how* to manage around this tight-fitting dress. Once I sat down, I could hear more details of the conversation.

"…apparently, it was the murder weapon," one lady whispered. "They found it near that dog park."

"You mean right behind his house?"

"That's what I understand, yes."

"Well, then that's it—the police should wrap this up quickly now."

I sat quietly, wondering if they'd known I was in there with them. Surely, they had heard me enter, but they chatted as though it was private conversation. Once I heard both toilets flush, the sink water turn off, the paper towels being wadded up, and then the door shut, I let out my breath. *Whose voices had I heard?* I hadn't recognized them.

Once I stood up, I struggled again to get all zipped back up. *Men never have this struggle!* I thought as I washed and hurried to get back to the table.

I leaned over Greg before I sat down, and whispered, "Did you happen to see who came out of the ladies washroom?"

He shook his head.

Dangit!

He leaned over once I'd taken my seat. "Why? What happened?"

I saw that everyone at the table was wrapped up in conversation so I whispered, "Two ladies were chatting about the murder weapon being found."

"Well, of course, we all know it was a revolver—we've known that from the first night," he said aloud. A couple of others looked our direction and I smiled at them.

Whispering close to his ear, "No. *The* murder weapon. The one *we* found."

His mouth made an O and he picked up his gin and tonic and took a sip.

"The police already let out that information?" he whispered, before setting his glass down.

"I guess. I thought they'd hold onto that a little longer—maybe get DNA back before telling the public. Anyway, that's why I wanted to know who they were. I couldn't see—and I didn't recognize the voices."

Our plates were placed in front of us. Banquet chicken that included steamed vegetables, potatoes, and a dinner roll. Fairly basic and not as grand as the first night, but still delicious.

I glanced across the room to find that Harold had sat at the table closest to the bar to eat his meal. It was then that I realized where he was standing earlier—the bar faced the bathroom hallway. I'd have to ask him—if he truly was such an amazing sleuth, then that type of detail would be exactly what he'd be watching for.

Within half an hour, everyone was antsy to get on with the search for clues. Greg found Britney, and I headed to the bar to talk to Harold.

"Ready? Or, did you want another drink?" he asked excitedly.

I shook my head, "No more drink. Hey, I was curious … before dinner was served, did you see when I walked in the bathroom?"

He nodded.

"Okay, did you see who walked out of the bathroom a few minutes later? Other than me…"

His eyes cast upward toward the ceiling. "I saw you come out … I do think there were a few others. Who was it?" his finger tapped his chin. "Ah, no, I can't remember."

So much for the super sleuth.

He wiped up the countertop really fast, leaving the rag behind and then giving us the go ahead. Shadow led the way to the staircase and we ascended six flights from the basement. Breathing heavily, he bent over and put his hands on his knees.

"Jeez, Libby. You take those stairs like there's nothing to it." He slowly stood up straight again, put his hands on his hips, letting out another loud sigh. "Okay, where do we start? End of the hall?"

I nodded, Shadow wagged, and we followed Harold.

"Looks like our strategy worked—almost everyone

else started on the fourth floor," I noticed as I peered into the first room. As we'd passed the others, I'd only heard voices of one other pair.

Shadow pushed her way into the room and went straight for the bathroom. Her nose quickly sniffed out the first note. Harold knelt down, and taped to the pedestal of the sink was a small piece of paper. He pulled it off, read it, and off we went to the next room, and on and on we went.

Harold, Shadow, and I made our way to each room along the fifth floor—ahead of one other pair, then down the stairs to the fourth floor. We were laughing and enjoying the chase when we ran into Greg and Britney in the stairwell. Both had found clues and had a difficult time containing their excitement. We all had a good chuckle and then proceeded on our separate ways.

After the final clue was found on the fourth floor, we stood staring at one another.

"I thought she said these were the only two floors that held clues?" I was confused. We both read the clue—it was leading us to the basement again.

"Maybe that was meant to throw us off?"

I shrugged. Shadow barked and nudged us to get going. We carefully navigated the stairwell all the way back into the darkened basement. Both Harold and I thought the clue referenced something to do with laundry so that's where we headed. As soon as we hit the bottom floor and opened the door, Shadow bounded down the hallway. I took it slower, trying not to become tangled in my long dress. It was curious to me why no one else was down here. Hadn't someone else found a clue yet that led them here—I still hadn't figured out how Cheryl managed to keep everyone heading in different directions. Seemed chaotic to me, but she was the expert at this after all.

We heard growling from Shadow. She was standing at the end of the hallway, looking through the threshold into the laundry room, before looking back at me with a look of 'you're taking too long!' Once I got closer to her, I saw her hackles up. She began barking loudly, her nose pointing straight ahead. I poked my head around the entrance and immediately jumped back, screaming.

Harold pushed forward. "What the …?" He rebounded nearly as quickly as I had, also breathing into the crook of his forearm and elbow. It wasn't an illusion or my imagination. We both saw, and smelled, the same thing.

A dead body.

CHAPTER EIGHTEEN

It took several more hours before the police completed taking everyone's statements. Greg still had his arms around me; he hadn't let go since receiving my text and finding us in the basement—with a dead man. Eventually the police had led us away from the laundry room and we had joined the rest of the mystery crew, who had gathered back in the ballroom. No one was allowed to leave.

Harold, shaken and subdued, stayed in his corner near the bar. Britney sat with us and couldn't stop crying. Mr. and Mrs. Brandish were also at the table next to us, when the lady removed her wig; I could tell for certain now that this was the hotel's assistant manager. I wasn't sure if the man I knew as Mr. Brandish in the mystery game was related to her in real life or not, but he was consoling her.

Cheryl paced the far end of the ballroom. She went to make a phone call and an officer stopped her; they had an angry exchange and then she went back to pacing. So many questions were running through my mind: *How had no one else detected Mr. Bill Longo's body before we did?*

I'd overheard an officer mention that it appeared he'd been dead for several days, which made sense. We had seen that rigor mortis had set in. So I wondered, *Had he been dead ever since his fictitious character 'died'? How had the hotel staff not found him while doing their cleaning rounds? Wait, I'd been in the laundry room since then ... impossible.* I answered my own question. *He hadn't died there—he was placed in that room tonight to be found. How sick!* Something else was nagging at me. I'd seen a shiny object protruding from Bill's shirt pocket when we found him. I hadn't wanted to touch anything. *Why did that thing seem familiar?*

I also couldn't figure out *why* Cheryl had fooled Harold into thinking that Bill had been arrested for Tricia's murder. *What was that all about? Why had she done that? That is, if Harold's not lying.* Nothing made sense to me and images continued to swirl around in my head. The only thing I knew was that Shadow had found two dead bodies since we had arrived in Jerome. Less than a week, two people dead. And the two victims used to be married to one another.

Chief Smith walked up to us, "Libby. Greg. You are free to leave now—thank you for your cooperation." He leaned over and petted Shadow, then looked over at Britney. "Ms. Barker, you may go too."

We all stood, collected our things, and headed out to the parking lot. Poor girl, Britney's eye makeup made her look like she'd been in a brawl, the way it was melting down her face. We walked her to her car—a beat up red older Chevy Malibu. I gave her a hug and told her to call us if she needed anything. We walked across the parking lot to Greg's Tundra and as I loaded Shadow in, I saw it. The dark blue Genesis.

"Greg, isn't that the car that was parked outside our place? Think it's the same one we saw in Prescott, too?"

He nodded slowly. I shut the truck's door, leaving Shadow inside, while we walked over to it. There was no one inside and the doors were locked. Greg snapped a photo of the car and its license plate with his phone's camera. We left; it was nearly two in the morning.

* * *

Later in the morning, Greg and I learned about the murder mystery weekend news as we sat at the café having breakfast. It was the buzz of the town; everyone was talking.

What was to be the finale of the *Sniper at the Speakeasy*, instead turned out to be Cheryl's worst nightmare. Nothing had been solved and now the site of the mystery weekend was a crime scene. The first time ever—Cheryl's mystery weekend finished without a winner. Police and forensic scientists were everywhere and Mrs. Brandish was told it would be that way the rest of the day. No new customers, and those who were checked in at the hotel were still in the process of being interrogated. The game was over.

I stepped out of the café and called Chief Smith, unsure what that meant for the massage appointments scheduled for the day. He said he'd let me know when I was cleared to return to gather personal effects, otherwise, it was off limits—the hotel was closed until further notice.

Greg and I sipped our coffee in silence, both lost in

thought. I noticed that Britney wasn't at the café, which was understandable, even if she had been scheduled to work.

"I don't think you've already said, but how did you guys end up in the basement anyway?" Greg looked up at me, inquisitive.

Snapping back to the present, "We had a clue—I don't remember what it said, but both Harold and I immediately thought *laundry*, so that's where we went."

"That's strange—we were told the search would be limited to the fourth and fifth floors."

"Yes, we thought that as well. But, then we followed the lead anyway." I shrugged, then looked up as the waiter set down my garden vegetable omelet.

We both thanked him after he'd delivered Greg's biscuits and gravy and asked if there was anything else we needed. We dug into the hearty breakfast and resumed discussion about the previous night once we left the café half an hour later.

It was a beautiful morning outside—slightly chilly, but our jackets kept us comfortable. We slowly walked back to the cottage to collect Shadow. Neither of us could sit— we were anxious and felt the need to do *something*. Once we walked in the small house, we could tell Shadow was feeling the same way so we made the decision to go to the dog park.

We walked the length of Main St., then when it veered into the loop, we crossed the street and ventured through a neighborhood before we arrived at the park. Before we got to the next intersection, we saw Nate in his front yard, several houses ahead.

Greg raised a hand to wave hi, then said to me, "I had

no idea they lived this close to the park." Nate waved back.

I waved too, saying under my breath, "Me either."

We got to the park and let Shadow off leash. She immediately ran to the far end, where she'd found the evidence the day prior. There was police tape up on the outer portion of the fence for a few feet in either direction, along the concrete block wall that was the barrier into the residential neighborhood.

"C'mon, Shadow … there's nothing left there to see," I said, tapping her head, trying to get her attention. Apparently, she agreed with me because she turned and trotted down the park's chain link fence, sniffing wildly the entire way.

I stopped in my tracks, remembering the bathroom conversation from the night before. Something about the murder weapon and 'behind *his* wall' … *whose*? The image of Nate waving from his front yard popped up. I turned around to size up the neighborhood we'd walked through to get to the park. From the road that intersected to either access the park or to travel into the neighborhood, I counted the houses in my head.

Greg, who had kept walking, now stopped too. "What is it?"

"How many houses down do you think Nate's home was?"

He started mentally counting. "Well, maybe three or four?"

"Yeah, that's what I was thinking too. Right behind where Shadow found the scissors…"

His eyes looked directly at the yellow tape, then up the wall where you could see the top half of the red tiled roof on the tan-colored stucco home. Slowly turning back to me, "What are you thinking, Libby?"

"The ladies in the restroom last night talked about the murder weapon being found right behind 'his' home," using air quotes to highlight my point.

Greg turned back and stared at the wall, then the ground where we found the supposed weapon, and then started shaking his head. "You think *Nate* or *Colleen* had something to do with Tricia's death?"

My eyes widened. "No. Not necessarily. Or, at least, I didn't know they lived there until now. Guess I'm connecting pieces and yes, I think I have more questions."

"Oh c'mon ... they are so nice. They can't possibly have anything to do ..." he trailed off as he watched the two and their little dogs walk down the sidewalk. Moving closer to me, he whispered, "You aren't going to say anything, are you?"

"No! But, I wonder if they know what was found here yesterday?"

We both waved enthusiastically to our new friends as they managed their dogs through the set of gates. Shadow had already run over to greet them. We met up with them in the middle of the park.

"Hey, guys," Colleen greeted. "Nate said he saw you walk this direction. Hope you don't mind if we join you?"

"Not at all. We're enjoying the gorgeous weather. Need something to keep our minds occupied." Greg said.

"Do you mean because of Bill's death..." her voice softened, eyes drifting to view the ground.

I put a hand on her shoulder to comfort. "Horrible shock for us all. I can't believe he was dead—in real life—this whole time."

Both Nate and Colleen eyed me suspiciously. He spoke

up, "Um, er," he shifted feet, then started again, "I'm not sure what you mean *in real life?*"

I explained, "Oh! The stupid mystery weekend. Right, you wouldn't know … but Bill played a character, Mr. Adler, who was killed the first night. We've been gathering clues to solve that and then found the actual Bill Longo dead."

Colleen gasped. "*You* found him?" Her hand slapped against her mouth in disbelief.

"Unfortunately. My partner in the game—and yes, Shadow and I—we all found him in the basement of the hotel."

"Oh, heavens!" she grimaced.

Nate, still shifting his weight from leg to leg, asked, "Do you … er, know *how* he died?"

I shook my head. "The police aren't saying much. And, it wasn't evident when we found him. Other than we know it didn't happen where we'd found him. I believe he was dumped there—during the game last night."

"What?" Colleen turned white; I reached out to help steady her. "That poor man." She turned away as she wiped tears from her face. Her attention was then held captive, looking to the far end of the park. "What's that? Nate—isn't that right behind *our house?*" She pointed and they both took off jogging that direction. All the dogs chased them and we followed.

When we caught up, we heard her saying, "What on earth?" as she kneeled down where the dogs were all sniffing.

Greg casually said, "Yep, Shadow found what the police think might be the murder weapon in Tricia's case."

Nate stayed near the ground, hugging his dogs. Colleen popped right up, "You've got to be kidding me? The murderer was *this close* to us!" she panted.

This time I wasn't close enough to catch her and she did go down—turned white as a sheet and fainted. The three of us knelt beside her as she came to.

"Want me to call the paramedics?" I asked Nate, pulling my phone from my jacket pocket.

"I'm fine, I'm fine," she whispered.

I still looked to Nate for the decision, worried about her.

He shook his head and we helped get her to a sitting position. Color began filling her cheeks again.

Taking their two dogs, Nate decided to jog home to get his car. She was too weak. We sat with Colleen and once we were assured she was better, Greg helped her up off the ground and we walked her slowly toward the entrance gates to meet Nate.

Trying to distract her, Greg asked, "I was curious, Colleen, that lawsuit with Tricia—had that been resolved? Did you guys win?"

She looked confused, then said softly, "Oh, well … it was only small claims court. We needed our money back for the butchered grooming and the subsequent vet bill. Ultimately, we wanted her shop closed down—she had no business being a groomer. Our court date would have been next week. Guess it's a moot point now."

"That must have made you both angry," he stated.

Eyeing him suspiciously, she said, "Are you saying 'angry enough to kill her'? Are you asking because of … that crime tape behind our house?" she hissed angrily. I'd never seen this side to her.

"Oh, no, no … it's only because I couldn't imagine our own baby being hurt. I'd be upset."

"Well, sure we were upset. We wanted a court to hold her accountable. You can't go around negligently caring for animals!"

Listening to this whole conversation, I found myself holding my breath waiting to see what car Nate drove up in. There was this nagging feeling, *what if he drove a dark blue sedan?* I breathed a sigh of relief when he rounded the corner in a white Corolla.

Nate appeared at the park's gate worried. He asked Colleen, "Everything alright, sweetie?" as he stared skeptically at each of us.

"They believe we had something to do with Tricia's death!" she yelled out.

Both of us, our eyes flew open, shaking our heads adamantly. "No! That's not what we thought!" we said in unison.

Nate turned on us both, his face beet red "Leave us alone! We mind our own business—we had *nothing* to do with that woman's death! *Nothing.*" He and Colleen quickly got in their vehicle and sped off.

In disbelief, I turned to Greg with a smirk. "Well, that went well, didn't it?"

CHAPTER NINETEEN

After leaving the park, we continued our journey. We hoped to get an update on the investigation, so we turned in the direction of the hotel. Once we began the ascent up the long drive, we could see in the distance the mobile command unit and numerous squad cars. Before we made it to the top, the coroner's van passed by us. Grief washed over me. Mr. Longo was never anything but polite and nice to us—I felt horrible for him, having no idea what he went through, and knew for certain he didn't deserve this ending.

Chief Smith was talking to a couple officers outside the hotel's lobby. Police tape encircled the entire drive-thru area in front of the hotel's main entrance. We also noticed at the far end of the building, where the hillside descended and ultimately led to the exterior ballroom doors, the staircase was blocked with the yellow tape and several fluorescent orange traffic cones.

The chief looked up to see us and called out, "Folks, this is an active crime scene. You can't be here."

"I remembered something from last night—" I called out.

He walked over. "What is it, Libby?" he asked as he also petted Shadow.

"During the dinner, I had gone to the restroom. I overheard two ladies talking…" I paused, swallowing hard, and realizing this was circumstantial and probably not related to the hotel's crime scene. "Anyway, they knew about the suspected weapon we found yesterday."

His eyes perked up. "We didn't release that information to the press. Who said this?"

"I couldn't see them. I could only hear them talking among bathroom stalls."

"Who leaked this?" His fists clenched and face blushed.

"Sir, they also said something about it being found … uh, 'behind *his* house'," I stammered. "We learned this morning that the house closest, behind the dog park, belongs to Nate and Colleen—the bakery owners."

His expression softened. "Yes, we know where they live. And, no, that's only a coincidence. Nate and Colleen are not involved."

"Okay. We wanted to pass along anything we remembered." I hesitated for a second, then added, "And, you do know about the legal case they had against Tricia, right?"

He didn't say anything, only waved us off.

Greg offered, "And, you know that Olivia …" he stalled, "uh, I don't know her last name, but Tricia's stepdaughter—she lives in Prescott. We visited with her yesterday. She knew nothing about Tricia's death … but we found it curious as to why she was driving that little yellow car around."

Chief Smith was listening intently. "She was informed about Tricia's death when we learned from the bank that Olivia was the co-owner of the car. What do you mean *she didn't know?* And, I swore the car was still in Tricia's garage."

Surprised, Greg and I stared at one another.

Why would she lie about that? When had she retrieved the car—before or after Tricia's demise?

"One more thing, Chief," I hesitated. "Another thing I've only now remembered. There was a metallic something hanging out of Bill's jacket pocket. I recognized it as being a piece of jewelry I had admired from the antique shop. Has that been taken into evidence?"

The chief looked perplexed. "Thanks Libby. I'll double check, but offhand, I don't recall seeing it."

* * *

Back at the cottage, both of us were exhausted. Sure, it had been a late night, but the tiredness was far more mental than physical.

"Do you think that Tricia and Bill's deaths were related?" Greg asked.

"I didn't at first, but now…" I sighed, "who knows!"

Shadow sat at my feet, looking up and following the conversation between us. That reminded me, "Shoot, we didn't give that license plate number over to the police or tell them about the blue sedan we've seen. It could be related."

Greg agreed, and looked up the non-emergency

number for the police department. As he spoke to them, I walked out onto the front porch. I dialed my friend.

"Hey JJ! Yep, we're having a good time in Jerome." I got him caught up on all the activities—including the deaths. "Yes, I know … everywhere I go. Yes, Shadow found …" I saw where he was going with this. "No, we're not trouble. We happened to be…"

He went on, relating all the various mysteries we'd been involved in over a short time. The client whose daughter went missing, our own spa that got broken into, Alexis and her neighbor both traumatized, my mother's neighborhood under surveillance, and then the drama at the recent retreat I went on. He had a point—*was I inviting trouble everywhere I went?* I cut him off mid-sentence.

"JJ—can you look up a license plate number?"

"Sure, Libby … what is it?" I read it off to him. I knew Greg was also trying to obtain the same information from the local police, but I wasn't quite sure they were taking us seriously. I was sure JJ could get the information back to us much quicker.

After several more minutes of listening how things were going back in Mesa, we said our goodbyes, and I went back inside.

Greg looked defeated.

"They aren't taking us seriously…" he said.

"Yep, *exactly* as I was thinking also. I've got JJ on it though…" I smiled. He took the few steps over and wrapped his strong arms around me, bending over to kiss me.

"And that's what I love about you, Libby Madsen— always one step ahead." He let his kiss linger this time. My mind swirled, *had he used the word* love?

Shadow whined. Our heads turned, laughing … poor pathetic face searching ours, she wanted love too. We called her over, knelt down to the floor, and wrapped her up in a hug. Longing for some much-needed rest, we curled up on the sofa and watched a couple shows on Netflix. I promptly fell asleep.

* * *

My phone startled me awake shortly before noon. It was Cheryl. She sounded frantic and wanted to talk. We agreed to meet her over at the Mining Town Brewery.

As we walked in, Monica tilted her head toward the far corner, "She's in a state…" she warned. "Can I bring you something to drink? Eat?"

"Water, please," I stated, and Greg agreed.

We took seats at Cheryl's table. Her energy was palpable. Monica arrived with the water and then promptly left, no doubt because of the look Cheryl gave her, which I read as, *Leave us alone.*

Greg started, "Cheryl, I can't imagine what this has been like for you. So sorry for your loss." She was caught off guard, squinting her eyes.

"My loss?"

"Well, yeah … Bill's death. We knew that you two…"

"You believed that rumor?" she quickly retorted.

My eyes quickly switched between her and Greg; I was confused. I asked, "It's not true then? You and Bill were never an item?"

"No! We did a lot of business together, of course. Me being part of the Chamber of Commerce, Tourism Department, and Arts Council. And, certainly, as the manager of one of the most recognizable hotels in Arizona—well, we'd have events to plan and organize *together*. But, any rumor of a relationship—that was most certainly Patricia's doing."

Greg nodded. "Cheryl, why have you asked us to meet you here today?"

"Oh! I am all in a dither over this mystery weekend … you've heard that we are not allowed back inside the hotel, right?"

I was stunned. A man died. He was a friend of hers, and she was only concerned with the outcome of the *mystery weekend*. And come to think of it, she had a similar response back when we all learned that Patricia had died. *What is wrong with this woman?* Greg glanced at me with a side-eye. *Uh, oh … was that my inside voice? Or, did he actually know me that well.*

He questioned her, "That doesn't exactly explain why *we* are here, Cheryl."

"Yes, of course not," she said in a softer voice. "I've asked you here because I need to find both of your partners. They are not answering their phones. I thought perhaps you could help."

We were momentarily confused and then realized she was speaking of Harold and Britney.

She clarified, "They seem to have disappeared. You wouldn't know where they are, would you?"

We both shook our heads. I felt irritated—*why couldn't she have asked for this over the phone? Did she honestly have to drag us out of our comfy place for this?* Then, I had an idea. "You know that Britney works at a veterinarian's office in Cottonwood, right?"

Either she hadn't known, or she'd gotten herself

so worked up that she had forgotten. Instead of saying anything, Cheryl pulled out her phone and started searching on Google.

Greg was curious and asked us collectively, "Does Britney live in Jerome, or in Cottonwood, then?"

I shrugged; I had no idea. Cheryl was still busy Googling and had tuned us out. I told Greg that Harold wasn't from Arizona—for all I knew, he'd already left town. I had no idea. In fact, last I saw him, he was at the far end of the ballroom, seated near the bar waiting for his turn to be questioned by the police. We never said goodbye.

"Won't the police know where everyone went—I mean, after being questioned, you'd think they'd have asked for that type of information."

Cheryl looked up from what she was doing. "Ah, good point."

"Why is it you are specifically looking for those two anyway?" I asked.

"I think they know more than they're letting on…" she whispered.

"About what? The conclusion to the *mystery weekend?*" Sarcasm poured from my words. Again, what could be so much more important than finding the killer, or killers, of Tricia and Bill?

She nodded slightly, then continued in a whispered voice as she leaned forward, "They were in cahoots—and Britney told me she knew who killed him."

"Killed Mr. Adler? Or, Mr. Longo?"

"Well, now I guess it's all one and the same, right?" she said dismissively.

My jaw fell open. "Are you kidding me, Cheryl? Why are you meeting with us, then—you need to tell this to

Chief Smith!"

"Oh, the chief isn't interested in our game. Never has been…" she sat back in her seat, checked her watch, and then abruptly stood up. "I've got to run!" and we watched her hurry out of the building.

I stared at the door as it came to a close. We could see her scurry across the parking lot and climb into an SUV. My eyes found Greg and we both sat shaking our heads.

"What on earth was that all about?" I asked.

He took his finger and made circles with it near his ear. "She is off her rocker!" Then he leaned in close to me. "Do you think she's having difficulties differentiating between the mystery game versus reality?"

I stared at him, contemplating his question. I was so confused—for the life of me, I had no idea. Regardless, I couldn't imagine Britney knew anything about the actual murders. *Even so, shouldn't we tell the police what Cheryl had said?*

Monica walked up then and sat at our table. "Do you guys see it, too?"

Our eyes questioned, but we remained stunned into silence.

She continued, "She isn't *riiight*…" Her southern drawl accentuated exactly the words that had popped into our minds. "Something is off with my aunt. I heard about Bill Longo, but what *exactly* happened last night?"

The connection between my brain and mouth stalled. Greg stepped in and walked her through the evening's events—at least from our perspective. My mind started to churn and I wondered where Cheryl had been all last evening, after the initial speech had concluded. In fact, wasn't that the case every night during the event? She'd give a presentation to kick off the evening's event and then she seemingly disappeared. Then, I remembered how Ted told us that he'd seen her fly by in her car on Main St.—the first mystery night; the same day Patricia died. *Where was she the night when Bill died?*

Monica couldn't glean anything from what Greg related. She hung her head. Then, carefully looking at us she quietly said, "I'm afraid of what's happening in our town. Have the police indicated whether they have leads on Patricia's death? And, then, poor Bill … do they know *how* he died?"

We couldn't answer her questions, but it cemented for me that we needed to learn who killed both Patricia and Bill. *Were they related? Or two separate horrible deaths?*

CHAPTER TWENTY

Once we were back at the cottage, I called Kirby and told her the news. She was horrified.

"Who would hurt Bill?" she cried. "He was one of the sweetest men I'd ever met."

"I know. In the short time I knew him, I felt the same way."

"Have they mentioned when the funeral would be?" she asked.

"I haven't heard anything yet. You're coming back when—tomorrow?"

"I think so, Libby. I'll let you know by the end of today for sure."

After hanging up, Greg asked if we were still planning to leave tomorrow. I thought hard about that before answering. "I don't think I can. I need to know what happened—and I feel like we could help. Shadow can help."

He nodded. "I'll have to call into work, see how things are going there. I'm not sure if I can stay or not."

"That's fine. I'll call Alex too—hopefully they won't miss me for a couple more days. Hopefully there's some way we can help in that time? At the very least, I'd like to come back for Bill's funeral—if that's what's planned." He agreed with that as well.

We each concluded our work calls and decided to stay through the funeral. With Kirby coming back, we needed to find a place to stay for the extra days. My friend's cottage was too small for all of us.

Shadow taking the lead, we set out for a walk about town. I'd seen a Bed & Breakfast a few doors down from the bakery so we tried there first. No vacancy. Maybe it wouldn't be as easy as we'd thought. We stopped at several other B&Bs as well as a small motel—no luck. This might take an online search later when we went back to the cottage.

In the meantime, we wanted to try and find Britney. We stopped in at the café shortly before two, and about the time they were due to close. She hadn't come in for the later shift, but we asked the manager where we could find her. He confirmed that she lived in Cottonwood and she'd requested the day off after the tragedy last night. He couldn't give us an address, but we tried several times to call her. No answer. We left concerned messages.

Since it was now afternoon, we walked up the hill to the hotel again and took our chances. Crime scene tape was still present and although there was less police presence, we found that there were still a couple deputies on patrol.

Chief Smith was nowhere around.

"Good afternoon, deputy," I called out as we approached the cruiser he sat in.

"Afternoon, Ms. Madsen," he looked down at Shadow and over to Greg and nodded to him as well.

"Any idea when we'll be allowed back in?"

"We should be wrapped up later tonight, then it'll be back open for business." He smiled.

"Perfect. We're looking for somewhere to stay tomorrow night. Kirby's coming back."

"Oh, you guys are planning to stay … even with Kirby returning?" He seemed surprised.

"Until the funeral. I assume family has been contacted? Would you be able to share next of kin information? We'd like to reach out with our condolences."

He looked a little nervous as he hesitated in answering. "Ah, well," he considered for a moment, "Oh heck, what can it hurt, you were friends with him … let me see, oh, right here," he pulled out his little notepad from the console, "Britney Barker; Only living heir."

How many more surprises can I take today? I thought as I tried to form my words again. "The waitress … from the café?" I asked, pointing in that general direction.

"Yep. You've met her then? Nice young lady." If I didn't know better, I'd say the officer had a crush on the twenty-something.

I didn't know what to say and obviously, Greg didn't either. *Britney was related to Bill? How had we not known about this?* I pictured that moment when Greg and she wound up in the basement laundry room and saw Bill's body on the floor. I couldn't remember her reaction. *I had no idea they were related.*

Greg answered the officer. "She was my partner in the mystery weekend."

He rolled his eyes, "Oh, that damn production! Cheryl has been on us every minute since we've closed down the hotel. She'll be relieved to get back in there tomorrow."

"So, have you talked to Britney since last night?" I asked.

"I haven't, but I'm sure others in the department got her statement and are helping her with resources for the arrangements and all."

A tingling sensation crept through my body—numbness, nausea. We should have stuck by her side last night instead of letting her drive off alone. I wish I'd known. *Why wouldn't she have said anything?*

CHAPTER TWENTY-ONE

Greg, Shadow, and I slowly walked back through town toward the cottage, lost in our own thoughts.

"She never indicated she was related to anyone in town," Greg softly said. "That one came out of left field."

"So, let's think back now, all the way to the beginning. First, Shadow's cactus wound festered and she referred us to *Tricia's Scruffy Solutions*. Then we learned she once worked at the grooming shop—and from her own words, 'didn't care much for the feisty little lady'. We found Tricia dead while we tried to retrieve Shadow, only to find that the police actually thought our dog could have … what, *bitten her to death*?" I scoffed.

Greg picked up from there. "Then we started the mystery weekend. Cheryl never hesitated to begin the festivities even though there had been a *murder*. And, now we learn that she and Tricia were *good friends*? Who did we learn that from?"

"Olivia … which I'm still considering lied out her…" I reconsidered, "well, I don't think she was completely honest with us. Or, perhaps we're falling too much for the town gossip—maybe she's the only one telling the truth!"

Greg nodded.

Shadow whined.

"What is it, girl?" She shook and carried on. I chuckled. *Was she actually agreeing with my assessment of Olivia? Or the town gossip? Nah.*

Greg stopped. "Wait, the whole conversation with Cheryl earlier … she wanted to *find Britney and Harold*. What did she say? Something about them knowing more…?"

"Good Lord, you think Britney and Harold had something to do with Bill's death?"

"I can't imagine. And, as Monica seemed to also think, Cheryl appears way more concerned about the mystery weekend than the real-life murders. She probably does think they'd figured out who killed the fictitious speakeasy owner."

I couldn't help but laugh out loud. It was simply ridiculous. "She was a bit wackadoodle earlier, wasn't she?"

Greg's eyes rolled.

We continued to walk the long way home. This route took us by the mining museum and then eventually back to Main St. before we'd turn off onto Holly St.

My eyes caught a flash of dark blue. A car was parked alongside the small museum building. From the other side of the street, we could only see a small portion of the hood.

"Is that the same car we keep seeing?"

Greg nodded yes.

"Wanna go see who it belongs to?"

We crossed the street and approached the museum. The sign that showed the hours indicated it was open, so we turned the handle and opened the door.

Lights were on, but it was a small, dim room regardless. There was a myriad of old mechanical tools hanging on every inch of one wall. Large posters showing a timeline and history of Arizona mining hung on another. Straight in front of us was a counter, but no one was behind it. A door in the back stood open so we figured whoever was manning the shop must have stepped outside for a moment.

"Hello!" an old man with a long white beard walked in and shut the back door behind him. "I'm sorry folks, I hadn't heard anyone drive up. How can I help you? Tours won't commence again until tomorrow, I'm afraid."

Greg introduced us and then said, "We saw a blue sedan—think it was a Genesis—parked out there. Thought it might be a friend of ours." He glanced around, "I don't see him in here though, so we must be wrong. You drive that sedan?" he asked.

"Oh no, I walk to work each day!" He sounded very proud of that fact. "That was Dale. He occasionally finds new artifacts for the museum and brings 'em on by." He pointed out the small window in the front door. "There he goes!"

We both turned only to see the tail lights moving off into the distance.

"Our mistake. We won't take any more of your time," Greg nodded to him and we said goodbye.

"Come back for a tour tomorrow!" he shouted out after us.

We missed seeing which direction the car took at the intersection once we were outside.

"If that is the same vehicle, I want to know why it was parked outside the cottage. I know he—or they—were watching the place."

"Where have we heard that name before?" Greg asked.

I couldn't recall and wasn't sure we had heard it before.

Later in the afternoon, I tried Britney's phone again. It went straight to voice mail.

* * *

By evening, we both were pacing around Kirby's place. Anxiety had set in; we needed to be doing something. We'd already scoured Kirby's home, ensuring it was cleaned in anticipation of her arrival the following day. Now we needed to find answers. Neither of us felt we could settle until we helped solve who killed the two people that we'd found dead.

We headed back to the brewery, after contemplating whether a nice steakhouse dinner would be preferable. No, we loved the brewery's food and the overall vibe of the place. Shadow stayed behind with a cookie, but only because we promised her a nice long after-dinner walk later.

The music was pumping louder than it had during our daytime visits. Most tables were filled, so we took Ted's suggestion of sitting at the bar instead. We both ordered the daily beer special and turned our swivel barstools to view the scene. You'd never know about the town's deaths by looking at the patrons. Of course, most were probably tourists so they wouldn't know. Still, I felt out of sorts with all the laughter—was it appropriate? I took a sip of my lager and turned to my handsome forest ranger. He gave me that sparkling wide smile of his—the one that makes his crystal blue eyes shine. Maybe it was okay to be out and enjoying ourselves, I decided. Or, maybe the beer was starting to inhibit the sad emotions.

"You look deep in thought. Care to share?" Greg asked me.

When I told him how inappropriate it seemed for so many people to be having such fun amidst the tragedies, he agreed with my sentiment. We sat quietly for a few more minutes until we caught sight of Britney. I waved my hand and called her over to an open stool next to us. She looked around the room first—perhaps she was meeting up with someone, I thought. Then she headed in our direction.

I stood up and wrapped her up in a hug. "I'm so sorry for your loss."

She pulled back slightly. "How'd you know?"

"Why hadn't you told us? I feel horrible about…" I drifted off when she held her hand up.

She lowered her head slightly, then accepted the hug from Greg. Then she looked between both of us and revealed, "Bill didn't know I was his daughter."

We both were caught off guard. I pointed to the empty stool; we all sat down. Ted came over and she told him she'd like a shot of whiskey.

"How long have you known he was your father?" Greg asked.

"I suspected for years, based on stuff my mom told me. I came here looking for him."

"But you never told him?" I asked.

"Once I got here, I wanted to get to know the man first. The last thing I wanted was to have him suspect I was here for his money. That's when I applied for a job with

Tricia. I hoped it would be a way to learn about both of them."

The room kept getting louder. Several tables full of people started laughing all at once; conversations grew in volume. The three of us huddled our stools closer and leaned in to hear her story.

"My mom was always cagey about who my real father was. She never wanted to talk about it when I'd ask. My stepfather was adamant that it wasn't a subject we needed to discuss—*ever*." She threw back the shot of whiskey and indicated to Ted to bring another. "By the time I was in high school, I wanted to know who my real father was. Snooping through my mom's stuff, I found some information—felt sure he was in Arizona. Then I set out online to research more." She received the next shot and knocked it down even faster. "Water, please," she said to another bartender.

After several reflective moments, she continued her story. She reminisced about all the family history research she'd done and how after graduation she knew she wanted to move to Arizona. She began slowly working her way through veterinary school in the Phoenix area. Then one day there was an announcement about the old haunted hotel in Jerome, having received a complete historic restoration, and a huge celebration surrounding the new grand opening. The picture in the article showed Bill Longo as the new manager. When she saw the picture, she felt inexplicably drawn to it. She and a friend decided to take a weekend trip to Jerome and check out the newest renovations of the hotel, hoping they'd witness a haunting. They were both into that. Secretly, she wanted to learn more about the hotel's manager.

Upon arriving in Jerome, she fell in love with the

small community. Britney knew that this was where she wanted to live—but questioned where she would work as a veterinarian ultimately. She still had years of school to complete, but she figured out she would live and work in Cottonwood and that'd be close enough. Most of the schooling was online for the time being, so she spontaneously made the decision and never looked back.

"How did you learn he was your father?" I asked.

"Actually, it was only confirmed for certain this morning," she bowed her head and wiped a tear from her cheek. "The sheriff's office called. They'd traced back to my mom—she told them where I was."

"Oh, wow. You were right all along, then."

She nodded her head. "I thought I had more time." She wiped another tear away.

"Why hadn't you told him your suspicions about being his daughter?"

"Mostly because of Patricia Simpson. I started working at her shop part-time because they were married once, and I thought I'd learn more about him that way. You know, to be sure I wasn't wrong. Again, I didn't want him to think I was after anything."

"How long ago was this?" Greg asked.

"Oh, gosh … nearly five years ago."

"And they divorced when?" I asked.

"Only about a year ago…"

Greg and I looked at each other. I couldn't remember if that added up to what we'd previously been told or not.

"Anyway, Tricia was a nasty wench. I learned that immediately. What I wasn't sure about was whether she was a liar. She told me stories that made me question whether or not I *wanted* Bill to be my father after all. I began thinking of him in an entirely different manner."

"Like how? What stories did she tell you?"

"Oh, how he cheated all the time. With Cheryl. How he'd been married *many* times prior. That he was not nice to Tricia. I couldn't believe that part—she insinuated that *he* was abusing *her*. All I'd ever seen of their interactions was the woman speaking *horribly* to him. I honestly didn't know what to believe. Then I learned that he asked her to move out. I stopped working for her not long after that—found a vet tech job in Cottonwood and tried to distance myself from the two."

"Cheryl told us herself she never had a relationship with Bill. They were only friends and business associates," Greg informed her.

She shrugged, then continued, "I started seeing them together—many places around town. My blood boiled thinking of everything Tricia told me—had he cheated on my mom, too? Had he abused her? Was that why she hadn't wanted me to search for him? I didn't know what to believe then."

"Sounds like you might have changed your mind?" I questioned.

"Honestly, I was still trying to figure all that out. I figured I owed him the benefit of the doubt. My heart was telling me that Tricia was the evil one, trying to convince people he was the problem. I still don't understand what her motive was in doing that—but I decided to try and get to know Bill. Once I did, I realized quickly he was the good guy. Now to prove whether we were related or not—I froze again and couldn't bring myself to tell him who I actually was or ask him about my mother. I don't honestly know why. But, now I feel I'll regret it the rest of my life.

Would that have changed anything? Maybe it would have altered the course—maybe he wouldn't have died." Her voice cracked and she looked away.

I put my arm around her. Greg reached out and patted her arm.

We all decided to order some food. The conversation turned lighter; she seemed to perk up slightly as we ate dinner. She wasn't sure yet when the funeral would be, but invited us to attend and we told her we wouldn't miss it.

Before we left, I asked her, "Do you know why Cheryl was looking for you earlier? She told us she needed to find you and Harold."

"Harold?"

"Yeah, the large Texan guy—my partner in the mystery weekend," I prompted.

"Oh, him! Why would she be looking for both of us?"

"Exactly what I'm asking you … she seemed rather insistent about it. Did she leave you voice messages too?"

"Oh jeez, I haven't checked my phone all day," she said, reaching into her purse and pulling it out. "Thirty-five missed calls?"

"Uh, we're a few of those, probably," I grimaced. "You can ignore ours now."

"Guess I better get home and answer some phone calls then." She stood up and gave us both hugs goodbye. We told her to call us if she needed anything—we'd help however we could with the arrangements.

I watched her walk away, feeling sad for her situation. She appeared to be a strong young woman, but from what we'd learned this evening, it appeared she was a girl suffering and in search of much more. Still staring out the exterior windows, I saw her stop abruptly, right before she would have climbed into her small red car. Perhaps someone had called out to her. Her head whipped around and before I knew it, she had disappeared into the dark parking lot.

"Did you see that?" I asked Greg.

"What?" he distractedly asked; figuring out the tip and pulling money from his wallet.

Maybe it was nothing. Then again, my stomach lurched. I had a bad feeling.

CHAPTER TWENTY-TWO

As promised, we took Shadow for a stroll before we turned in for the night. Remembering what the deputy had told us, we once again walked up the all-too-familiar hillside to the hotel and sure enough, it was open.

I walked up to Mrs. Brandish at the front desk and asked about availability for the next night. Hopefully, the funeral would be held by the weekend and we'd only need to stay an additional few nights. Once that was set, we headed down to the basement to make sure Kirby's room was all cleaned up and ready for her return. I also wanted to double check the appointment schedule since I hadn't had access all day. Certain there were some clients that required rescheduling, I was determined to leave the transition back to Kirby as seamless as possible.

Descending the staircase, I had to catch my breath. Memories of last night came flooding back—Harold and I coming down the staircase, Shadow running ahead barking, and then the horrific sight of Bill in the corner by the washer. I shook it off and was grateful that I wouldn't have to visit the basement ever again. *Was it a wise idea for us to have booked a room in the hotel? Maybe we should have tried harder to find somewhere else?*

Greg broke through my thoughts. "Bet it'll be nice not to come down here anymore…"

"How'd you know that's what I was thinking?" I smiled.

Shadow started to bark. *Oh no, not again.* She stood and pressed her paws against the door to the therapy room. I went to unlock it, but Shadow pushed her way through. *It was unlocked? Again?* The place was a disaster—the counters had everything turned over or thrown off onto the floor. Several glass candle holders were smashed; shards were everywhere. I grabbed Shadow's leash and held her back. The heavy mechanical massage table was turned over. Drawers were wide open and the contents thrown out. I looked over to the counter where the laptop was yesterday. It was gone.

"What the …." I stopped. "Did the police leave it this way?"

"Why would anyone have reason to be in here anyway?" he asked.

"Good question."

I pulled my phone from my jacket pocket and called the police.

* * *

"Miss Madsen. This is becoming a common occurrence." Chief Smith walked in, glanced down at Shadow, who was keeping my feet warm, and petted her.

I glared at him. "Is this how your officers typically leave things?" I looked around the room, still horrified at the mess I'd have to clean up.

"My department had no reason to come into this room," he informed me.

"Then, who?"

He shrugged. "Guess that's what we're here to find out now." He motioned for one of the officers to come to him. "We'll move down the hall; please gather fingerprints and look for anything else out of the ordinary. Take pictures."

The chief ushered us to the ballroom. I was so sick of this room, but we sat down at one of the tables, hopefully for the very last time. I wracked my brain trying to think of why someone would trash Kirby's massage room. It made no sense. She wasn't even in town and I couldn't imagine her upsetting anyone enough to do the damage they'd done. Then it hit me. *Hadn't I been told a couple times now that I ask too many questions? Had I caused this? Was this a warning?*

Chills ran down my spine.

* * *

Eventually, we were allowed to leave the hotel and we made it back to Kirby's place. How many late nights in a row could I handle? Apparently, not many—I was exhausted and fell right to sleep when my head touched the pillow.

It didn't last though.

* * *

Around three in the morning, a loud crash jolted us out of bed. Shadow barked furiously. The moonlight cast shadows through the bedroom window. I could make out Greg slipping into his pants stealthily. He motioned for me to stay quiet and tiptoed from the room.

I began carefully pulling on my sweatpants, grabbing in the dark for my sweater, when I heard him call out "Who's there?" Of course, no one answered. Shadow still barked intermittently but seemed to settle once Greg was nearer to her.

"Hon!" I heard him yell.

Adrenaline spiked.

I ran out to the living room, where he'd already turned on the light. Through the living room window and only inches from Shadow's crate, I saw what appeared to be a large brick. My eyes followed the apparent trajectory and I stood, mouth open, staring at the large gaping hole in Kirby's front window. Following the path back to the crate, I noticed a shiny field of tempered glass strewn about the room.

Greg bent down to pick up the brick.

I went to Shadow. There were pieces of glass in her crate as well. I opened the door and carefully guided her toward the bedroom until we could clean up.

"Wonder no more," Greg broke the silence, startling me.

"What's that...?"

He held up the brick, which had a piece of ragged paper attached. "A clear warning: *Get out of town!*"

"How rude!" My opinion of small towns was beginning to change.

Once again, we picked up the phone and called the police.

* * *

It was Officer Tan who arrived this time, about twenty minutes later. Searching both inside and outside, he and his partner slowly and methodically collected evidence.

Greg's ears burned red; I saw it begin to spread down his face and present as splotches, almost rash-like down his neck. The frustration of listening to the officer's account of events was too much. He'd had enough; he'd been silent too long.

"You mean to tell me that you think that brick *with that note* is a harmless prank by teenagers?" Abruptly, he turned away from them, running his fingers through is hair. "After all that has happened within the last few days—Kirby's spa being broke into and trashed, the murders in town, and all. C'mon guys! This was a targeted attack!"

Office Tan held back for a second. Then softly said, "Greg. I realize you're upset. Please—let's discuss this rationally. Is there anyone you suspect? Someone who may have threatened either of you?"

Greg and I began to put our heads together, throwing ideas out while Tan's partner continued collecting prints and Tan patiently listened and took notes. The list was fairly short: Nate—maybe Colleen, too—they were upset with us now. Cheryl could be, too. Britney was aware that we knew Bill was her father—was that something that had upset her? It'd been mentioned a couple times that I ask too many questions—who had said that? Well, the chief for one. Who else though?

Then, Greg snapped his fingers. He went to the bedroom and came running back. "You need to find out who owns this car—it's a newer model, dark blue, four-door,

Genesis. I called it in earlier—or was that yesterday—can't remember, but I would bet you this is our brick thrower!"

Officer Tan took Greg's note. "And, why do you think that?"

"We came home from a walk; someone was casing the place and that was the car."

"How do you know that?"

"Well, it was parked out there," he pointed to the smashed window. "We came walking up and it sped off."

"No interaction with the driver then?"

"No. Shadow barked at the car—he, or I suppose, *she*, or maybe even, *they*, drove off. It had dark tinted windows, we couldn't see who the driver was.

I remembered something else. "We also saw it at the museum, and when we were in Prescott having lunch." Considering what we'd learned during those encounters, I turned to Greg who continued to pace. "The museum guy—he mentioned a name! What was it?"

We couldn't come up with it.

"Okay. We'll run this plate number and see what we get." Officer Tan was ready to go.

Another epiphany struck me. "Oh! We also saw the car at the hotel. During the mystery weekend—I think I actually saw it there two different nights. It has to be a participant's car, right?" I remembered I owed JJ a call; I was surprised he hadn't returned my request for the license information.

"Thanks guys. We'll take what we have here. I'll let you know what we find out. You said Kirby will be back later today?"

We both nodded. "We'll be moving up the hill to the hotel today."

"Oh, so you're staying on longer then? I'm surprised; figured you'd want to get out of here by now." He grinned.

"We've been invited to Bill's funeral ... we'll leave after that."

He rounded up his partner and they left. We spent the next hour cleaning up all the glass. Greg found some ground-covering plastic in Kirby's shed and did his best to temporarily patch the window. I dialed JJ's number, but it went straight to voicemail.

I couldn't believe that happened on our watch.

* * *

It was moving day. We changed all the bedding and linens—washing and putting everything away before Kirby got home. We were pleasantly surprised when she arrived earlier than we'd expected. Shadow alerted us.

I stepped out onto the patio. "Welcome home!" I reached out and gave her a big hug.

"Libby—look at you!" She pushed back slightly. "You have not aged a day! And, what, it's been at least five years since we've last seen each other? Probably way longer."

"You're too kind, my friend. And likewise, looks like therapy careers might be doing us both good!"

Kirby glanced behind me. "Aww, this must be Greg!" She gave him a hug. "And Shadow!" She knelt down and could barely hold onto the excited Labrador. So much for the handshake—she was simply too enthusiastic.

We couldn't wait much longer; I could detect Greg's uneasiness. "Uh, Kirby ... there was an incident early this morning," he stated.

Kirby's eyebrows knitted together when she looked at

him. "What's wrong?"

We walked her into the living room, pointing to the window facing the street.

"Those damn kids!"

"Well, we're not so sure about that," Greg said." We have filed a police report and you'll want to get with your insurance." He explained the few theories we had given the police to follow up on.

"You can't be serious? I don't know anyone with a blue sedan—" She walked to the kitchen and set down her purse on the counter. "But, who knows. I'm still in shock over our groomer. And, then of course, Bill. Have you heard anything more about how he died?"

We both shook our heads.

Looking around, she said, "Wow, you guys outdid yourselves—I don't think this place has ever been so clean."

"I feel horrible about that..." I pointed back to the window.

"Not your fault. The police will get to the bottom of it. I'll call State Farm today." She turned to the refrigerator. "Had breakfast yet?" she asked. When we both indicated no, she started pulling things out. "Well, it'd be brunch by now seeing that it's nearly eleven. Hey, you've hardly used what I left for you."

"We've actually been enjoying your local restaurants," Greg mentioned. "That Mining Town Brewery is amazing."

As she started cracking eggs into a bowl, she nodded in agreement. "Ted and Monica are great. I go there occasionally."

She made vegetable omelets, straight from her garden, and we updated her on the town's happenings. I asked about her dad; her brother was there now to help. He was making great progress. She was happy to hear we found the bakery and befriended Nate and Colleen. Then we had to tell her that we thought we blew it. She was surprised to hear how Nate responded so strongly and said she'd stop by to see if she couldn't smooth things over. Certainly, it was a misunderstanding. I wondered privately—*could Nate have been so angry with us that he threw a brick through the window?* No. *That'd only hurt Kirby; why would he do that to her?*

We finished brunch and chatted for a couple hours, then Greg and I decided it was time to give Kirby her space and we should check in at the hotel.

CHAPTER TWENTY-THREE

Greg agreed to meet me at our room on the fourth floor. He took our luggage up in the elevator; Shadow and I took the stairs. The door was propped open with a suitcase; I was surprised that he'd beat me there. He apparently had much better luck with my brass-gated nemesis.

The room was cozy. A queen-sized bed covered with a blue and gray quilt, small desk with an antique lamp, and an armoire for our clothing. There was nice space beneath the desk for Shadow's crate, I pointed it out to Greg and he went to work. I walked into the bathroom—basic pedestal sink, bathtub and shower combination, and a toilet in the corner. Only enough room for one person, but it would do.

I sat on the bed, then flopped backwards—sprawled out. *Was this such a great idea to stay?* I was utterly exhausted.

Deep down I knew we should stay for the funeral—supporting Britney, Kirby, and the nice townies we'd met. But, there was a different part of me that wondered if we were better off leaving. The warning was clear. There was someone who clearly did not want us here. Didn't appreciate us snooping around. Thought we were too close to the truth.

I sat up abruptly. *That was it! We must be too close. To what? Whoever murdered Tricia … or was it Bill's death that had spooked someone into issuing us warnings?* That didn't make sense though—I wasn't sure we'd figured anything out yet. And, we still had no idea what happened to Bill. That's when I remembered there should be a press conference soon. *Would they hold that at the police station—or maybe at the hotel?*

I stood up and went to the window which overlooked the guest parking lot. There were a few vans that had pulled in since we'd arrived.

"Hon, I think the press conference is being held here today."

"Really? Here? I'd think it'd be at the police station."

"Look—" he came over and peered out the window.

"I'll be right back," I announced. "I'll find out what time." I left Shadow and Greg to continue unpacking.

Behind the front desk, I found a young girl—I think Bill had introduced her to me as Laurie. I casually walked up and asked, "Press conference being held here today?"

Her large brown eyes pooled, she nodded her head slowly. "I still can't believe it, Libby."

Surprised that she remembered my name, I then noticed from her nametag that I was correct with hers, so I reached out. "I'm so sorry for your loss, Laurie. He valued you—" The tears spilled over, but she quickly wiped them away as the front door opened. It was Cheryl.

"What in God's name is happening out there?" she bellowed coming into the lobby.

Laurie and I both rolled our eyes. I grimaced and moved over to Cheryl, trying to protect Laurie from dealing with the lady.

"Press conference," I simply stated.

"Well, what on earth for?"

Was she truly that clueless? "Uh, Bill's death … here at the hotel."

She didn't skip a beat. "Ugh. They should do this down at the police station. Bad for business—"

"Cheryl, the hotel manager died—in the hotel he manages no less. I—"

"Even more reason why!" she shrieked. Turning away from me, she gave Laurie a look, stuck her nose in the air, and stomped over to the elevator. She became impatient, punching the button when the car didn't immediately appear. Finally, it made its way to the lobby. "Oh great, we're still letting dogs in here?!" The look she shot over to Laurie was meant to kill.

Cheryl angled herself so she wouldn't come into contact with Shadow as they exited. Thankfully, Greg had the leash taut. Cheryl struggled more with the elevator gate, then the buttons, before she descended to the basement.

Greg caught on to my irritation, "Cheryl having another spell?" Both Laurie and I busted out laughing. I walked back over to the front counter, Greg and Shadow followed. "What time is the press conference?"

Laurie answered, "As soon as the chief arrives—slated for about half an hour from now."

"And, how are you doing? I'm so sorry for your loss."

She welled up with tears again. "Thank you. You two are so nice. Yeah, I'm hanging in there, but I can't believe they reopened so quickly afterwards. I could have used a couple days off." She looked back to the elevator. "That was Cheryl's idea. That woman is all about money and nothing else. No sympathy or compassion whatsoever, I swear!" She choked on her words. I went around the counter and pulled her into my arms. Poor girl.

Greg waited, then asked, "Why would that be Cheryl's decision?"

We didn't understand his question.

"To keep the hotel open or not…" he explained.

Laurie's eyes widened, "Oh! Well, sure, you're right, it's not Cheryl's decision—actually, it's another dude … um, Doug Lister. The Chamber guy. She has such influence over him. And, she seems to *always* be the one here, getting into our business. I'm sure Mrs. Banter can't stand her either, but she's better behaved than me."

"Even so. Bill managed the place. I don't understand what the Chamber of Commerce has to do…"

"Doug Lister owns this building," she clarified.

Flashbacks of seeing Cheryl, Doug, and another gentleman at a table in the Mining Town Brewery the other day appeared. They had been in deep discussion. Then, she had called us over to introduce—I couldn't recall what the interactions were specifically, but remembered it seemed fairly benign. *What was I missing? Were they all in cahoots to get Bill out? Or, worse—to kill him? If so, why?*

Greg apparently had a similar thought. All he said to Laurie was, "Interesting." Then, he tilted his chin toward the door. We excused ourselves and told her we'd check in on her later.

Outside the lot was filling up with media vans. I recognized several well-known stations from Phoenix, but Tucson, Flagstaff, and Prescott had plenty of representation as well. Camera operators were setting up their equipment and correspondents were busily staking out their real estate claim for the best possible shot. It was a flurry of activity.

We walked around the side of the hotel. Greg stopped me.

"Are you as uncomfortable as I am with the fact that Cheryl appears to have taken over immediately following Bill's death?"

I nodded. "Especially given her role at the Chamber and Doug Lister being the owner of the building. I had no idea."

"I wouldn't say it means either are responsible for Bill's *death*, but with her bizarre behavior—which Monica even noticed—red flags are going off in my brain. Am I wrong?"

"I think the cause of death will answer a lot of questions."

"Or create a lot of questions—could go either way."

We decided to casually walk our dog back inside the hotel and hang out inside the lobby until the press conference began. We hadn't made it but only a few steps in front of the building, when a young reporter ran over with her cameraman. *Oh geez.*

"Excuse me!" she called out. The small woman struggled to run in high heels. "Can I ask you a few questions? Are you guests in the haunted hotel?"

Greg stepped in front me. Shadow sat and held her paw up.

"Oh, how cute!" the new reporter exclaimed, leaning over to shake her paw.

So transparent, I thought silently. *She's trying to win our trust through our dog.*

Greg started, then stopped when the reporter turned to her camera man and asked if he was getting the shot. Greg held his hand up. "No. You may not interview us on camera. Please turn it off."

The reporter turned to her guy and nodded. The light went off on the camera.

Greg then said, "Look, we barely checked in—not even an hour ago. Had to take the dog out..." he looked down to Shadow. "We have nothing to say. We don't even know why you're here."

The reporter explained the hotel manager's body had been found in the hotel. She stopped for a second, then added, "Our sources say he was found by a black Labrador and its owner." The 'gotcha' moment was the same classic reporting we saw every night on the news.

Greg held his hand up again as soon as he saw the camera's light flip back on. "No comment." He put his arm around my shoulders and shuffled us into the hotel lobby. Thankfully, they didn't follow—the police must have set clear boundaries.

"Oh, great. We're going to become part of this story, aren't we?" I asked him. "And what source told them Shadow found the body?"

He shook his head. We took our seats in the lobby and waited for the police to arrive. I picked up one of the many binders and tried to divert my attention by reading about hauntings instead.

CHAPTER TWENTY-FOUR

Chief Smith arrived and the media circus began. We snuck out and did our best to fade into the Halloween-decorated background outside the lobby doors, where we could hear what was said, but we couldn't be seen. He began by updating the press on the sequence of events from two nights before. Enduring criticism for withholding information until now, he cautiously maneuvered around reporters' questions and informed them the department had been waiting for results of the autopsy, therefore until now, there was nothing to report. Then, we learned that after medical examination, it was determined Bill died from coronary thrombosis.

One reporter yelled out, "Are you saying no foul play then?"

"He died from a heart attack. The investigation is ongoing—we're not commenting, other than from the coroner's report."

Another reporter attacked. "Is that because you suspect he *didn't* die here at the hotel? Can you confirm whether he died in the hotel's laundry room?"

"Ladies and gentlemen, I've told you all I can for now. This is an open investigation. When we have more to report, I assure you, we will."

Hordes of reporters all started shouting at once—including asking whether this death was related to his former wife's. Chief Smith turned and walked inside the lobby. Before the vultures spotted us, we hastily snuck inside ahead of him.

He turned to us and shook his head, "Can you believe those people?"

"Somehow they know Shadow was the one who discovered his body," I related. "That reporter with KNBE rushed us earlier, too."

Chief Smith's face turned beet red; his fists clenched. "There's a leak. How would they know where the body was found, who was present, or when it was discovered? We have not revealed any of that information publicly."

"Is it true that Bill died prior to the night we discovered him?" Greg gently asked.

The chief nodded his head.

"Any leads on where he'd been in those few days?"

"None. But, we're still looking for Harold—don't have his last name. Several of those interviewed told us he was the one to remove the character's—uh, Mr. Adler's—body from the ballroom the first night of Ms. Basque's production." He carefully peeked out the window. "Wish these vultures would leave! I've got work to do!" His hand went up, signaling a deputy to come closer. Soon after, he said goodbye to us, and his entourage got in the elevator, headed to the basement, then out to the alternate parking lot.

That was a surprise. I struggled to remember where Harold had told me he was during the time of the acted murder. I thought he'd said the bar, but too many things had happened since then.

We took the steps, wanting to hide in our room until the press left.

When we opened our door, we stood there dumbfounded, taking in the scene of personal belongings scattered everywhere. Someone had been in our room.

* * *

The call from Kirby came shortly after we'd cleaned up our clothing and toiletries, putting them back into the drawers and hangers they'd been strewn from. I told her what had happened. This time we decided not to call the police; they already had too much to deal with. She said she'd be right over; she was checking to see if the coast was clear so she could get into her business.

Once she arrived, we met her downstairs in the basement and put our heads together—who were these warnings coming from? First the massage room, then Kirby's home, and now our hotel room. *Why?*

"We've got to help them find Harold!" Greg startled us. Kirby and I whipped our heads around when he spoke.

"Where do we start?" I asked.

"Mrs. Brandish," he didn't hesitate.

"Don't you think the police have already started there?"

He shrugged. "It's *somewhere* to begin."

I agreed. Kirby informed us that she'd got herself a new laptop and needed to get to work, but she offered to help later, if needed. We agreed to meet up for dinner later that evening—this time a nice steakhouse dinner.

We walked out of our room, double and triple checking the door lock to make sure it held. *Had someone actually broken in?* There had been no sign of it looking at the doorknob; if so, they had a key. *Or, was this one of the pranks the ghosts pull?* Had we not experienced the vandalism at Kirby's house, I could almost convince myself ghosts were trying to run us out of the hotel. Surely, they'd also had enough of all the mystery weekend fun, too.

At the front desk, Mrs. Brandish was busily typing away on her computer. Her face appeared slightly swollen and her voice indicated her sadness as well.

"Good afternoon, Libby. Greg." She leaned over the counter and looked down. "And, Shadow … how may I help you?"

"How are you doing, Mrs. Brandish? There's been a lot to take in, hasn't there?"

She nodded, keeping her composure. After a long pause when it was clear she wasn't going to add more.

"We've been looking for Harold … is he staying here at the hotel for the mystery weekend?"

"Harold?"

"You know, my partner for the mystery … bartender?"

"I vaguely remember a large man at the bar, but never interacted much with that character. Seems the police are looking for him as well. I told them the same thing—no one named Harold is, or was, registered here."

Since that was a character name, then of course, that made sense and was obvious he hadn't registered at this hotel or she'd know. However, you'd think that Cheryl would have some master list; she'd probably know where he was staying. We thanked Mrs. Brandish and then stepped outside. I pulled out my phone and tried reaching Cheryl. No answer.

From our earlier research, we already knew of all the motels and B&Bs in the area. We decided to set out to find Harold. He had to be staying around here somewhere.

"We don't even know what name to be asking for, how's this going to work?" I asked him as we walked up to a lovely place called, *Molly's B&B.*

Greg waggled his phone. "This is how…" he showed me a picture. It was a selfie of Britney, Harold, and us, all dolled up the second night of the mystery weekend. I gave him a smile and a big kiss. I'd completely forgotten we'd ever taken the photo.

After the third place we'd tried, the girl behind the counter said he looked familiar. But, he wasn't staying at their motel. She struggled to come up with where she'd seen him before, but never succeeded. I left my cell phone number, asking her to contact me if she remembered or saw him again.

It hadn't taken us long to exhaust the Google list before we found ourselves sitting at the bar, talking with Ted at the Mining Town Brewery. If only I hadn't been so hesitant to befriend Harold initially, maybe we would have traded numbers. Or, I would have learned more about the man.

It was late afternoon and, apparently the slow time for the business; we were the only customers. Monica came and sat down beside me.

"You guys see the press conference?" she asked us.

We nodded, filling her in on our new accommodations, and how the press discovered us.

"Shocking he died of a heart attack," she said solemnly. "The police mentioned they are still investigating so it must mean there's more to it."

We didn't divulge our conversation with the chief earlier.

Instead, I asked, "Monica, the first night of the mystery weekend, Cheryl left the hotel. Ted saw her drive by at some point, so we know she had left—and we think it was during the game itself. Does she typically only stay to get it started?"

She was shaking her head before I could finish asking. "No! She stays from beginning to end. Always. That production is her baby."

Greg and I glanced at each other.

"Does she routinely lend her vehicle out to others?" Greg asked.

She considered for a moment. "Uh, I'm not sure about that. Doesn't seem like her…"

* * *

We had another hour before meeting Kirby for dinner, so we continued to walk around town, testing theories with each other. Frustrated, I knew we were going around in circles—and not related to our walk.

Shadow stopped suddenly; her ears perked up. I held tighter to the leash. As abruptly, she turned her attention in the opposite way and pulled me. We began walking back the way we'd come—past the antique shop. She plopped her bottom down and stared at me.

"What is it, Shadow? This shop is already closed…"

Greg pressed his face to the window, looking for Chris inside. No lights were on and there was no indication of anyone around.

Shadow wouldn't budge.

"C'mon, girl … let's go!" I tried prompting her.

She stood, then jumped up and put her paws on the side of the building. If the windows were lower, I'd think she was trying to look in.

Greg reached in his pockets. "Cookie?" he offered her.

That got her attention. She accepted the treat and then Greg coaxed her into moving by promising we'd come back when the store opened. *Had she actually understood all that?* I was shocked it worked.

We continued along the road, up the hillside, past the mining museum again, when we both suddenly stopped and Shadow began barking. I quickly tried to shush her.

Olivia and Harold were standing outside the museum arguing. Loudly. He glanced over at us, and his eyes got huge. He quickly jumped into a vehicle, grinding the starter, tires squealing, as he bolted away. Olivia stood there dumbstruck—her arms flailing. "Dale! What the f—!"

It was the blue four-door sedan. The Genesis we'd been seeing around town.

CHAPTER TWENTY-FIVE

Greg and I started across the street toward the girl. She ran.

Shadow took off, pulling me along; Greg sprinted after Olivia. Not able to hold onto the leash any longer without getting pulled to the ground, I let go.

"Shadow!" I yelled, dashing to catch up.

One block ahead, we found the girl on the ground. Shadow had a paw on her back and Olivia laid perfectly still.

"Get her off me!" she sounded terrified as we approached.

"Why did you run from us, Olivia?"

She scrunched her face, looking up at me—there was no recognition.

"How do you know my name?" she spat.

"Olivia, we met you the other day in Prescott," I reminded her.

Greg had grabbed Shadow's leash and moved her aside.

Olivia stirred and moved to a sitting position, leaning up against the brick front wall of the antique shop. "That's right. Should have recognized her..." she tilted her head sideways at Shadow.

Greg asked again, "Why did you run away from us? And, where did Harold go in such a hurry?"

"Harold?"

What had she called him earlier?

"Who is Dale?" I asked.

"Dale is my brother!"

"Was he the one who left you at the roadside?" Greg asked.

Her head fell forward. "That's him ... can't believe he left."

"Maybe you should start from the beginning ... what are you doing in town? And, what were you two arguing about?"

"See! I knew you were cops! Asking too many questions..."

I knelt down next to her. "Olivia, we witnessed you two fighting. We're concerned about you. That's all." I tried reaching out for her arm, but she abruptly moved it.

"I don't need y'all's help! What don't you understand about that!" she shouted and stood up. "Leave me alone!" She ran.

Shadow lunged to chase her again, but Greg held her tight. Then he reached out to help me up and we followed the direction she went. Shadow tugged my arm; we looked up and down each street we passed. By the time we made it to the bottom of the hill, close to Kirby's place, Shadow resigned herself to losing the scrappy young woman so we gave in.

"Well, we learned a few new things," I started. "Harold is Dale. Olivia's brother, Dale, to be precise. And the blue sedan belongs to him."

"It makes sense that's why we saw the Genesis at the hotel a couple times. But, I still want to know what he was doing casing Kirby's place. And, was he the one who threw the brick?"

"Wonder what they were so worked up about back there? Looked intense. But, *if* either of them had anything to do with Tricia or Bill's death, why would they even be in Jerome? Why come here? Why aren't they thousands of miles away by now?"

"Yeah, not sure they're involved with that—but both are sure acting guilty of something." He pulled out his cell phone. "I'm going to update the chief. If nothing else, we have the Prescott address for Olivia—has to be where Dale is staying."

As he related that information to the police, we made our way back to the hotel. When we walked up to our door, Shadow started barking. Shushing her, I stuck the key in the hole and turned it.

Inside, our jaws dropped—all our belongings were scattered everywhere, *again*. Every drawer pulled out and turned over. I immediately ran to get Mrs. Brandish. Someone with a key was responsible for this—that door was locked!

CHAPTER TWENTY-SIX

While we were cleaning up for dinner with Kirby, my phone rang.

"Hi JJ! You're on speaker phone," I answered.

"Still chasing ghosts?" he asked with the all too familiar hearty laugh of his. "Oh, and good afternoon, Greg!"

Greg said hi, then, "Think ghosts are chasing us, if anything."

"JJ, I think we found the owner of that sedan," I informed.

"Oh, okay. So you know it's registered to a Patricia Olivia Simpson, then."

My heart lurched. Greg stopped in his tracks. "What?"

"Yeah, that's what I was calling about. Department of Motor Vehicles records show that it was last registered to

Patricia Olivia Simpson … 539 East Ave."

"That's interesting because the police didn't recognize that vehicle. If it was hers, surely they would know that. Plus, we'd only ever seen her zipping around in the little roller-skate of a car."

"Roller-skate?" JJ was confused.

"Smart car," Greg said.

"Ah, yeah. I show recent records transfer on a Smart car from Patricia to Olivia and Dale Chavez."

"Chavez? Are you certain?"

"That's what it says…"

Greg and I stared at each other. I would never have thought either one as being of Hispanic heritage. Had to have been one of Patricia's many husbands' last names.

"When are you guys coming home?" JJ asked.

We explained and got all caught up with family news before we had to cut the conversation short and get to dinner.

* * *

After filling up on a delicious surf and turf dinner, I noticed that Doug Lister and another gentleman were being escorted to a table near ours. He nodded in recognition as he passed by us.

Kirby was surprised. "You've met Mr. Lister, too?"

"Cheryl introduced us," I said. "Do you know him?"

"Oh, he's become quite powerful around town. He and Cheryl both."

Dessert was served—beautifully designed small patisserie-style works of art. The slice was multiple alternating layers of cake and mousse. Chocolate and raspberry with a small orb placed on top within a cloud of whipped cream. The waiter instructed us to break the sugar glass dome with our spoon. When we did, a gooey red substance coated our dessert. Each of us were in heaven as we savored the sweet treat with a hint of raspberry-lime tartness.

Loud voices penetrated my thoughts as we listened to Kirby. That was the first thing that caught my attention and made me look their direction. Thankfully, we saw it coming—fists were flying between the two men. Quickly, we stood, getting out of their way. Mr. Lister was thrust over into our table, dishes crashing to the floor.

I was thankful I'd finished that wonderful dessert—or I'd be plenty mad right now.

"You son of a ..." his tablemate yelled. "I'll see that you *never* do business here in Jerome again!" The man stomped out of the restaurant.

Several waiters came running.

One young man helped Mr. Lister up off the floor. Two others asked if we were okay. They efficiently shuttled all of us out of the main dining area, through a swinging door, and into the hallway leading to the restrooms.

As they fussed over Mr. Lister, who had coffee all down the front of his white business shirt, he began to lose patience. "I'm fine!" he retorted.

I asked, "What was that man's problem?" Rolling my eyes, I added, "How rude to behave that way in a place like this!"

"He's not happy with my plans for the former groomer's shop." Using the rag the waiters provided, he continued to work on his shirt and trousers. "That witch bent his ear about me, too," he grumbled.

Greg and I both caught the anger searing from him.

"Anything we can do to help?" Greg asked.

He grumbled some more, then pushed past us. That was the last time we saw him.

Kirby spoke up. "What is happening with our town lately? I'm embarrassed. No one typically behaves this way. I've always been proud of our community and how everyone gets along."

We paid our bill—which was greatly discounted by the manager after the scuffle—and left the restaurant. Walking with Kirby toward Holly St., we said goodnight and turned off a couple blocks before her street to take the hillside steps. There was no hurry; it felt good to walk off the huge meal.

Mrs. Brandish was at the front desk and signaled us over when we entered the front doors. The grimace she displayed had us approach her cautiously.

"Shadow has disturbed your neighbors upstairs. You are going to have to keep your dog quiet. This will be the last warning."

"What? She's never..." Her expression stopped me cold. She didn't want excuses, she wanted us to do something about it. "Yes, ma'am. I apologize and, of course, we'll keep her quiet."

We hurried upstairs. With all the exercise Shadow had done since we'd arrived in Jerome, I couldn't imagine that she would have done anything but sleep while we were away.

Greg opened the door to find Shadow outside of her crate.

"We had latched it," I said immediately. Then, I realized our stuff was spread all over the room again. I knew instantly that Shadow had not done it. *But, who had?*

I called down to Mrs. Brandish, letting her know about another break-in. "Have you talked to your staff about our earlier complaint?"

She huffed. "No one has gone in your room since you checked in. They all assure me of that." I clearly received the protection message; her staff was not going to be blamed.

"Then how do you explain the mess?"

"I don't know, Ms. Madsen. There are many occurrences in this hotel that I cannot explain."

That's when it hit me. *Were spirits the cause?* I sure wished Shadow could talk. *What had she seen? What was she barking at earlier? Perhaps the mischievous little boy I'd seen earlier in the trip?*

We put on Shadow's halter, the 'bra' and leash, and took her out for an evening stroll to release her pent-up energy.

* * *

The night had cooled significantly, making me wish I'd added another layer for the stroll. I checked my watch because the town appeared to have completely shut down. No cars were about, all the businesses we'd passed were closed, and it was eerily quiet.

Greg appeared subdued.

"You've been awful quiet," I stated. "Is something wrong?"

"Something doesn't feel right."

"Well, yeah … the whole trip has gone a bit haywire, hasn't it?"

"Aside from that," he started. He stopped unexpectedly. "Quick, over here," he pulled me and Shadow to the side of a building, disappearing into the darkness of an alleyway. My eyes followed his, as I leaned around him to see.

"That's the antique shop, right?" I asked, viewing the building across the street and a few doors west of us.

He nodded, putting his finger over his lips.

Then my mouth formed a huge O when I saw a man emerge from the building and put something into a dark-colored vehicle. That wasn't the surprising part—I was most interested in the little yellow car that was tucked into the alley next to the shop. I pointed it out and he nodded his head.

We continued watching quietly. Shadow couldn't see from her position in the darkened space and, thankfully, she hadn't noticed anyone. A large man with black clothing and a stocking cap walked quickly from the alley to the trunk of his car multiple times.

I whispered in Greg's ear, "What's he moving?"

He shrugged. We needed binoculars.

I gasped. Greg shushed me. "Oh geez, I think—uh, that is the man who watched us having lunch with Olivia that day in Prescott."

Greg's face twisted, looking confused. I'd never told him about that.

"Look," I pointed. "That *has* to be Olivia, right?" The young woman also dressed in dark clothing, emerged from the lane and threw something into the trunk.

He nodded, then pulled his phone from his jacket. He snapped a few pictures, but in the darkness, they were too grainy and not helpful. I held up my finger and pointed down our alley, mouthing 'be right back.' I took Shadow's leash, vanishing further into the darkness until I was certain we wouldn't be detected.

From behind a large brick building several businesses farther away, I felt safer to make a call. I dialed, then whispered. "There's a burglary happening at the antique shop—" I struggled to hear the dispatcher as a raucous diesel semi-truck's engine brakes sounded coming down the hill. After answering several questions in what felt interminably long, I hung up and walked back.

Greg was nowhere to be seen.

CHAPTER TWENTY-SEVEN

I peeked out around the side of the building; across the street, both cars were gone. *How had I not heard them leave? Where had Greg gone?*

We cautiously emerged out onto the street and Shadow's ears perked up, her nose high, sniffing the air. There was no sign of Dale or Olivia anywhere. Something caught my eye in the middle of the street. We cautiously walked over to it, constantly looking over my shoulder, anticipating danger. I bent down. *Oh nooo!* It was Greg's phone.

"GREG!" I panicked, shouting and praying he'd answer.

I heard vehicles coming and I quickly pulled Shadow back into the alley. The police cruisers pulled up in front of the antique shop; I was relieved to see them.

"They were right here—" I exclaimed, pointing to the ground I stood on. "And now I can't find Greg!"

Officer Tan took me aside while the others approached the building. "Tell me exactly what happened."

I told him everything: the makes and models of the vehicles, whom I suspected the people were, and most importantly, they needed to find Greg. I handed over his phone. Another vehicle approached and squealed to a stop. Chris jumped out and ran to the front door, opening it for the police.

Once Officer Tan followed the others inside, Shadow and I bolted down the street calling for Greg. Shadow pulled aggressively, and I kept screaming for my boyfriend. Horrible thoughts ran viciously through my mind—*had Dale kidnapped him? Maybe he took off chasing the large guy?* But that didn't explain both cars disappearing. Sprinting along Main St., I realized I was not going to find him. I crossed the street and we made our way back to the police.

"Who said you were released?" Tan was annoyed.

"Am I under arrest?" I retorted.

"No."

"Then, I'm free to do as I please. Who is looking for Greg?" I could be saucy when required and I'd say this was the time for it.

Officer Tan spoke into the radio. "Chavez, you copy?" When the officer replied, he gave instruction on surveilling the area, repeating my description of Greg: six-foot tall, roughly two-hundred pounds, brown hair, blue eyes, wearing black slacks, a blue sweater, and a brown jacket.

Shadow jerked the leash and took off into the store.

"Shadow!" I called out, running after her.

Inside, Chris' arms were flailing and his voice was animated—the thieves had made away with a new load of items that Bill Longo had brought in several days ago.

"Shadow!" I yelled out again. This time Chris and the officers were staring at me. "Sorry…" I said, scooting by them.

I found her at the back of the store. An officer was also back there taking prints off the door. On the floor, she was pawing at something sticking out from a shelving unit. I knelt down and saw a conspicuous white cloth protruding from underneath the bottom metal shelf. I signaled for the officer. With gloves on, she reached down and pulled out a large sheet—I recognized exactly where it'd come from—the hotel's insignia prominently showing. We both also recognized something else that fell when she shook it. Bill Longo's business jacket—with his nametag still pinned on. And, the Celtic brooch with the beautiful pearl also fell out of his pocket.

The officer called for her partner. Together, they cuffed Chris and read him his Miranda rights.

CHAPTER TWENTY-EIGHT

I called Kirby and she picked Shadow and me up.

"What do you mean Chris was arrested for Bill's death?"

"Well, I'm not sure of the specifics, but he's definitely been pulled in for more questioning. I mean, why would hotel sheets and Bill's clothing be hidden in the antique shop? What explanation would there be?"

"And, Greg … disappeared?"

"I think Dale and Olivia saw him—"

"Who?"

"The guy was my partner in the mystery game. Olivia—well, long story short, both are Tricia's stepchildren."

"And, why would they have something to do with Greg disappearing?"

"Because we witnessed them stealing from Chris' shop?"

Her eyes grew huge. "So, you were with him? How'd you get separated? This is nuts." She turned the corner, apparently heading for the hotel.

Urgently I asked, "Would you mind driving me around town? I feel like I need to be doing *something* to find him. The police say they are … but *are they?*"

She understood and we wound our way through the small community several times. No sign of the vehicles or of Greg anywhere. I filled her in on everything since we'd last seen her.

"This is going to be a big ask," I began. "I know where Olivia lives. Can we drive over to Prescott?"

Kirby's head turned. "Prescott?"

I nodded, my eyes pleading with her. "I can't think where else they'd have gone. And, I certainly don't think they'll be there for long. I identified them and the police surely will be following up on that."

"Sure. Let's go!"

* * *

Slightly over an hour later, we were casing Olivia's quiet neighborhood. No signs of police presence anywhere so apparently we had beaten them there. Or, they were too focused on Chris' interrogation and ignored my pleas for help. As we approached from several houses away, I asked Kirby to turn off her headlights. We parked and watched. I couldn't see cars parked outside her home. That didn't mean they weren't in the garage, however.

"I want to see if there's any sign of life inside that

house." I looked into her backseat at Shadow. "Can I leave her here with you?—I think I'd be more stealthy that way."

She nodded. I told Shadow to sit quietly and I got out of the vehicle. As I walked away, I could already hear her whine. Poor Kirby.

When I got within one house away from Olivia's, I cut through the neighbor's lawn and over to the side of the brick home. I stood quietly in the shadows listening. Chills shot up my spine, making me quiver. The stillness unnerving, I moved silently toward a small window and tip-toed to see in. I could vaguely see beyond the bathroom I was staring into, and there was a distant light on in the house. *Had they left a light on? Or, were they indeed here?* I couldn't wait to find that out.

Moving to the front of the house, I gingerly climbed the front steps praying no motion sensor lights, cameras, or creaky steps would be triggered. Hunkering down low beneath the large picture window, I took a seat, catching my breath and listening intently for noise inside. After several seconds, I cautiously raised myself up to peep through the window. Sensing someone in that room, I darted down beneath the window's edge. *Who, or what, was that?* My pulse quickened. Sweat formed on my brow; my stomach felt sick.

I ventured another look. Slowly. Steadily, I peered in the window. There was no movement, but my instincts were correct. There was a man in a chair. I squinted harder—a man was *tied* to a chair. My eyes adjusting to the darkened interior, now I could see his mouth was covered. Silvery covering—duct tape. Then, I made out the whites on the pair of eyes. They were wide and pleading.

It was Greg!

I ran back to Kirby's car, startling her when I banged on the window to unlock the door. Shadow barked. I climbed in, careful to not slam the door, drawing attention to ourselves.

"He's there! Greg's in there!" I exclaimed, pulling the phone from my pocket. I called the police. Now we were in Prescott jurisdiction and they didn't know the story. Impatiently, I quickly explained. As they asked me endless exhaustive questions, I wrote down Chief Smith's number on a receipt I found in Kirby's console. I motioned to her—*call him!* We both feverishly spoke, trying to get someone to act *now*.

Then I saw the garage door opening at the brick house.

"Hurry! They are leaving!" I spoke into the phone, telling the dispatcher. "No, I don't know if he's with them! Hurry!"

The little yellow car backed out of the driveway and pulled away. From our position, I couldn't tell if the other car was in the garage or not. Shadow began barking.

"Shhhhh…" I didn't actually think anyone would hear her from inside their homes, but even so, we didn't want to be discovered.

"Should we follow that car?" Kirby asked. We heard answers from both phones' speakers, "NO!"

I couldn't stand it any longer; I had to know whether Greg was still there. I told Kirby to stay on with the police departments and I got out of the car. I ran back to the house, up the front steps as quietly as I could, and peered into the front window again. No lights were on this time. I strained to see in the darkened room, but it was impossible to tell if he was still sitting there. I sat down, back against the wall, pulling in deep breaths of the cold air with my eyes closed. After another second, I slowly moved up again trying to see in. My eyes fixated on where I'd last seen him. Then, there it was—a movement. He was trying to bounce up and down in the chair!

Where were the police?

Then everything went black.

CHAPTER TWENTY-NINE

The first thing I saw was a wooden shelving unit and staring at me was a red cardinal. It was fuzzy—my vision, not the bird. *Was it porcelain?* I couldn't be sure. Before that thought was complete, my heart started racing. I had no idea where I was or how I got here. Then I sensed movement from across the room.

"Good morning, Libby," the familiar Texan voice sounded.

Morning?

I could tell it was still pitch black out, but I had no clue how much time had passed. *Where were the police?* Inside the home there was only a faint distant light. Maybe from the kitchen or a hallway. My eyes found Harold … oh yeah, *Dale*, sitting on a sofa, sneering at me. I twisted my head from side to side, looking for Greg. He was to my left. Smiling made impossible from the gluey gray patch over my mouth, I lifted my brows in recognition. Uncomfortable, but unable to twist my torso at all, pain shot through my arms that were bound behind me and to the wooden chair. My eyes found what looked like cord around each ankle and chair leg, anchoring me in place.

"What were you doing snooping around my house?" he goaded me, knowing I couldn't speak.

My eyes questioned, *his house?*

"Lookie who we found spying on us earlier…" his head tilted toward Greg. That was also the first time I realized he held a gun. He kept alternating, pointing it at each of us. "Now, what do you think you two are doing? Couldn't leave well enough alone, could you?"

My heart pounded. I never suspected Harold capable of this—full of himself, yes. This? No. And what else was he capable of? Murder—Tricia's or Bill's? Or, both?

I heard a distant sound. *Finally! The police have arrived.* Then a door slammed, causing me to jump. Olivia's voice sounded.

"Dale!" she yelled.

"In here, sis … gotta see what I found," he chuckled.

I heard footfalls coming down the hallway. Then, "What the hell?" she hissed. She walked right over to me and kicked my chair. "WHY ARE YOU TWO FOLLOWING US?" she screamed in my face.

"Settle down, sis … we're just having a nice visit."

"Well, I suggest you get them loaded in your trunk. We've gotta get out of here, there's not much time left."

"Did you get what you needed from storage?"

"Yes! You dumb lug! We wouldn't be in this position if you'd stayed in Texas like we discussed!"

His face turned varying shades of red. He stood, grabbed her by the collar, effortlessly picking her up to his six-foot-two height. "What did you call me? All *this* is YOUR fault—not mine!" he spat, then dropped her to the floor with a loud thump.

Greg and I looked to each other.

Olivia got up, brushing herself off. "Me? My fault! You're the one who killed Tricia!"

Dale looked over at us realizing her revelation. We didn't react. He walked over and pulled her into the next room where they proceeded to scream at each other. We enjoyed the audible show.

"I did NOT kill her," he shouted.

"I drove by, saw your car there … drove around the block to find parking and by the time I went in, she was dead and your car was gone. Explain that, Dale!"

"No, no, no … you have it all wrong. Is that what you've thought this whole time? That *I* had something to do with *her death*? She was as alive and fiery as I've ever seen her when I stormed out of there."

Greg and I both lifted our eyebrows at each other, waiting in anticipation for the rest of the story.

"Dale, blood was everywhere! And that *dog* … wait, do you mean the dog actually killed her?" her voice got softer and we leaned in to hear better.

"The dog? No! Well, I honestly don't know actually … but *I did not touch her.* She came after *me*! Swinging those scissors around, pointing them at me, she threatened *me*. I know she's crazy as a loon; you can't stop her when she gets like that!" We could hear him pacing around. "I can't believe you— thinking I killed her!"

"You were supposed to scare her into dropping her

damn lawsuit!" She stomped her foot loudly.

"Yes, and I *tried* ... she's scary though."

I chuckled to myself, envisioning an expression he had several times during the mystery weekend. The enormous man was a wuss!

"So, *Dale*, you mean to tell me that I've been freaking out all this time for *nothing*! That I never had to take the murder weapon to save *your bacon*!" She screamed. Then, we heard her pause. "And, *why* did we take those two as hostages then?" she hissed, trying to make herself unheard. "I thought I was protecting *you*, but if none of that is true, *why* are we here?"

"Okay, Olivia. You need to calm down! I have no idea what you're talking about. You took what murder weapon? You're speaking nonsense! And, those two—he's here because he saw us stealing from the antique shop—and she's a little snoop."

They became quiet and my pulse quickened again. Those two were in trouble regardless— multiple crimes have been committed—*what would they do with us? And, how long does it take the police? Jeez!*

Greg and I jolted when we heard her shrill voice again.

"Dale, shut up! Did you hear that?" She came running into the living room and looked out the front windows. "I swear I heard a car. We've got to get out of here!"

"Let's go then—leave these two." He looked over and for a second, I saw the Harold that I'd been partners with. As quickly, he soured again, face distorted, and pointed his gun at us. "Or, we can kill them!" he sneered.

I squeezed my eyes shut in anticipation.

"No, you idiot! We're not killing anyone!"

I peeked open one eye and cautiously looked upward.

Seeing the black metal pistol pointed directly at me, I immediately squeezed them shut again.

The two kept arguing. When I looked up again, Dale had moved a few feet away; they appeared distracted. Movement from Greg caught my eye. He tilted his head toward the window. Squinting, I caught a brief glance; something stirred the bushes beyond the front patio. I carefully twisted my head back to Greg, lifting my eyebrows in question. Were we both imagining the same thing—*the police have arrived and this could quickly get out of hand now.*

"You were the one who came up with the brilliant idea of stealing back Tricia's heirlooms from the shop!" she yelled.

"They could be valuable—we are the heirs! They are ours! I don't consider that *stealing…*" he shouted back, glancing over to us. Our heads bobbed back and forth watching the tennis-like shouting match. *Thankfully, they were plenty distracted and hadn't detected people outside*, I thought, trying to keep up with their revelations.

"Then why didn't you *ask* for the belongings?"

"I don't know…"

"The witch kept our family in court for years! Why not ask for them during the settlement? I got my car back that way…"

He looked genuinely surprised that it could have been that simple. Poor Dale.

"Forget that! We've got to get out of here—on the road to Texas before…" Something grabbed his attention. I'd heard it too. Shadow's bark.

Trying to divert him, I started squirming in my chair, making noise. Shouting with duct tape over the mouth was impossible, but it had the desired effect. Dale turned away from the window, walking toward us. My eyes pleaded with him to remove the tape.

"Oh no, you don't … no way," he hissed.

"C'mon, Dale. Help me grab the rest of the stuff! They aren't going anywhere…"

This time it worked. The two went to another room. We heard them rummaging around and at least one of them opened the door into the garage. It slammed.

Greg and I kept our eyes on the windows. Not long after our captors had left the room, I saw movement outside again. We began to shuffle in our chairs, creating movement they might see from outside.

The garage door slammed again. Each time, I startled, wishing the police would end this. I looked to Greg worriedly; he tried his best to visually comfort me from a distance and all bound up.

A huge explosion sounded and everything that came next appeared in slow motion.

CHAPTER THIRTY

Dale's enormous forearm wrapped around my torso, effortlessly picking me up along with the chair. "I'll shoot her! Back away!" He yelled out to police as they entered the room.

I heard someone scream, "She got away!"

Then, "Go after her!" shouted from another officer.

The heat emanating from Dale's arm made me sweat. Beads dripping from my brow, stinging my eyes, which I couldn't wipe. My vision blurred but I could see the shapes of two officers at the entrance to the room about twenty feet away.

"Get back! I mean it!" Dale was shaking. His heartbeat strong and pulsating through his arm that had slipped closer to my throat. The constriction was unbearable, the pressure in my eyes throbbing.

"Dale, you aren't going to win this. You need to let her go and drop your weapon." The officer's voice was steady and emotionless. "Now. C'mon. This doesn't end well for you."

"I didn't do it!" I felt his entire body shudder.

"Didn't do what, Dale?"

"I didn't kill Tricia!" he hissed.

The officers shared a glance. "Is that why you think we're here?" the calm one asked.

"That, and breaking into the antique shop…"

"Dale, we only want to see these two…" his head tilted to both Greg and me, "safe and back home tonight. They're innocent bystanders here. We can talk through everything else."

The heat fired up in Dale again; more sweat poured into my eyes. His body quivering as I tried to blink away the saltiness, he screamed, "There's nothing to talk about!"

"It's okay, Dale. No need to get angry. You see, there's been a slight misunderstanding—let's calm down, let these folks go, and we'll clear everything up. I'm sure then you'll be on your way."

To prison, I was hoping.

There was a loud crash. My head felt like it split open. Searing pain shot up throughout the left side of my body. Commotion throughout the room confused me and I clenched when the gunshots went off. The ringing in my ears was unbearable.

CHAPTER THIRTY-ONE

Opening my eyes, and then shielding them from red flashing lights, I saw Greg's face smiling down at me.

"Hello, sunshine," he softly said as he swept hair from my face.

My eyes stung as I blinked away tears. "What happened? Where are we?" I tried to raise up to see.

"Lay back down, Libby. We're in an ambulance—soon headed to the hospital. You are alright."

I closed my eyes letting the tears stream down the sides of my face. "Where's Dale?"

"Oh, he's going away for a long time."

"Where's Kirby? Shadow?"

"They're headed back to Jerome. Kirby will keep

Shadow until we make it back. Don't worry—everything is being taken care of, sweetie."

* * *

Morning light shone softly across the sheet and blanket. I blinked several times before I saw the hospital room clearly. Greg was snoring in a reclining chair in the corner. There were machines beeping and whirring. An IV line attached to my right arm—I followed the tubing upward where I saw a bag of clear fluid, slowly dispensing one drop at a time. Something was around my right shoulder, I turned my head to see and the pain radiated down that arm. I reconciled the fact I now had a cast on my arm and in a sling. *What happened?*

The door opened and in walked Chief Smith. I tried to smile, but it came out as a groan.

"I know, Libby, not exactly the person you'd like to see so early. I'm happy to hear you'll be okay," he whispered, smiling at me.

"Chief Smith, can you tell me what happened?"

Greg stirred, then quickly sat up once he realized the police chief was standing there and I was awake. He stood, came over to my side, and kissed my forehead. "Are you sure you want to do this now?" he asked me.

I nodded. "Yes, I can't remember much. I need to know what happened."

The chief pulled up a chair. "Libby—you, Greg, and Shadow led us to the all the answers surrounding both Tricia's and Bill's deaths. Thank you."

My eyes flew wide open. "How?"

He filled us in on the investigation. After Tricia's autopsy came back and revealed that a dog bite was *not* the cause of death, they began looking for a sharp object—figuring it could be a tool used for grooming. Then we found the scissors in a bush at the park. Those scissors were determined to be the murder weapon—the depth of the wound along with the measurement of the blades matched exactly. All the nearby neighbors willingly cooperated and not only turned over their DNA samples, but also their home security camera footage.

"Nate?" I asked.

"All cleared—neither Nate or Colleen's DNA or fingerprints were found on the weapon."

I breathed a sigh of relief; they were nice people. Then I remembered what Olivia had confessed—she was the one who took the murder weapon from Scruffy's! I told the chief everything I'd heard and he went on tell us that they had caught up to Olivia. She and Dale were both in police custody and still being questioned. So far, they're talking—and had already admitted to many things. Specifically, trespassing, breaking and entering, felony theft, kidnapping, and tampering with evidence. However, the chief believed they were not responsible for murder. In fact, according to the forensic experts—now that they had the weapon—they believed it could have been self-inflicted.

"Suicide?" Greg was shocked.

The chief nodded and said, "More likely, an accidental death. According to Dale, who was the last person to see her alive, she was extremely agitated and flailing those scissors about in a threatening way. It looks like she tripped and fell … impaling herself on the scissors."

I pictured when she tripped over Shadow at the bakery that day. *Oh, jeez! Was Shadow ultimately responsible for her death then?*

I rapidly pushed those thoughts from my head, trying to pay attention to what Chief Smith was telling us. He went on to explain that Olivia and Dale were half-siblings from one of Tricia's previous marriages. Of course, we knew they were her stepchildren, but I hadn't been aware of the rest. They shared the same father, and years prior to ever having met Tricia, the siblings had learned about one another and had become quite close. That much was true of what Olivia had divulged to us. The chief shared what a resentful and angry young woman she was—we agreed, witnessing it firsthand. She'd had enough of Tricia's relentless court cases trying to keep their father's inheritance away from them, after he'd so carefully set up a will and trust. She was set on fighting her to the end.

As the chief spoke, I couldn't help but remember Olivia feign surprise that Tricia was dead. Memories were coming back from the night before as well. I remembered her saying she went to the shop and found her dead. *Had she told the police that part?* Maybe that was part of the ongoing interrogation.

"You believe that neither of them killed her then?" I asked.

"Again, we're still investigating. Those two are thick as thieves, and they certainly are not innocent. But, from what we've learned so far—both from them, and forensics—I do suspect it was an accidental death."

"Wow," Greg stated. "I didn't see that coming."

I cleared my throat. "You said earlier we helped you solve both these cases..."

"Yes. Are you sure you're up for this? You look quite tired, Libby," he said, lowering his voice.

I nodded. "I'm fine. I want to know about Bill."

"Well, you led us to the antique shop ... I should state,

Shadow found key evidence," he sighed, leaned back in the hospital chair, then began again.

We had already learned the official cause of death was a heart attack so that part wasn't new. Beyond that, the police focused their efforts on *where* and *when* Bill had died. It turned out that it was most likely when the gun went off at the mystery weekend dinner ball.

"But, you said he didn't die from a gunshot wound. Plus, they were blanks … it was a game."

"Yes. After interviewing everyone, we learned that Dale … uh, Harold as you knew him in the mystery production … was scripted to pick up Bill and carry him from the room with the character-acting detectives. He did as his role dictated, but earlier under interrogation, he admitted remembering that night Bill must have been a great actor—he played dead extremely well.

"He swiftly carried him from the room and into a storage area and then rejoined the party. Never realizing there was a true emergency, he left Mr. Longo where he truly believed he'd get up and go home … or back to work … or whatever."

My pulse quickened. *We all continued that night, answering detective questions and playing a game while a man died in a closet? That was sickening.*

He proceeded to tell us that within an hour, Cheryl realized something was wrong. She freaked out and left the venue in a panic. When she returned hours later after everyone had left, the body was gone.

"You've questioned Cheryl now too?"

He nodded. "Oh yeah. We started asking about Mr. Longo when you came in that morning thinking he'd been arrested for Tricia's murder. Of course, we'd had him on our radar—he was an ex-husband. Well, turned out they never officially married, but that's not the point. We still needed to find him and learn more. By that point, he was nowhere to be found."

"Did you learn why she sent us to you—she's the one who said he'd been arrested, you know? I wouldn't have thought she'd want police involvement at all."

He shook his head no. "She hasn't said anything about that."

Greg jumped in, "What did she do when Bill's body was gone?"

"She contacted Doug Lister to get his assistance—both knew it was bad for business. She was particularly concerned about optics if anyone learned the hotel manager died during her mystery weekend. Once the body went missing, she and Doug conspired together for damage control."

"Did you learn what happened to Bill's body from there?" I asked.

His eyes widened. "That's where you—uh, Shadow—helped us again. Chris Dougherty, antique shop owner, has been spilling all the beans since we arrested him last night."

Greg was dumbfounded. His voice softened, cautiously questioning, "Chris had something to do with Bill's death?"

"With the movement of a corpse, yes."

Greg and I looked at each other in amazement—*never saw that coming.*

The chief explained how Bill and Chris had an earlier altercation related to some monies owed. Bill had loaned Chris a substantial amount and then began questioning him when several payments were late. Apparently, Chris was not great with money. He got involved in a large Ponzi scheme, hadn't used the loan to save his business as he indicated. The two became embattled; it was witnessed by numerous people in town. Including Cheryl.

When she approached Chris to help him out of his financial troubles, of course, he went along.

"Late at night, after everyone had already left, she convinced him to gather sheets from one of the washers at the hotel, roll the body in it, and they planned on dumping him miles away from here."

"That doesn't explain why he was actually found in the laundry room, does it?" I stated.

"He's still divulging—but the gist I got was that Chris had a change of heart. The guilt was killing him, he knew Cheryl and Doug basically owned him now, and somehow, he figured he could pin it all on Cheryl."

I couldn't believe everything I was hearing. This was incredible. I thought all these people were close friends and neighbors. Now, we were learning that they had no respect for the living or the dead. It was disgusting.

"Why didn't Chris call the police? I mean, that should have ended his concern about paying back the loan." Then Greg snapped his fingers. "Wait, also how did the hotel sheet and Bill's jacket get into the antique shop?"

The chief sighed. "First, his financial problems— illegal Ponzi scheme and being associated with a bunch of thugs—he felt he couldn't risk being found out. He'd scammed Bill as well. And, as Cheryl convinced him, too many people saw their nasty fight. She frightened Chris into disposing of the body and all their troubles would be gone. That's his story anyway." He took a sip of his coffee. "I suspect Cheryl had something to do with the sheet and jacket ending up at Chris' shop. She wasn't too happy with our questioning. She *knew* Shadow would find the evidence if she stuffed it under a shelf."

"But, hold on a minute … surely Cheryl, or Doug, knew Bill hadn't actually died of a gunshot wound. His death wasn't *actually* caused by the mystery weekend festivities. So, I don't understand why they went to all this trouble. I mean, they actually brought *more* attention to the tragedy. No wonder she's been a basket case."

His head tilted curiously. Then, he added, "Again—business optics. At least for Cheryl and Doug. Chris was certain he'd be blamed. Libby, stupid people and ridiculous choices is what it all boils down to. You can't make sense of their actions."

"Poor Mr. Longo."

Greg squeezed my hand a little tighter, feeling my pain. "So, you actually believe that he died of a heart attack when the fake gunshot sounded? Certainly, someone would have recognized signs of a heart attack, right?"

"I hear what you're saying, but the coroner said specifically it was an aortal tear—he was dead instantly. He couldn't have been revived. And, they said it could have been a lifetime issue with his heart. Whether he knew about it or not, no one can say. It simply was a horrible tragedy." The chief's eyes cast downward.

"But, Cheryl, Doug, and Chris are all in trouble regardless, right?"

"Oh yeah. Many issues with the decisions they made. No, they didn't kill anyone, but nevertheless, they will be going to jail for a while. Tragic ending for all."

I tried to turn over slightly to relieve pressure on my left hip and winced in pain.

The chief stood. "Libby, you need rest. I hear they'll

release you in another day or so."

The timing was perfect; the chief left and the doctor took his place.

CHAPTER THIRTY-TWO

Two days later, late afternoon, Kirby and Shadow came to get us from the Prescott hospital. I had learned from Greg that Dale had dropped me from his six-foot-two height after the police busted into Olivia's home and he refused to surrender. The fall left me with numerous injuries on my left side: a broken arm, bruised ribs, bruised but thankfully not broken hip, and various contusions along my face and head, including a huge purple and black shiner. I was a mess and my sweet pup seemed to understand that. Since I was in a wheelchair, she approached me cautiously when they greeted me outside the front doors of the hospital.

"Wow!" Kirby exclaimed. "I'm so sorry, Libby."

"Hey, not your fault." I attempted a smile, but grimaced instead.

Once they got Shadow and me settled and buckled into the back seat, Greg jumped into the passenger side and Kirby drove us home.

Kirby filled us in that Nate and Colleen had reached out to her. They felt horrible about what happened to us—they'd heard through the grapevine as had everyone in town. Monica was disgusted with her aunt's behavior. Ted couldn't believe his ex-girlfriend was involved at all, but had acknowledged he realized he dodged a bullet with her.

"Maybe my memory isn't good, but I can't understand how Bill's body got *back* to the laundry days later for us to find him."

Greg reminded me what the chief had said. "It was all Cheryl and Chris' brilliant plan to make it appear he'd worked himself to death."

I shook my head. "Stupid! People were in and out of the laundry all the time."

"Yes, but remember … we're not dealing with logical people. To be able to have done that at all—we're not talking rational thinking."

"Such a shame," Kirby added from the driver's seat.

Greg twisted slightly in his seat. "Hey, Kirby—whatever happened related to the brick thrown through your window? I forgot to ask the police about that."

"Oh! That was a brilliant Dale maneuver, apparently, to try and scare you two out of town."

"And, your massage room? What about our hotel room?"

"I don't know about those …" she quietly said. "They may never know."

"Mrs. Brandish indicated ghosts were responsible," I chuckled.

She looked at me through the rearview mirror. "Do you believe that?"

I shrugged. "Hmm … Not sure."

We crested the mountain and drove quietly into the small town. It was Halloween, kids dressed in all types of costumes, from princesses to monsters. Kirby carefully navigated the streets, watching cautiously for the ghouls and goblins running amok. My thoughts went back to Kirby's question. Remembering the ghostly young boy I saw at the hotel—it was quite convincing.

I'd have to say after my stay in Jerome, I probably am a believer now.

Thank you for taking the time to read *Spooky Shadows*.
If you enjoyed it please tell your friends, and I would be
so grateful if you would consider posting a review.
Word of mouth is an author's best friend, and very
much appreciated.
Thank you,
Jennifer Morgan

What's next for Libby and Shadow?
It's a ski trip to Taos, New Mexico, for Libby, Shadow,
Greg and their friends. The wedding of Greg's friend is
the main purpose, but of course a mystery very quickly
presents itself and Libby and Shadow are drawn in to
solve it. Don't miss Book 6 in this "impressively original
and deftly crafted"* series!

**Midwest Book Review*

Let's connect!
Website: www.jenniferjmorgan.com
Email: jennifer@jenniferjmorgan.com
Facebook: facebook.com/profile.
php?id=100076154359528
Twitter: twitter.com/JenniferJMorga3
BookBub: bookbub.com/profile/433830544
Goodreads: goodreads.com/user/show/148099219-
jennifer-morgan

**Get a free book from Jennifer—
Scan the QR code to find out how!**

Books in the Libby Madsen series:
Shadows in the Forest
Spa Shadows
Shadowed Treasures
Shadow Retreats
Spooky Shadows
The Christmas Fairy – a holiday novella

www.ingramcontent.com/pod-product-compliance
Lightning Source LLC
Chambersburg PA
CBHW050150120726
47903CB00002B/562